The

FIGARO
MURDERS

The

FIGARO
MURDERS

LAURA LEBOW

MINOTAUR BOOKS

NEW YORK

THE FIGARO MURDERS. Copyright © 2015 by Laura Lebow. All rights reserved. Printed in the United States of America. For information, address St. Martin's Press, 175 Fifth Avenue, New York, N.Y. 10010.

www.minotaurbooks.com

Library of Congress Cataloging-in-Publication Data

Lebow, Laura.
 The Figaro Murders / Laura Lebow.—First edition.
     pages cm
 ISBN 978-1-250-05351-0 (hardcover)
 ISBN 978-1-4668-5619-6 (e-book)
 1. Opera—Fiction. 2. Murder—Investigation—Fiction. 3. Vienna (Austria)—History—Fiction. 4. Austria—History—Joseph II, 1780–1790—Fiction. 5. Mystery fiction. 6. Historical fiction. I. Title.
 PS3612.E28F54 2015
 813'.6—dc23

                                                      2014040987

Minotaur books may be purchased for educational, business, or promotional use. For information on bulk purchases, please contact the Macmillan Corporate and Premium Sales Department at 1-800-221-7945, extension 5442, or write to specialmarkets@macmillan.com.

First Edition: April 2015

10 9 8 7 6 5 4 3 2 1

IN LOVING MEMORY
OF MY MOTHER

The

FIGARO
MURDERS

Prologue

The paper crackled as it hit the flames. From his place on the deep sill, the boy watched from behind the heavy golden drapes as it melted into the fire. He tried to keep perfectly still. They mustn't find him here.

How he hated these people, this house! Why had Papa made him come? It wasn't as if he really needed the position. His future had been decided at his birth. Why did he have to spend every day reading those dull books? It was no fun, none at all. Everything here was boring.

He stuck his finger in the collar of his shirt to loosen it. Why did they make him wear this uncomfortable uniform? He wasn't a servant. The trousers were too tight. He wriggled quietly on the sill, pulling the crisp white shirt from his waistband. The shirt was wrinkled. He'd hear about that. He was expected to take care of his own clothes here. But why should he have to? Why should he clean his room? Didn't these people know who he was?

He missed home. Everyone there loved to take care of him, to treat him the way he should be treated. Heinz pressed his clothes and helped him dress, and Liesl made his bed and cleaned up any mess he chose to make. Renate, the fat cook, always had a sweet for him when he visited the kitchen. He missed them all—but especially Mignon, the little chambermaid, who willingly put down her broom and let him undress her whenever he wanted.

"Promise me you won't speak of this to anyone," a voice said.

He heard a sharp laugh. "Don't worry about that. I don't want this getting out either. We'll keep it to ourselves." Two sets of footsteps sounded, and the door closed.

The boy drew back the drape. Now *that* was interesting. Those two—one always telling him what to do, as if their stations were reversed; and the other, always looking at him as if he were some kind of worm. If he told Papa what he had just heard—Papa wouldn't want him to stay here. He'd be able to go home.

As he glanced at the little notebook in his lap, he recalled his tenth birthday. Maman had hired a puppet company to come all the way from Venice to entertain him. What was the play they had put on? Something to do with two sets of lovers, a servant who causes all sorts of misunderstandings— it had been funny, he remembered that. Afterward, the master had let him climb up above the stage, to see how to work the puppets. The great lady in the play had worn a dress of red satin, just like Maman's. But the puppet was made of wood. She was not soft to touch, and did not smell of French perfume like Maman.

Now *he* could play the puppet master. He could pull a string here and make this one jump with joy, or slacken a string there and make that one collapse in sorrow. A snatch of music entered his head. It could be fun. And later, when it was finished—he would go home, to Maman and Papa.

The boy parted the drapes, climbed off the sill, and went over to the desk. He dipped a pen in the inkwell, and wrote a few notes in the little book. Yes. He *would* tell what he had just heard. It was the right thing to do. But not yet. No. Not quite yet.

PART I

The Amorous Butterfly

One

Tuesday, April 18, 1786

Four acts. Fourteen arias—twelve complete, two more to write.
I waited as a cart laden with firewood trundled by, then I
crossed the busy square. *All six duets are finished.* I turned the
corner and began to pick my way down the dung-strewn
street. *Three long ensemble pieces, one for each act except for—*
    "Sir! Take care!"
    I looked up. Two enormous black beasts hurtled toward
me. My walking stick clattered to the ground as I threw myself against the wall of the nearest building. I clung to the
cool, hard stone as the carriage raced by.
    When the pounding of the horses' hooves had receded, I
reached down and retrieved my stick. My cloak was splashed
with dark stains. I raised the right sleeve to my nose and
sniffed. At least it was only mud. Sighing, I calculated how

much it would cost to have my cloak cleaned. There are days when I hate this city.

I've lived in Vienna for almost five years, but I've yet to become accustomed to the traffic. There seems to be a horse for every person in the city, and a vehicle for every two. The narrow streets are filled to overflowing with the gilded carriages of wealthy noblemen, the sturdier coaches used by bureaucrats and merchants, and the rickety wagons driven by laborers and peddlers. As a foot traveler, I put my life in jeopardy every time I leave my lodging house.

Lately, I've found myself longing for Venice more and more—for its dense maze of alleys and passageways; its serpentine canals; its broad, light-filled piazzas, where people from all walks of life mingle. The pace of life there is more civilized. But I could not go back. Vienna was my home now, and I was obliged to make the best of the opportunities Fortune had presented me.

It was with great relief that I turned into the small street where Johann Vogel had his barber establishment. When I reached the shop at the end of the street, though, the door was closed, the shutters drawn over the windows. I frowned. It was unlike Vogel to close on a weekday, especially when there was plenty of business to be had from the bureaucrats who toiled in the Hofburg offices a few blocks away. Vogel's establishment was popular among the Viennese. He was one of the new breed of men in the city who had left positions with the court or with noble houses in order to offer their services to the public in small shops and offices.

I knocked on the door with my walking stick. "Vogel!" There was no response. "Vogel! Are you there? It's Lorenzo

Da Ponte." No response. Damn. I scratched my chin. I desperately needed a shave. The deathly quiet of the shop was unusual. On a normal day one could hear the barber singing in his loud bass all the way down the street. Vogel was a burly, jovial man who would do anything for his customers. If you desired a new wig and did not want to pay the prices charged by the *friseurs*, he could find you a cheap one; if you were ill and needed to be bled, he could provide leeches at a low cost, sparing you the expense of calling on a surgeon.

I knocked and called one last time, and when there was no answer, turned to leave. I had not taken but two steps when a low moan came from inside the shop. I stopped. A moment later, another moan, followed by what sounded like a loud sob. I returned to the door and pressed my ear against it, but all was quiet once more.

"Vogel! Are you in there? What is wrong?"

A loud shuffling sound came from behind the door. A moment later, the bolt was drawn back and the door opened a crack. I could not see anything within, for the interior of the shop was pitch-black, and the sun in the street too bright. I pushed the door open with my walking stick and entered. The one-room shop was quiet and cool. A loud thump came from the edge of the room, followed by a thud. As my eyes adjusted from the sunshine outside, I made out the heavy form of my barber slumped in a chair in the back corner. I dropped my stick and soiled cloak on the floor and hurried toward him.

"Vogel? What is it? What is wrong?"

His head sagged as he clutched his arms together over

his chest and rocked back and forth, moaning loudly. I leaned over him and placed a hand on his shoulder.

"Are you ill? Shall I send for a physician?" I asked.

He ceased his rocking and looked up at me. Fat tears coursed down his cheeks. He drew a large handkerchief from his pocket and blew his nose. "Oh, Signor Abbé. It is terrible." He took a deep breath and began to weep again. "I have lost my shop, signore."

"What do you mean?" I looked around me. The small room had been stripped almost bare. The shelves contained none of the customary gleaming bottles of tonics and lotions, and the barber's chair in the center of the room—the latest model, Vogel's pride and joy—sat lonely in the shop, draped with a large cloth.

"I don't understand," I said. "I thought business was good."

Vogel blew into the handkerchief again. "Yes, it is," he said. "But I am only making enough money to cover the rent and my living expenses, and to put a little bit by toward my wedding day."

"Then how have you lost the shop?" I asked.

He stretched his arms in front of him and looked down at his hands. Even in the dim light, I could see his face reddening. "I am going to prison, Signor Abbé," he whispered.

"Prison! What have you done?"

"Debtor's prison, signore." He looked up at me. "I borrowed some money from a lady in order to start up the shop. Now she wants full payment, and I cannot—" His voice broke. "I cannot pay her." He began to weep again. The handkerchief dropped to the floor.

My heart swelled with compassion for him. "What do you

THE AMOROUS BUTTERFLY → 11

need?" I asked. "I have a bit of money set by. I could cover the loan for you and you could repay me at your leisure."

"Oh, Signor Abbé, you are truly a man of God," Vogel said, grasping my hands. "But it is too late. The lady has already received a judgment against me. I am to go to prison today."

"Surely if I paid her, she would petition the court to reverse the judgment. How much do you owe her?"

He reached to the floor and picked up the handkerchief. "Four hundred and ninety-two florins, signore," he muttered.

I winced. That was nearly my annual salary as poet to the Court Theater. "I'm sorry, Vogel," I said. "I'm afraid I can't handle that much. How long is your sentence?"

"One whole year," he said, shuddering. "Now I will not be able to marry my Marianne. While I am locked away, she will find another man." He buried his large face in his hands and sobbed.

I placed a hand on each of his wide shoulders. "Try to compose yourself. There must be something we can do to prevent this," I said.

Vogel pulled away from me and rooted through his pockets, drawing out another handkerchief. "There is nothing to be done, signore," he said, blowing his nose again. He sighed. "I thought I had found a way to get the money, but if I am in prison—"

"A business deal?" I asked.

He shook his head. "No, nothing like that. You see, signore, my mother died last week."

"I'm so sorry."

"Thank you, Signor Abbé. In a way, it was a blessing that

God took her. She had been suffering for a very long time," he said. He stood up and reached for a cloth that sat upon a nearby pile of boxes. "Oh, it is a long story, signore. I shouldn't keep you from your business."

"Do you have time to give me a shave?" I asked. "You could tell me about it while you worked."

He nodded, crossed to the front of the shop, and opened the shutters. The afternoon sun flooded the forlorn room. He pulled the cloth off the barber's chair and invited me to sit. "Give me a moment, signore, to heat some water."

As he headed out the back door of the shop, I moved my cloak and stick to the top of a pile of boxes and settled into the chair. "Who is the lady who lent you the money?" I asked as he returned with a bowl of water. He placed a cape around my neck and pushed the chair into a reclining position.

"She is called Rosa Hahn," he said. He dipped a cloth in the water and placed it over my face. The warmth seeped into my skin. "She is the housekeeper where I used to work, the Palais Gabler."

I nodded as he pressed the cloth around my face. After a few seconds, he removed it, rolled up his shirtsleeves, and covered my face with lather. "Hold still, signore." I relaxed as the rhythmic scraping of the razor plied my skin. "You may remember, I used to work as valet to Baron Gabler. My fiancée, Marianne, is lady's maid to the baroness. When I decided to open the shop, Miss Hahn was eager to lend me the money. She is an older woman, never married. I'll admit, I flirted with her a little to get the loan." He sighed. "I should never have taken the money from her, I know. But I told myself the loan would be a good investment for her."

A warm tear hit my cheek as he began to weep again. He leaned his head down to wipe his eyes on his shirtsleeve. "I had no idea the cost of running a business would be so high. I have not been able to pay Miss Hahn on schedule. Both Marianne and I pleaded for more time, but she refused."

"But I don't understand," I said. "How does all this concern the death of your mother?"

"Turn your head a bit, signore." He pressed my head against his burly bare arm. I studied a large purple birthmark just below his elbow. His forearm was covered with large freckles. Coarse hair tickled my nose, and I fought back the urge to sneeze.

"As my mother lay dying, she told me that I was not her natural son. She and my father had adopted me as a newborn, thirty years ago."

"What? They had told you nothing about it all that time?" I asked.

"Not a word. I was shocked, of course. I tried to ask about my real parents, but by then, she was too far gone to answer my questions. I doubt that she even heard me." His deep voice broke. I reached over and patted his free hand. "She passed away the next morning. When I was cleaning out her things, I found something odd." He replaced the damp cloth, now cool, on my face. I heard his heavy steps cross the room.

"You see, signore—this box." I pulled the cloth off my face and sat upright. Vogel was holding a plain carton the size of a lady's hat box. "I found this hidden deep in the cupboard where my mother kept her change of clothes." He thrust the box toward me. "I believe this belonged to my birth mother. The contents look valuable."

I reached for the box. A loud knock sounded at the door. Vogel started. The box fell onto my lap.

"Johann Vogel! Police! Open up!"

The barber began to tremble. "Oh no, Signor Abbé, they are here to take me to prison." He had picked up the cloth I had removed from my face, and now began to wring it between his large hands. "Please, signore, please. Help me."

I took the cloth from him and wiped the remaining lather off my face. "But what can I do?" I asked.

The pounding at the door resumed, this time much louder.

"You know so many important people, signore," he said quickly. "You are educated, cultured. I am sure my real parents were rich, perhaps even of noble birth. Could you find them for me?"

My mouth dropped. Nobles? "But that seems like an impossible assignment," I said. "Do you know anything at all about them?"

"No, signore. I just have the things in this box."

"Vogel, open up! Now!"

"Please, Signor Da Ponte, take it and see what you can find." He hurried to the door and flung it open. Two constables entered.

"You are Johann Vogel?" one asked.

The barber stifled a sob. "Yes, I am."

"Take your things and come with us."

Vogel took a deep breath. "I am almost ready. Please, sirs, let me finish with my last customer." He returned to the chair and leaned over me, wiping my face with a dry cloth. "Please, Signor Abbé." He lowered his voice. "Please, you are a kind and generous man. Take the box. Go to the Palais Gabler and speak to my fiancée, Marianne Haiml. She will tell you everything we know."

"But I have no idea where to begin," I protested. "And the odds of finding your parents after all these years are slim."

"Please, signore. At least talk to Marianne. I feel in my heart that my parents are still alive, and that they are rich."

One of the constables grabbed Vogel's arm and pulled him toward the door.

"Wait, I need my bag," Vogel cried, pointing to a large gripsack sitting in the corner. The other constable heaved a sigh and lifted the bag. As the three reached the door, Vogel turned and looked back at me. "Please, signore. I will give you ten percent of any money I get from my parents, if you find them for me."

My heart surged with pity as I stared into his broad, decent face. Words came out of my mouth before my brain had a chance to advise caution. "All right, I will see what I can find. But do not get your hopes up too much. Your parents may both have died in the last thirty years."

"I know, I know. But I must try to find them," Vogel said. The constables pulled him outside. I grabbed my cloak and stick, hefted the box, and followed them out, closing the door behind me. Vogel nodded down at the pocket of his coat. I pulled out the key to the shop.

"Keep it for me, Signor Abbé," he said. "Please. Go tomorrow, talk to Marianne. Find out what you can. My life's happiness depends on you!"

"Come on already!" The constables pulled Vogel down the street to a waiting carriage.

"Wait, Vogel!" I called. "I did not pay you for the shave!"

He turned toward me. "It is an honor to shave you, signore," he shouted. "You can pay me by finding my real parents."

"But wait—are you sure your mother never told you anything—"

The constables pushed him into the carriage, threw his bag after him, and jumped in. The door slammed, and a moment later the carriage rolled away. The street was silent again. I placed the box on the ground and locked the door to the shop. A pang of anxiety shot through me. What had I gotten myself into? I did not have time to investigate this fantastic notion of Vogel's. I was up to my ears in work. I sighed. The poor man was desperate. I wanted to do anything I could to help him. I pocketed the key, picked up the box, and walked slowly down the street.

The Graben was busy as I headed toward my lodgings. Long and wide, lined with apartment buildings, the street was the gathering place for fashionable Vienna. I joined the throng, this time taking care to stay close to the buildings so as to avoid the fancy carriages taking the fine ladies out to the Prater, the popular park at the northeast edge of the city. The crowd was mixed: government workers heading back to their desks after dinner; lackeys in the liveries of the great houses running errands for their masters; and minor noblemen dressed à la mode, hoping to see and be seen by the rest of society. Around me I heard chattering not only in German and French, but also in Italian, Greek, Polish, and Magyar.

I passed the Trattnerhof, the most famous address in Vienna. It was a large apartment house, built by a wealthy businessman who had come to the city as an inconsequential printer thirty years before, earned the favor of Empress Maria Theresa, and become the official publisher of all of the schoolbooks in the Holy Roman Empire. Trattner's publishing empire now encompassed five printing plants, a paper factory, and eight bookshops. He entertained the cream of society in his personal apartment, which took up the entire second floor of the building. I gazed up at the façade, which was decorated with what to my eye seemed an excess of furbelows. Two huge telamones flanked the doorway, and high above the street, a row of tall statues on the balustrade watched to make certain that passersby bestowed upon the building the admiration to which it was entitled.

A few minutes later, I turned into the portal of my own, more modest building. After arranging with my landlord's wife to have my cloak and handkerchief cleaned, I climbed the stairs to the fourth floor. My salary at the Court Theater, where I was responsible for editing all the librettos— the texts—of the operas performed and for coordinating production details, was a decent amount, and I was able to embellish it by selling libretto booklets at performances and by taking on commissions to write operas myself. Nevertheless, Vienna was an expensive city—a pair of silk stockings cost five florins!—so I tried to cut my costs as much as possible. I would much have preferred to live on a more desirable floor lower in the building, but the rents were very high, so I did not allow myself to complain about the long climb of four flights of stairs I made several times a day.

I unlocked the door and crossed the small room to place Vogel's box on my writing desk. The girl who cleaned for me had already been in to make up the bed, sweep, and refill the water jug on my basin cabinet. I selected a few pages of the libretto I was writing and stuffed them into my satchel, then pulled Vogel's box toward me and took off the lid.

I gasped. Was this some sort of prank? Was my barber trying to make a fool of me, with his sad tale of missing parents? I stared into the box. A white, furry dead animal lay curled inside. I forced myself to lean down and sniff. There was no foul odor, so I took a deep breath and plunged my hands into the box, pulling out the unfortunate beast. To my surprise, it was very light. I quickly threw it onto my desk and examined it, then laughed in relief. It was not a dead animal at all, but a fancy lady's muff. I picked it up and turned the silky fur around in my hands. The muff, colored a pristine white, looked expensive.

I reached into the box and pulled out a small book. Its leather cover was soft and worn, mottled with dark spots. The book's spine was engraved with tiny golden fleurs-de-lis, but displayed no title. As I opened it and gently turned the pages, the familiar musty aroma wafted toward my nose. I sneezed. The book was a French grammar, of the type students use when learning the language at school. I had purchased one myself when I first came to Vienna, for everyone connected with the court and high society conversed in French instead of German. I turned to the frontispiece, then to the inside back cover, but could find no writing to indicate the owner of the book, nor even the date on which it had been published.

The remaining object in the box was a small ring, its band

dull and discolored, but possibly solid gold. A pronged setting held a small, rosy gem in the shape of a heart. A diamond? A betrothal ring, perhaps? I studied the inside of the band for engraving, but could see nothing because of the discoloration. I ran my finger lightly around the inside, but felt nothing but smooth metal. I laid the ring on my desk and considered the three objects. Perhaps Vogel's idea about his parents was not as far-fetched as I had believed. A muff of fine fur, possibly white fox; a leather-bound book; and a gold and diamond ring: these had surely been the possessions of a wealthy lady, a countess perhaps, or even a princess.

Questions tumbled through my brain. What had led such a woman to give up her newborn son? Why had she chosen to give him to the Vogel couple, people of humble origins? And why had she sent these valuable items along with the babe? Had she hoped that someday he might try to find her?

I returned the muff to the box and ran my fingers over the worn leather cover of the book. I did not remember much about my own mother, who had died giving birth to my youngest brother thirty-two years ago, when I was only five years old. Yet even today, when I hear a certain lilt in a woman's voice or see her lips form a soft smile, I feel a stirring of recognition, an awakening of an inchoate, bittersweet emotion deep within me.

The bell in St. Peter's Church next door chimed the hour. I started. I had grown so intrigued by Vogel's mystery that I had lost track of the time. I had work to do at the theater. I laid the book and ring on top of the muff and replaced the lid on the box. I pulled my second cloak, a frayed one I usually saved for bad winter weather, from the cupboard, stuffed a clean handkerchief in its pocket, took up my satchel and stick, and descended to the street.

The street had quieted while I had been up in my room. The government workers had returned to their offices, the ladies had vacated the city for an afternoon of pastoral recreation, and the rest of Vienna was sleeping off their dinners. At four o'clock, the promenade would begin anew, but for now, I and a few stragglers were able to walk about in peace.

I quickly made my way down the Kohlmarkt to the Michaelerplatz, the heart of imperial Vienna. At this hour the large expanse was almost empty. To my left, the stately portico of St. Michael's Church was deserted, its tall wooden doors closed. In front of me, the monumental dome of the Spanish Riding School marked the threshold to the great halls, apartments, courtyards, and gardens of the Hofburg, the emperor's residence and home to the government of the empire. Nestled under the dome was my destination, my place of employment, the Court Theater.

Two men in their mid-sixties stood in front of the theater's doorway, deep in discussion. They had not seen me. I lowered my head and took a sharp right, hoping to skirt the edge of the plaza and duck down a side street until they had left.

"Signor Da Ponte! Signor Poet!" a high, nasal voice called.

I groaned. Damn. There was nothing I could do but turn back. I approached the pair and bowed to the taller of the two. This was Count Franz Xavier Rosenberg, high chamberlain to the emperor and also, more important to me, the director of the Court Theater, and thus my supervisor. His steely eyes took me in from head to toe. He grimaced slightly as his eyes alighted on my shabby cloak. He himself wore a deep purple court suit cut in the latest fashion, the coat made of fine satin. He graced me with a curt nod.

"Tell us, Signor Poet, how is your latest project proceeding?" the nasal voice asked. "The opera with Mozart?"

I struggled to keep dislike from showing on my face as I turned to the speaker, the Abbé Giambattista Casti, my most guileful enemy. Like me, Casti was a poet and a priest. Unlike me, he had enjoyed a celebrated career all over Europe. Monarchs, aristocrats, and connoisseurs of modern poetry delighted in his satirical style and the lubricious subject matter of his rhymes. After many years at the courts of St. Petersburg and Tuscany, he had settled in Vienna a few years ago, hoping to use his friendship with Count Rosenberg to win a post with the emperor.

"It is going very well, signore," I said. "We have dress rehearsal in two weeks."

"Is Mozart pleased with your translation of the Beaumarchais play?" Casti asked.

As I took a moment to measure my response, I studied him. His wispy hair was uncombed, and as usual, he wore a rumpled satin cloak. A long, dark hair sprouted from a mole on his right cheek. "I am not translating the play, signore," I said. "I am adapting it. You see the difference, I am sure?"

"Adapting it? Like you did for your last libretto, the one for Martín? What was it called, *The Grumpy Curmudgeon*?"

My cheeks grew hot. My opera with the Spanish composer Martín had been a hit just a few months ago. Casti knew the correct title perfectly well. *The Good-Hearted Grump,*" I said.

"Ah, yes. A nice translation of the Goldoni play, but would you really call your work original?"

I glanced at Rosenberg as I fought to bite back a retort. The theater director's face was expressionless, but I saw a gleam of amusement in his eyes. "The public loved my libretto, signore. As you recall, that opera sold out every performance."

Casti fixed his beady eyes on me. "You are right, it did. Martín is a very talented composer for one so young. His music was sublime."

"I believe—"

Rosenberg coughed. "I trust you and Mozart are taking care with the text," he said. "The emperor was reluctant to allow you to use that play."

"Yes, *Figaro* was a sensation in Paris," Casti said. "I've read it. The emperor was wise to ban its performance here."

Mozart and I had written an opera based on the most notorious play on the Continent—Beaumarchais's *The Marriage of Figaro.* In the play, a nobleman carries on affairs with his female servants while his wife flirts with a teenage boy. A servant openly expresses his belief that he is the social equal of his master. The emperor had allowed the play to be printed in Vienna, but had banned its performance in any of the city's theaters because of its vulgarity and impropriety.

"I've cut all the objectionable parts out," I said to the count. My voice grew tighter. "We are focusing on the human aspect of the material—the characters' yearnings for love and respect, for reconciliation and forgiveness." Rosenberg just stared at me.

"Ah! The human aspect!" Casti said. "Yes, I see now." He sighed. "I hope the emperor isn't disappointed with the final product. You must admit, you and Mozart took a great risk deciding to write the opera without his prior approval."

Mozart and I had been so sure we could make a successful, acceptable opera out of Beaumarchais's play that we had written it without a commission. My enemies have big ears and mouths, however, and one went running to the emperor with the tale of our deed. I had been summoned to explain myself and I had described the libretto to him, and then had sent for Mozart, who had played some of the arias he had already completed. The emperor had been delighted with our work and had ordered Rosenberg to put the opera on the theater schedule. It had been a bad day for Casti and Rosenberg.

"As I said, I've read the play," Casti continued. "It seems to be challenging material from which to make a comic opera."

As if Casti knew what made good theater! In my position as theater poet, I am the first to read librettos that are to be performed. I had read several of Casti's. He had an elegant style, to be sure. His lyrics were beautifully worded and sparkled with wit. But his plots dragged, his dramatic structures were absurd, and his characters were clichéd. I strained to hold my temper, and bit off the snide retort that was forming on my lips.

"Thank you for your concern—"

"Be careful, Da Ponte," Rosenberg said. "Remember, you are on shaky ground with this opera. I worry that your career here won't survive another debacle like the one with Salieri."

I tightened my fingers around my stick. Antonio Salieri was the court composer. My first assignment had been to write a libretto for an opera to be composed by Maestro Salieri. I had heard he was a gentleman of good taste and artistic discernment, so I had proposed a number of possible subjects and left him to choose. Unfortunately for the opera and for me, he had selected the work that was the least suitable for adaptation to opera—a play called *Rich for a Day*.

Casti nodded. "Yes, *Rich for a Day* lasted only one poor night in the theater." He tittered. A glob of spittle had formed at the corner of his mouth.

"That play was extremely difficult to adapt," I snapped. "There were not enough characters. The plot was much too slender to fill two hours of theater!" I had worked on the libretto for several excruciating weeks, only to have Salieri request "minor changes" that involved deleting most of the plot that I had created. The composer had then set what remained of my verses to that shrieky music he had admired on a recent trip to Paris. It was then that I had learned the most important truth about theater in Vienna: if an opera is a smash, the libretto is considered, at best, a frame surrounding a beautiful painting. The composer receives all the credit. The words are unimportant. But if the opera is not well received, why, then the words become paramount—in fact, so very important that they can cause the failure of the work all by themselves!

Casti looked at me with feigned sympathy. "How unfortunate for you, Signor Poet, that the court composer looks elsewhere for his librettos. How long has it been since you last worked together? Four years?"

I clenched my teeth. My hands began to shake. "It's not my fault—"

"Gentlemen, gentlemen, please," Rosenberg said.

After *Rich for a Day* had quickly closed, Salieri had sworn that he would never work with me again. I had heard from friends that Rosenberg had advised the emperor to dismiss me and appoint Casti to my post. My beloved sovereign would not play the game, however. He encouraged me to try again, and since then, I've had a few successes, most notably my recent collaboration with Martín. I hoped that my opera with Mozart would erase Vienna's long memory of my failure with Salieri.

"Thank you for your concern," I said to Casti. "I'm sure my new opera will be a success." I bowed to the count. "If you will excuse me, sir." He nodded his dismissal, and the two started off toward the Hofburg next door.

As I opened the heavy door to the theater, Casti's high voice rang out, mocking me. "I'm thure my new opera will be a thuccess." Rosenberg laughed.

I stood in the empty foyer of the theater, trembling with anger. I took a deep breath to calm myself. I needed to get to work. *Figaro* must succeed. I couldn't bear another failure.

Two

The next morning I rose early, hoping to call on Vogel's fiancée before she started work. The sun was shining as I crossed the Graben to my favorite coffeehouse, where I found a seat at one of the long, crowded tables. I liked this establishment because it was frequented by government clerks and merchants, not theater people, so I could enjoy breakfast without the need to engage in idle chatter or gossip with my colleagues. Most of the patrons today were either talking quietly with their neighbors or had hidden themselves behind various newspapers. I nodded greetings to a few of my fellow regulars and ordered coffee and a roll from the harried waiter.

I reached across the table for a pile of political pamphlets that had been left behind by a previous customer. The emperor was an enthusiastic disciple of the liberal ideas spread by the French *philosophes*. One of his first acts upon ascending to the throne had been to eliminate government censorship of the press. The result had been a steady stream of monographs from the city's printers, most either praising or condemning the emperor's ambitious reform program.

A serving boy brought me a bowl of coffee and a large crescent roll. As I blew on the brew to cool it a bit, I shuffled through the pile of pamphlets, studying the titles. "The Emperor Must Restore Pensions!" shouted one in large typeface. Before she died, the old empress had bestowed generous lifetime pensions on thousands of aides, servants, favored ladies, and the other flunkies who cling like barnacles to the rich and powerful. One of the emperor's first acts had been to revoke them all, for fear that they might drain the treasury dry.

I tore off a small piece of soft roll and chewed it. It was freshly baked, buttery and yeasty, with the proper hint of cinnamon. I sipped my coffee and ate small bites of the roll as I took up another pamphlet. Titled "Equal Punishment for the Modern Era," it praised the emperor's reform of criminal law. Under the empress, aristocrats had not been subject to the same severe punishment for crimes as were the middle class and peasantry. I had heard about several cases where a nobleman had committed theft, fraud, or even murder, and had escaped trial. Since the emperor's reforms, everyone was subject to the same penalties for commission of a crime.

I took a final sip of my coffee and rooted around in my pocket for some coins. As I placed them on the table, a voice shouted behind me.

"I'm telling you—Joseph is a follower of Luther!"

I swiveled in my seat to find the source of the noise. Two corpulent men in expensive suits, merchants by the look of them, sat two tables away from me. One of them, most likely the one who had shouted, was red in the face.

"Keep your voice down," his companion said. "That's nonsense. The emperor is merely holding the modern view. People of all faiths should be free to practice their religions."

"But to let Protestants have the same rights as Catholics?" Red Face sputtered. "It's an abomination! Why should they be allowed to join our guilds, or to own property? Why, one snatched a warehouse I was eyeing right from under me, just last month!" He grunted. "Most of them weren't even born here!"

"You're looking at it the wrong way," his friend said. "Joseph was smart to order toleration of the Protestants. We need people from other parts of the empire to move here to Vienna. You've said yourself that the Protestant areas are filled with skilled laborers."

Red Face opened his mouth to speak. His friend held up his hand to stop him.

"Our economy needs these people. We have to give them the same privileges we Catholics enjoy, so they will be loyal to the emperor. Don't worry. Our religion will always be the official religion, and no Protestant can hold a position in the government."

Red Face laughed. "You and Joseph both—you are so naïve, Hans! These people are not loyal to Joseph. They worship Frederick, the King of Prussia. The emperor is just asking for trouble, I tell you. The religions shouldn't mix. And I still think he is a secret Protestant." He waved away his companion's protests. "Don't even waste your breath trying to convince me otherwise."

I snorted to myself as I reached for my cloak, satchel, and stick. I knew the emperor well, and there was no better Catholic in all of Europe. I shook my head as I left the coffee-house. I admired my sovereign's attempts to bring the empire into the modern age, but he really shouldn't allow people to make such ridiculous, undeserved criticisms of him.

The morning had warmed, and my cloak felt heavy as I walked through the marketplace in the Freyung, where the cooks of the great houses were fastidiously selecting food-stuffs and piling their purchases into the waiting arms of small kitchen boys. A few moments later, I entered the most fashionable part of the city. The quiet streets were lined with the homes of wealthy noblemen and merchants—solid, heavy mansions trimmed with an extravagance of columns, cartouches, and corbels; pedestals, pilasters, and paterae. At the end of a small side street I found the Palais Gabler. I laughed as I studied the building. In Venice, only the magnificent homes of the doge and the bishop were called "palaces." The rest, no matter how large, luxurious, or expensive, were designated merely as "casas"—houses. Here in Vienna every nobleman called his home a "palais," whether it was a truly grand mansion or just a large residence, as was the case here.

The façade, made of stone the pale yellow color of French champagne, was designed in the restrained style that had become popular over the last ten years or so. Simple milky-white pilasters alternated with tall windows beneath an entablature tastefully decorated with floral-engraved cartouches.

I walked through the central archway into a courtyard paved with cobblestone. The white accent color of the street façade was prominent here, but there were no ornaments except for a row of small quatrefoil windows that lined the building directly beneath the roof. Below them were two stories of large windows, several of which stood open to the fresh spring air. A small fountain set into the left-hand corner of the courtyard bubbled gaily in the morning sun. Directly ahead of me was a large wooden door topped with a plain stone arch. To my right was a smaller door, reserved for tradesmen and servants. I hesitated for a moment, shook my head, and knocked at the main door.

Several moments passed. I knocked again and then again. Finally, as I was about to turn away, the door was dragged open by a girl in her mid-teens. She wore a fashionable English-style housemaid's uniform, but her apron was crooked, and her straw-colored curls had been hastily tucked under her cap. The top ribbons on her bodice were undone, and I could see the curve of her right breast, which had become loosened from her undergarments. She stared at me blankly with sapphire-blue eyes.

"Good morning. I would like to see Miss Marianne Haiml, please," I said. I fought the urge to stare at her breast.

"Marianne?" Her voice was breathy. "Yes, please, sir, come in."

I stepped inside and looked around me while she pushed the door closed. The foyer was small and intimate, its floor inlaid with black-and-white stone in a checkerboard pattern, its walls covered with pale gold brocade silk. A large mirror, set in a wooden frame simply painted with pale green and gold flowers, hung on the wall to my left. Below it sat a simple bench of white marble. The girl motioned for me to precede her up the stairs. I mounted a few steps. When I did not hear her behind me, I turned. She stood in front of the mirror, tidying her bodice. As I watched, she leaned forward to peer into the glass. Obviously pleased with what she saw there, she gave a small smile. I wondered what kind of household the Baroness Gabler ran, that she would allow such a disheveled, odd girl to open the door to guests.

I coughed, and she turned quickly, picked up her skirts, and ran past me up the stairs.

"This way, sir," she said. At the top of the stairs, she turned to the left. I followed her down a short passage to a closed door. "You may wait in here, sir," she said. "I will send Marianne." She turned and ran down the hall before I could pull off my cloak and hand it to her. I turned the knob and entered the room, leaving the door ajar, and sighed with pleasure. I was in the baron's library, a large room paneled in dark wood, its walls lined with tall bookcases. To my left was a wall of tall windows with deep, high wooden sills and heavy drapes of soft golden velvet. The middle two windows stood open, letting in the morning sun, which danced off the leather-and-gilt bindings of the books on the shelves. To my right, a fireplace with a marble mantel carved with rosettes sat cold. I dropped my cloak on one of the richly brocaded armchairs, placed my satchel and stick on the floor, and began to peruse the baron's collection.

"Where are you, you—"

I jumped as a man ran into the room. He stopped in surprise when he noticed me. "Oh, I beg your pardon," he said. "I did not know anyone was here." He looked at me with friendly, curious eyes set in a square face. He appeared to be a few years older than me, and was about the same height. His accent was Italian, one that had been changed by many years living in Vienna. "Are you waiting to speak to the baron?" he asked.

"No, I am here to see Miss Haiml," I said.

"Marianne?" He came over to me and extended his hand, peering into my face. "I am Tomaso Piatti. Forgive me, have we met before?"

I shook his hand. "I don't believe so. My name is Lorenzo Da Ponte."

He held on to my hand, and shook it up and down once more. "Da Ponte? The theater poet? I knew you looked familiar! I've seen you at the theater." He continued to pump my hand up and down. "Signore, it is an honor to meet you! I saw your latest opera, *The Good-Hearted Grump*—why, I have never laughed so hard. Martín's music, of course, was wonderful, but your libretto—it was masterful."

My cheeks warmed with pleasure at his praise.

"Come, signore, sit, sit." He finally let go of my hand, and pointed me toward a small sofa. "No one has offered you anything? Let me ring." He pulled a rope hanging on the wall next to the fireplace.

"I am fine, thank you," I said, as I settled onto the soft sofa.

"But what are you doing here? Are you planning to use Marianne in your next opera?" His eyes twinkled.

I laughed. "No. I am here with a message from her fiancé."

He sobered. "Oh yes, poor Vogel. He used to work here. We were great friends. He was very helpful to me, helping

me move instruments and set up for recitals. I am the director of music for the household, you see. I teach the baroness, and arrange concerts here in the house, when the baron
entertains."

"From where in Italy do you come?" I asked.

"Bologna. I grew up there and was fortunate to attend the
conservatory there." He drew up his shoulders. "It is world
famous—I'm sure you have heard of it."

I nodded.

"When I finished my studies, twenty years ago already,
I came to Vienna to make my name as a composer. Perhaps
you have heard some of my work?"

I shook my head.

"Most of it is for the church service."

Then I certainly wouldn't have heard any of it, I thought.
A slight cough sounded at the door. I turned to see a tall,
handsome middle-aged woman wearing a dress of plain gray
linen, decorated only with a crisp white collar. The skin on
her thin face was pale and almost flawless, not covered by
the cosmetics most women of her age used. The few lines
around her mouth were set in a disapproving frown.

"Rosa!" Piatti gestured toward me. "This is Signor Da
Ponte. He has come to see Marianne and was left alone in
here. The girl did not take his cloak or offer any refreshment."

I pulled myself to my feet.

The woman eyed him coldly for a moment and turned
to me. "I apologize for Antonia, sir. I am Rosa Hahn, the
housekeeper here. May I take your cloak?"

Ah, Vogel's creditor. "I am very pleased to meet you,
madame," I said, giving a slight bow. I usually find that the

unexpected courtesy warms women of the lesser ranks, but this one did not thaw. "There is no need to apologize. I will hold my cloak. I only expect to stay a few more minutes."

"Perhaps some coffee and a pastry, Rosa?" Piatti asked.

A flash of anger crossed her face so quickly that I thought I might have imagined it. She gave Piatti a tight smile. "Oh, I am sorry, Signor Piatti. The baroness has been ringing for you for ten minutes now. She is ready for her lesson, and sent me to find you."

I saw a gleam of satisfaction in her eyes as Piatti reddened and glared at her. "Yes, well, then," he said, turning to me and offering his hand. "Signore, it was a pleasure to meet you. Perhaps we could meet and talk some other time? I would love to hear about your work."

I shook his hand. "Of course. You can find me most days at my office in the theater. Anyone who is about can direct you."

He smiled. "I will look forward to it." He bowed, and with a final glare at the housekeeper, left the room, closing the door loudly behind him.

Rosa Hahn looked after him, gave a grim smile, and turned to me with a puzzled expression on her face. "You are waiting for Marianne, sir?" she asked.

Before I could answer, the door opened, and a young woman entered. My mouth dropped at the sight of her. My eyes took in soft, light brown curls framing a face ornamented with clear, intelligent eyes; a long, thin nose; and soft, pink lips. She wore a dress in the English fashion, probably a cast-off from her mistress, with no apron or cap to betray her status as a servant. A scooped neckline trimmed with white lace framed her lovely white throat, and drew my eyes to her vivacious bosom. My gaze traveled the pale green silk down to her narrow waist. From there, a green and yellow striped skirt cascaded over her shapely hips, ending at her thin, well-turned ankles, covered in white silk stockings. Finally, my eyes rested on her small feet, which were clad in yellow satin slippers dyed to match the skirt.

She came to me and curtsied. "I am Marianne. You asked to see me, sir?"

Before I could reply, the housekeeper grabbed her arm and pulled her toward the door. "Should you be entertaining a guest in the library, Miss Haiml?" she hissed.

Marianne's eyes widened. Her cheeks flushed. She opened her mouth to speak, but quickly clamped it shut. She took a deep breath and said, "I did not invite him here, Miss Hahn. Antonia told me only that I was wanted in the library."

The older woman stared at her. "Next time, remember your place. This is the baron's library. You are a servant in this house, despite your inappropriate friendliness with the baroness. You would be wise not to forget that." She released her grasp on Marianne's arm, bade me good day, and departed.

Marianne closed the door. "Decrepit old bat," she muttered under her breath. She turned to me.

"Are you the Abbé Da Ponte? Johann told me you would be coming to see me." Warmth surged through my chest as she smiled at me.

"Have you seen him? How is he?" I asked.

Her smile faded. She bit on her lower lip. "I saw him last

evening, signore. He is very upset. I could tell he was trying not to cry in front of me. But the prison isn't as bad as I expected it would be. His room is clean, and there is only one other man with him." Her mouth turned down in disgust. "The food looked awful, though."

I nodded toward the closed door. "That was the lady who has put him there?"

She sat on the sofa and beckoned to me to join her. "Yes. I warned Johann not to borrow any money from her, but he wouldn't listen. He was too excited about starting the shop."

"It does seem like a great deal of money," I said.

"Yes. But he needed that much—the rent is very high, even for that one little room. And he had big plans. He wanted to have shops all over the city, with barbers working for him. I told him to wait until the first shop made some money, but he didn't want to. He tends to jump into things," she said, chewing on her lip. "Miss Hahn offered him the money at a low interest rate, and he couldn't resist. I told him she was after more than just a return on her investment. I knew she wanted him." She laughed. "Imagine, an old crone like her thinking she could interest Johann!"

"What led to the court suit?"

"Johann spent all the money getting the shop set up. He bought that fancy chair, and ordered all sorts of lotions and—what are they called?—pomades to sell. In the beginning it took a while for customers to find him. And not everyone likes the idea of going to a shop for a shave." She picked up a porcelain figurine of Harlequin from the small table at the end of the sofa. "He wasn't able to pay the interest to Miss Hahn. At first, she was willing to give him more time, especially when he turned his charms on her." Her lovely face set into a frown. "Whenever he came here to see me, he would bring her a little gift—a posy of flowers, some candies from the market."

"That must have been difficult for you," I said gently.

Her expression changed. "Oh no, I knew what he was doing." She laughed brightly. "Did you think I was jealous? Of her?" She shook her head. "Johann and I were betrothed two months ago. That was when she started to make trouble for us. She demanded that Johann pay all the interest he owed at once, and part of the principal, also. Of course, he couldn't pay any of it. We both tried to talk to her, but she was very rude. She wouldn't even listen. A few days later, Johann got the court summons." She took a deep breath. "You know the rest."

"Do you believe she is willing to pay to keep him in prison the whole year?" I asked. The emperor had reformed the debtor laws, limiting sentences to just one year and replacing the dank, miserable prison with a modern facility. Under the new law, the plaintiff at court was required to pay a fee to cover the cost of incarcerating the debtor. If the plaintiff failed to make regular payments, the prisoner was released.

"She's so hateful toward us, I believe she will," Marianne said sadly. She turned the small figurine in her hands. "Our only hope is to find his real parents—then he will have money to pay her back, and we can marry." She looked up at me through lush brown lashes. "We are both grateful for your help, Signor Abbé."

A deep feeling of warmth and tenderness rushed through

my blood as I looked at her. What a charming young woman! No wonder Vogel was worried about spending a year away from her. I found myself determined to do anything I could to help the unfortunate lovers. I stood and walked over to the fireplace. "Tell me, why is he so certain his parents were aristocrats? Because of the things in the box?"

"Yes," she replied. "I haven't seen them myself, but he told me there was a beautiful jewel and an expensive muff. He also said that all his life, he has felt that he might have some noble blood. His tastes are expensive, and he's always felt he is better than most of the other valets and barbers he has known."

I winced. I often felt that way myself, and I knew for certain that my parents had not a drop of noble blood between them. "Does he have any other evidence to support this idea?" I asked. "I will try to trace the items in the box, but I must warn you, the odds are slim that I will be able to find their owner after all this time."

She hesitated. "Yes, there is one more thing," she said. "I haven't told Johann this. It would only upset him more. There is a boy here—a young man, really, in his teens. He is a page to the baron. His name is Florian Auerstein. His father is Prince Auerstein—perhaps you've heard of him?"

I nodded. The prince was from one of Vienna's oldest families. He owned one of the largest, most opulent palaces in the city, and I had heard that his country home made his dwelling here look like a hut in comparison. He was a patron of many of the composers in the city, and frequented the opera.

"Florian has hinted to me that he has information about

Johann's birth," Marianne continued. "He probably overheard something while he was in his father's house, some rumor about another noble family whose baby was kidnapped and sold for adoption thirty years ago."

"Vogel thinks he was kidnapped from his birth mother?" I was astonished.

"Well, that is the most likely explanation, isn't it?" she asked. "Why would any noble lady have to give up her child for adoption?"

I shook my head in disbelief. "Why hasn't this Florian told you what he has learned?" I asked.

Her cheeks colored. She lowered her eyes and rubbed her finger on the little Harlequin figurine. "He wants me—he wants certain favors from me in exchange for the information," she said in a low voice. She looked up at me, her eyes pleading. "Please, signore, don't tell Johann. He'll be so angry. Perhaps you could talk to Florian? You are much more clever than I. I am sure you can find out what he knows."

My heart stirred again with the desire to help her. "When can I speak to him?" I asked.

"He—"

A bell on the wall jangled loudly.

"Oh! The baroness wants me. I must go." She set the figurine on the table, rose from the sofa, and smoothed her skirt. "I will speak to Florian and find a time for you to return. Where can I reach you?"

I told her my address. She repeated it and ran to the door as the bell clanged again. "Can you find your way out, Signor Abbé?" she asked.

"Of course," I said.

She came to me and took my hand. I bent and kissed hers. She smelled of freshly cut roses. "Please, Signor Da Ponte. You are the only one who can help us. Please find Johann's parents. My happiness is in your hands." She ran out of the room.

I sighed as I watched her go. Vogel was a lucky man! As I turned to take my cloak and stick, my eyes caught the gleaming books on the shelves before me. Surely no one would take offense if I lingered a few moments to survey the collection? I crossed over to the nearest shelf and ran my fingers over a row of books at eye level. The leather felt soft, warm from the sunlight. I smiled when I saw that I had chosen the shelf that contained the baron's poetry collection. I scanned the titles on the book spines: Dante's *Divina Commedia* and *La vita nuova;* Ariosto's *Orlando Furioso;* Tasso's *La Gerusalemme liberata* and a few volumes of his *Rime;* a collection of poems by Metastasio, the imperial poet who had died just after I had arrived in Vienna. I pulled out a volume by Petrarch, my favorite of the great Italian poets.

The beautifully bound book felt substantial in my hands. As I opened it, my mind traveled back to my first experience with the printed word, back in Ceneda, where I had been born. Fathers, of course, are notorious for giving little attention to their young children, but to be fair, after my mother died, mine had spent most of his waking hours toiling in his leatherworking shop in order to feed three young mouths. Thus my younger brothers and I grew into adolescence with little supervision and no formal education. I was a quick-witted child, curious about everything around me, burning for knowledge, yet, I am still ashamed to say, I did not learn to read or write until after age ten. The children in the town snickered at me, calling me "the brilliant dunce." I laughed along with them, but to this day, my cheeks burn when I remember their teasing.

One day, when I was about thirteen, I climbed up to the attic of our small house to explore. To my astonishment, I discovered a treasure trove—a carton of dusty, yellowed books, left there by a previous generation of the family. I dragged the box down to my room and hid it under my bed. Thereafter, I read whenever I had the opportunity. I pored over volumes of medieval romances, collections of country tales, and tomes of ancient history. My favorites, however, were the slim volumes of poetry, which I had studied for hours. I must have read each book in the box four or five times.

The soft rustling of the drape in the window drew me back to the present. I turned to the first page of the Petrarch, and read aloud. "'You who hear in scattered rhymes the sound of these sighs . . .'"

"'You who hear in scattered rhymes the thounds of these thighs,'" a loud voice said. I jumped and turned toward the window.

"Who is there?"

"The thounds of these thighs. The thounds of these thighs," the voice mocked me. I put the book down, crossed to the open window, and pulled back the heavy drape. A slim boy of about sixteen sat cross-legged on the deep sill. He wore the breeches of a livery uniform and a rumpled, untucked white shirt.

"Who are you?" I demanded. "Have you been eavesdropping on me this entire time?"

He grinned. "Yeth, I have," he said. He pushed me aside, climbed down from the sill, and threw himself into an armchair. He tilted his head to one side and studied me.

"What is your name?" I asked.

He raised his voice to mimic mine. "What ith your name?"

I gritted my teeth. "I am Lorenzo Da Ponte. You must be the Auerstein boy—Florian, is it?"

He cocked an eyebrow and grinned again. "Must I be? I think I must be!"

"Why didn't you make yourself known before?" I asked. My right hand balled into a fist. I took a step toward him. "What gives you the right to listen to private conversations?"

He did not answer, but instead jumped out of the chair and darted over to the fireplace. He began to bounce from foot to foot. He was not tall for his age, and his delicately sculpted features and long, curly hair gave him a girlish appearance.

"What do you know about Johann Vogel's parents?" I asked. "Why won't you tell Miss Haiml what you know?"

His mouth curled downward. "She will not play with me," he said sadly.

I fought the urge to go over and shake him. "Aren't you the son of a great prince?" I asked. My voice rose. "It is not very chivalrous to exploit the unhappy fortunes of an innocent woman to gain advantage over her."

He waved his hand in the air and gave me a bemused smile. "She is the one with the advantage over me," he said airily.

"What do you mean?" My voice shook with anger.

"I love her."

My cheeks grew hot. I went over to him and wagged my finger in front of his pert little nose. "You love her! Liar! What do you know of love? You are just a boy. She is a grown woman, engaged to be married."

He wriggled away from me and moved to the sofa. "Yes, she is," he said, "but she cannot marry unless I help her. So she must love me back."

I lunged at him, but he jumped from the sofa and began bouncing around the room, humming a tune I did not recognize. "See here," I said, trying to corner him. "Tell me what you know, so I can help her." I stopped still and put my hands on my hips. "If you really love her, as you say you do, you would want to make her happy."

"Of course I love her!" He threw back his head and whooped. "She is a woman! I love all women!"

My patience with this young fool was nearing its end. "Sit down and speak to me seriously," I snapped. "What have you heard about Vogel's birth mother? Did you overhear some gossip in your father's house? Tell me!"

He stared at me for a moment. A sly smile formed on his lips. "Say, do you like riddles?" he asked.

"Riddles! I don't have time for games. This is a serious matter! A man is in prison!"

"Try this one. What am I? See if you can guess!"

I was close to losing my temper completely. Only the fact that I was in a stranger's home, and that Marianne believed this boy knew something of use to us, prevented me from throttling him then and there. I let out an exasperated sigh.

"Listen. I have no body. I have no soul." He peered at me. "Can you guess it?"

"I don't know."

"Here's a bit more. No one can see me, but everyone can hear me."

"I don't have time—"

"You are really stupid. All right, I'll give you one more clue. I can be brought to life only by man, as often as he wishes."

I tried to grab his arm. "I told you, I don't want to play games."

"My, you are a dense, irritable person! Since I feel sorry for you, I'll give you another hint, but this is the absolute last one. I die a moment after I am born. Go ahead, take a guess!"

I forced myself to take a deep breath to calm the pounding of my heart. "I don't know," I said.

"You can't figure it out? You must be an imbecile. Well, then, you lose! I'll tell you. I'm a fart!" He collapsed in the armchair, giggling.

I looked at him with distaste. "Very funny," I said. "Now that you have had your amusement, will you tell me what you know about Vogel's parents?"

He sighed loudly. "You are so boring! But all right, I'll tell you."

I let out a breath of relief. Finally I was getting somewhere with this annoying boy.

"You should look for the woman," he said.

"What woman? Vogel's birth mother?"

"The woman who spilled the wine." He giggled loudly.

I slapped my hand against the wall in frustration. "Spilled

the wine? Is this another one of your stupid riddles?" I shouted. Once again I attempted to grab him, but he twisted away and darted toward the door. Something fell to the floor.

"Come back here!" I shouted. I ran after him, but I was too late. I crossed into the hallway and looked both ways, but he had disappeared.

Heavy footsteps sounded near the stair landing. They were too heavy to belong to the boy. I retreated into the library, my hands shaking with rage. I stood at the window for a few moments, trying to regain my composure. It had been foolish of me to lose my temper. My anger would do nothing to help Marianne and Vogel.

As I walked over to retrieve my things, I tripped over an object on the floor. I leaned over and picked up a small notebook, tied closed with a ribbon. It must have fallen from the boy's pocket. Probably a collection of his asinine riddles. I heard the same heavy footsteps, this time from the hallway. I quickly shoved the notebook into my satchel. I would give it to Marianne the next time I saw her. I stood at the door until I heard the footsteps retreat down the hall, then quietly let myself out.

I stopped by the theater and worked for a few hours, then returned to my lodgings for dinner. My landlord set an ample and appetizing table, and my fellow boarders included instructors from the university, musicians from the court orchestra, and the occasional writer or philosopher passing through the city. The talk was lively and the food flavorful. Afterward, I went up to my room, determined to put the finishing touches on the *Figaro* libretto.

I worked steadily for a half hour, then my concentration began to wander. I thought back to my visit to the Palais Gabler, to Marianne Haiml's bright eyes and warm smile. My stomach clenched as I recalled my exasperating conversation with that irritating boy. I had let him get the better of me, and in my anger, I had been unable to learn what he claimed to know about the circumstances surrounding Vogel's birth.

My eyes fell on Vogel's box. I pushed my papers aside, pulled it over, and dug out the ring. A little polish would make it gleam. Again I wondered about the woman who had worn it. Had it been given to her by her husband upon the joyous news of her pregnancy? Or had it been a gift from a lover? Perhaps that was why she had given away the baby, to avoid a scandal.

I returned the ring to the box, replaced the lid, and moved it onto the floor beside my chair. I reached for the aria I had been editing. I scratched a few minor changes onto the paper. A moment later, my mind turned again to the boy, Florian Auerstein. What had he meant when he had told me to find "the woman who spilled the wine"? Spilled what wine? Had he been referring to Vogel's christening, perhaps? Why would anyone in the Auerstein family know anything about that? Had Vogel's birth mother been a member of that noble household? I shook my head to clear my fancies away. The boy was a flighty tease. He had been trying to goad me into anger. I shouldn't dwell on what he had told me. It was probably just nonsense.

I returned to my work. A few moments later, I threw down my pen in frustration. I was getting nothing done today. I was too distracted by Vogel's mystery. I went over to my cupboard and pulled out my cloak, took up my stick and the box, and headed out into the Graben.

I turned right and headed into the maze of streets behind St. Peter's Church. A few minutes later I entered the Jewish Quarter, a small area of narrow streets crowded with medieval buildings housing small shops and moneylenders. The old empress had hated the Jews, and had done everything in her power to drive them from Vienna. Her son was much more broad-minded, however, and soon after he ascended the throne, he ordered a loosening of the restrictions on Jews. They were now free to worship in their own homes, but they were not allowed to build synagogues or, for that matter, to own land.

I passed a small group of older men in dark caftans and with long beards, but also saw a few younger men wearing modern clothing. At the end of the street, I entered a small pawnbroker shop. The proprietor, Michael, was deep in discussion with a middle-aged man dressed in a fancy silk suit even more out of style than my own. Several items lay on the counter. Michael looked up and nodded a greeting to me and returned to his customer.

"I can only give you ten florins for the snuffbox," he said.

I put Vogel's box on the floor and walked around the shop to see Michael's latest acquisitions. I could not help but overhear the conversation.

"Only ten? But it is solid gold! It is worth at least a hundred florins!" the customer said.

"It isn't solid gold—it is plated," Michael replied. He pointed to a glass cabinet in the corner of the shop. "Look how many snuffboxes I already have," he said. "But you are a good customer, so I'll give you fifteen florins for this one."

The customer's voice grew pleading. "Are you sure you can't go up a bit more? This is the most valuable thing I have left."

"I'm sorry, sir, I wish I could. But I cannot."

My survey of the items on offer in the shop told me that many of the aristocrats of Vienna were financially overextended. I studied a display of gold saltcellars and inkwells, then moved over to the jewelry section of the shop, where Michael kept a large collection of gemstones in a locked glass cabinet. A few watches sat on top of the glass. I picked up one with a gold case engraved with delicate arabesques. I sighed. I would love to have it to wear with my court suit, but I too was overextended, and if I did not want to dip into my meager savings, I would have to wait until I received payment for the *Figaro* libretto before I bought myself anything new.

After a few moments, the customer, realizing that he was not going to cajole Michael into giving him a better deal, gathered up his florins and left the shop.

"I'll be with you in a minute, Signor Abbé," the pawnbroker called as he carried his purchases into the back room. I placed Vogel's box on the counter and removed the lid.

Michael returned, a frown on his face. He waved toward the door. "That one, always arguing with me," he said. "Every week."

"Gambling debts?" I asked.

"No. He is one of those who lost his pension when the old empress died. He lives off the money I pay him for his family's collection of baubles." He peered into the box. "What have we here, signore?" he asked.

"A small favor, please, Michael. I am in need of your expertise." His eyebrows rose with curiosity. I removed the muff from the box and laid it on the counter, then brought out the ring and the book. "A friend of mine recently lost his mother. He found these things in her cupboard after she passed away. He would like to know if they are of any value. I thought you could tell him. You are the man to come to for authentication of valuables." I had known Michael since I had arrived in Vienna, and I knew that an appeal to his pride and professional inquisitiveness would entice him to help me.

He puffed out his chest. "Yes, well, as you know, Signor Abbé, I have studied on my own for years. Let me see what you have." He picked up the muff. "How old does your friend believe these are?"

"About thirty years."

He ran his fingers through the fur of the muff, turning it over and over, looking at it carefully. "You must understand, Signor Abbé. I am not an expert on furs and fabrics."

I nodded.

"But I think I can safely say that this muff is of no real value. Most of the ladies' trappings in that time were made of ermine or white fox. This hair does not feel like either of those to me." He laid the muff to one side and picked up the ring.

"My friend believes this might have been a betrothal or wedding ring," I offered, as I watched him turn the ring in his fingers. "I noticed myself that the jewel is shaped like a heart."

He looked up at me and laughed. "Ah, Signor Abbé, you are the sentimental type. This is not a heart. It is just a badly cut piece of glass."

"Glass? My friend was certain it was a valuable gem."

"No, sir. I don't even need to use my glass to see the poor quality. Here, have a look. Do you see how cloudy the jewel is? It is not a real gem, it is an imitation. The ring itself—it is brass, not gold. This is nothing but a cheap piece, something you could buy for a few coins from a vendor in the street."

I tried to keep my disappointment from my face. "What about the book?" I asked, pushing it toward him. He ran his fingers over the leather cover, then opened it, turned a few pages, closed it, and handed it back to me. "Again, signore, it is of little value. Such books were common at the time—all the ladies had one. This one is an inexpensive version. The leather is too thin, and the stamping on the side is not real gold." He smiled at me apologetically. "I'm afraid your friend will be disappointed. These things will bring him no money."

I sighed as I placed the items back into the box. "He will be sorry to hear that," I said. "He was hoping to use them to trace the woman who owned them."

"That would be a difficult task, Signor Abbé. Those things could have belonged to any number of women. I can tell you this, though. No lady of noble birth would own items of such inferior quality. Most likely they belonged to a shopkeeper's wife or even a servant girl."

I nodded and pressed a coin into his hand. "Yes. Well, thank you anyway, Michael," I said, taking up the box. "I appreciate your help."

"Come back soon, Signor Abbé," he said, his eyes full of mischief. "I noticed you admiring that watch—shall I set it aside for you?"

I hesitated, thinking again about how good it would look with my suit. Perhaps I could afford it. After all, I had the *Figaro* fee coming soon, and I had already agreed to write another libretto for Martín. But I had promised to send my father more money. Two of my young stepbrothers were entering the seminary in the fall, and my father could not afford the tuition without my help. I shook my head. "No, Michael, thank you, but not now. If it is still here in six months, though—" We laughed.

Disappointment washed over me as I carried the box down the street. I did not look forward to telling Marianne and Vogel that I had already failed in my investigation. If the items in the box had indeed belonged to Vogel's birth mother, she had not been the aristocrat he had imagined. The best he could hope for was that she had been a servant who had been seduced by a nobleman. But how to trace such a man? As Michael had said, cheap trinkets like those in the box were sold in markets all over Vienna. The box grew heavy in my arms. I shifted it and trudged down the street toward the Graben.

Three

That evening, I joined the crowds of well-dressed Viennese milling around outside the Court Theater. The emperor had been twice widowed, and when he ascended the throne, the social life of the court ceased to revolve around the dances and parties his mother had loved, and now centered around the opera. The theater was the place to see and be seen, and most of its patrons were so busy conducting business affairs, flirting, or arguing with one another that they paid little attention to the performance, ceasing their chattering only when the prima donna sang her arias.

I spent some time supervising the sale of copies of the evening's libretto in the lobby. The performance had already begun when I slipped into my seat in the fifth row on the main floor. As theater poet, I tried to attend every performance, whether I had written the libretto or not, whether the performance was a premiere or a repeat. Tonight's opera was by Casti and Salieri, a revival of a work that had premiered last

year. Since I had heard the opera several times already and
did not consider it all that good, I allowed my attention to
wander from the stage to the main hall of the theater.

To my right, up on the second tier, boxes reserved for the
emperor and his closest advisors were festooned with red and
gold bunting. The royal box sat empty tonight, as did its im-
mediate neighbor, that belonging to Joseph's chancellor,
Prince Kaunitz, the second most powerful man in Vienna.
A third box belonged to Count Rosenberg. His party was
small, just a few friends and the omnipresent Casti, beam-
ing and nodding as his poetry was performed.

I turned my gaze to my left, again to the second tier, where
a box close to the stage was reserved for the librettist and
composer of the work being performed. Because Casti never
left Rosenberg's side, tonight the box was occupied only by
Court Composer Salieri and his wife. I studied Salieri's suit,
which looked to be a three-piece set of dark green wool. From
my seat on the main floor, I could just pick out the elegant
embroidery—gold thread, I guessed—around the cuffs and
collar of the coat. The suit must have cost over eighty florins. Salieri could easily afford it. He had held the well-paid
position of court composer for the last seven years. He, his
wife, and their five children lived in a large house in the best
part of the city, and I had heard that he possessed a wonderful art collection, although I personally had never been
invited to see it.

As my eyes wandered over that side of the theater, a flit-
ting movement from the box next to Salieri's caught my attention. The box was occupied by a young woman dressed
in a white gown. She sat stiffly at the front center of the box,

alone, toying absently with a fan, staring down, not at the stage, but at a spot near my seat. Despite her direct gaze, I sensed that she was looking at no one in particular, but that instead her eyes were unfocused and her mind was miles away.

Her auburn hair was loosely bound up by a small jeweled tiara, not tightly drawn under a large feathered hat, as was the current style among the ladies. A few tendrils had escaped from the headdress and tumbled to join the white pearl earrings hanging from her lobes. The effect was an aureole of warm spun copper about her small head. Her face was a perfect oval, her neck long and graceful. Yet her skin was deathly pale, its ashy color relieved only by two spots of rouge on her cheeks. She wore an expression of utter melancholy. I wondered who or what had caused her such misery.

Loud applause erupted as the first act came to an end. Everyone around me rose and headed toward the lobby to purchase punch or wine. I remained in my seat, turning to look at the woman again. Her expression was unchanged.

"Lorenzo!" I stood as Mozart approached. "Are you enjoying the performance?" he asked, his eyebrow cocked.

I laughed. "As much as I can," I replied. I put my hand on his arm. "Wolfgang, look at the woman in the box next to Salieri's. Do you know her?"

"The one in white? No. I've never seen her before," he said. "Whose box is that? Do you want me to run up and ask the countess? She knows everybody." Countess Thun was the wife of one of the emperor's closest advisors, and had been one of Mozart's patronesses since he came to Vienna from Salzburg.

"No, no," I said. "It's not important." I looked past him. "Where is Constanze tonight?"

"Carl had a little cough, so she wanted to stay with him. She's heard this opera before. She said once was enough for her!" We both laughed again. Mozart's eyes narrowed as he looked at someone behind me. "Here comes the court composer," he said in a low voice.

I turned and gave a slight, automatic bow. "Good evening, Signor Salieri," I said. Mozart merely nodded at his fellow composer and turned his attention to digging his watch from his coat pocket.

"Good evening, gentlemen," Salieri said. The court composer was actually a year younger than me, but looked older. His lips turned downward, giving him an air of sad experience, and his dark eyes always looked tired and bored. I looked at the suit. I had been right, the embroidery was gold thread. I sighed to myself, thinking how much better than Salieri I would look in that suit.

"How does your work proceed?" he asked.

Mozart looked up from his watch. "Very well," he said. "We have dress rehearsal in two weeks. I am almost done with the composition. Lorenzo has written a wonderful adaptation of the play," he added.

Salieri glanced at me and turned back to Mozart. "Yes, I'm sure it will be excellent," he murmured. "I hope you will have no delays. I am looking forward to hearing it, but as you probably have heard, I am leaving in July for a year in Paris."

Mozart caught my eye. I frowned. Delays? What did he mean? We were due to premiere in three weeks. By July we should be well into our tenth or twelfth performance.

Salieri hesitated. "May I, as a friend, of course, offer you both some advice?"

Mozart began to fiddle with his watch fob. His face grew red.

"If it were I who was working with such a delicate subject as the Beaumarchais play," Salieri continued, "I would take pains to include Count Rosenberg in all of my artistic decisions. I've found him to have excellent judgment as to what will please the emperor, and—"

"We have already spoken to the emperor about the opera," Mozart said in a cold voice.

"Yes, yes, of course. You had one interview with him, I believe—"

"Lorenzo!" A familiar voice cried behind me. A moment later I found myself enveloped in a hug from my dearest friend, Vicente Martín. He gave a nod to Mozart and Salieri. "When are we going to meet?" he asked me in his rich Valencian accent.

"Soon," I said. "A week, maybe two. After that I am all yours."

"Good! I have a lot of ideas and I'm eager to start writing." His dark eyes twinkled. "We should go out again soon. You've been a hermit. Rosita was asking for you just the other night." Martín was a bachelor like me. The wife of the Spanish ambassador was his patroness, and he and I had spent many evenings enjoying the charms of her lady's maids. I had found the raven-haired Rosita to be a nice diversion from the pressures of work.

Martín smiled, nodded at the three of us, and was off to

the next group of friends. Salieri looked after him. "An exuberant young man," he said with a sniff. He turned back to us. "As I was saying, the emperor is fixed in his likes and dislikes. The count can give you valuable guidance as you proceed, so that you will have no problems over the next few weeks. I would hate for you to discover, at the very last moment, that His Majesty has found something in your libretto of which he cannot approve."

I heard Mozart's jaw snap shut. His fist clenched around his watch fob. His face was redder than I'd ever seen it. I tried to catch his eye, but he was staring at his watch. I took Salieri by the arm and led him away a few steps. "Please do not worry on our account, Signor Court Composer," I said. "We have everything under control. We appreciate your advice, though." I turned to Mozart, whose eyes were bulging. "Don't we, Wolfgang?" He forced himself to nod.

"Well, all right, then," Salieri said. "Good. Now I must return to my box for the second act. Good evening, gentlemen." He turned and headed toward the stairs to the second tier.

Mozart exhaled loudly. "May I? As a friend?" he said, mocking Salieri's Veronese accent.

I placed my hand on his arm. "Don't worry," I said. "Let's make this opera the greatest that Vienna has ever heard. That will shut him up."

He took a deep breath. "It will, it will." He turned to go back to his seat. "Oh, Lorenzo, I almost forgot. I have a few more changes for you. I'd like to finish this week. I still have

that quartet to write for Hoffmeister." The music publisher
ran a popular shop that sold chamber music to the public,
to be performed in private salons.

"Yes, and I have to start working on the libretto for
Martín. I've put him off for a few months already."

"Good, then come to me tomorrow, anytime." I watched
as his small figure headed to a seat in the back of the theater. The orchestra began to play the opening music of the
second act. I settled into my seat, but before I turned my attention to the action on the stage, I looked up to the box next
to Salieri's. The woman in white had disappeared.

The long day had tired me, but although I went to bed right
away, I could not sleep. I lay staring at the ceiling, my mind
full of the day's events. Even though Michael had told me
the items in Vogel's box were of no value, I wanted to know
more about the woman who had given them away with her
newborn son. The ring, book, and muff must have been treasures to her, the only gifts she could give the baby. But why
had she given him up?

I turned onto my side and punched my hard pillow, trying to find a comfortable position. My thoughts wandered to
the Palais Gabler. What a strange group of people I had met
there! Marianne Haiml was beautiful and charming, to be
sure, and the music teacher—Piatti, I believe he had said his
name was—seemed to be a man of learning and good taste.
But that annoying boy, the waspish housekeeper, and that
fey chambermaid!

I closed my eyes and took a few deep breaths, trying to
lull myself to sleep. An image of the woman from the the-

ater came to my mind. During the last act of the opera, I had looked up several times to see whether she had returned, but no one had appeared in her box the rest of the evening. I wondered again what or who had caused the sadness I had read on her face.

I turned the pillow over again and pulled the bedsheet over my shoulders. Stop thinking about her. Go to sleep. But I could not help myself. I set free my imagination and envisioned my fingers running through her loose, lustrous curls; my hands caressing her soft, pale face; and my words persuading her lips into a sweet smile. A familiar, joyful yearning spread in my heart, and after a while, I slept.

My dreams took me back to my childhood, to my neighborhood in Ceneda. I was ten years old, already a leader among the boys of my age, admired for my knowledge and wit. I stood in the middle of a circle of friends and recited a poem I had heard in church and had quickly memorized. As I finished, the boys my own age applauded, and I flushed with pleasure. The local butcher's son, an older boy with a domineering swagger, approached me and, with a sly grin, held out a book to me, demanding that I read a passage. I demurred, saying that it was someone else's turn to be the center of attention. He pushed the book into my trembling hands. "Go ahead, read to us," he said loudly. The younger boys all looked at me expectantly. My mouth grew dry as I looked down at the words, which were unintelligible to me. My heart thumped in my chest. The older boy and his friends began to laugh. They began the familiar chant. *Brilliant dunce. Brilliant dunce.* The butcher's son grabbed a heavy stick and began to beat it against the trunk of a nearby tree. *Brilliant dunce. Brilliant dunce.* I stood red-faced with humiliation as he pounded out the rhythm with the stick, louder and louder.

"Open up," a voice yelled. I sat up straight in my bed, wide awake but dazed, my heart racing. The room was pitch-black.

"Signor Da Ponte?" I heard the tremulous voice of my landlord. "Are you there? Signor Abbé, please open the door, quickly." The pounding resumed. I rose from the bed and stumbled through the darkness to the door. As I opened it, a draft of cold air blew into my room. I shivered. My landlord, his nightdress clutched around him for warmth, stood there holding a lantern. Beside him were two men dressed in black uniforms. I peered at them through the dim lamplight. One was short and heavy. He held another lantern. The other man was of medium height, loose-limbed, with a week's worth of beard on his face. He stepped forward, pushing my landlord aside.

"You are Lorenzo Da Ponte?" he asked.

"Please, gentlemen, may we step inside?" my landlord asked. The lantern shook in his hands. "The other tenants—"

The heavy man turned to him. "You may go. Don't worry, we won't be here much longer." The landlord flashed me a look of pity and scurried away.

The tall man pushed me back into my room and stepped in. He grabbed the front of my nightshirt and pulled me so that my face was inches away from his. I gagged at the smell of his breath, a mixture of fermented cabbage and stale beer. "Police," he said. "Get dressed."

By now I had recovered my senses. "What is this? What do you want with me?" I asked. He pushed me aside. I stumbled and fell to the floor. My pale, bare legs splayed out from beneath my nightshirt.

My cheeks grew hot with shame as the two officers laughed. "Get dressed," the heavy one said. "You are coming with us."

"Where? Why? Where are you taking me?" I sputtered.

"You'll find out soon enough."

I pulled myself up and hobbled over to my cupboard. My hands quivered as I put on a pair of breeches and a shirt. I pulled on my stockings and shoes. "What do you want with me?" I asked again. "There must be some mistake. You have the wrong person."

"You are Lorenzo Da Ponte, the theater poet?" the heavy officer asked. I nodded. He put the lantern on my basin cabinet and quickly moved toward me. He grabbed my shoulders, spinning me around. Pain shot through my right elbow as he pulled both of my arms back. His partner pulled a length of cord from his uniform pocket, and together they bound my hands behind my back.

"You are under arrest," the heavy officer said. He clutched my arm and dragged me to the door. My legs shook violently and my bladder began to fail me. I feared my heart would explode from its pounding.

"Under arrest? That's not possible! For what?" My voice squeaked. The heavy officer pushed me forward as the other closed the door. They flanked my sides and each took one of my arms. I winced in pain as they pulled me down the hall toward the stairs.

"I demand to know what this is all about!" I cried. "You can't do this! Under arrest? For what crime?"

We stopped at the top of the stairwell. The tall officer leaned into my face and smiled. My stomach heaved as his foul breath washed over me. I bit my lip to avoid crying out as he squeezed my arm tightly. He laughed and spat the words into my face.

"For murder."

Four

I stumbled several times as I was pushed down the stairs and into the street. The Graben was dark and deserted. The street lamps had been extinguished hours before; no lights shone from the windows of the apartment buildings. The only sound was the whimpering of a prostitute in an alcove nearby. The wind bit through my thin shirt. I shivered as the officers dragged me to a waiting carriage.

"My cloak—" I said hoarsely.

"Shut up and get in," the heavy officer said. He opened the door of the carriage and shoved me inside. Pain shot through my shoulder as I fell onto the floor. The carriage sagged as he climbed in after me. He pulled me up and pushed me onto the hard seat. His companion followed and slammed the door. The carriage rolled down the dark street.

"I demand to know what this is about!" I said. My voice shook. "Who is it you think I murdered?" Neither officer answered. I turned my head and looked out the window. The streets were dark, but I knew this route well. We were headed toward the Hofburg Palace.

I hunched my shoulders in an effort to stay warm. A few minutes later we reached the Michaelerplatz. The carriage veered to the right, drove past the theater, and headed around the corner toward the labyrinth of buildings occupied by the empire's ministerial offices. The carriage entered a courtyard and stopped. The taller officer opened the door and climbed out. His partner pushed me after him. I fell out of the carriage, crying out as my right knee hit a jagged stone on the ground.

"Come on," the taller officer snarled. My eyes filled with tears as he grabbed me by my injured shoulder and pulled me up. I took a deep breath, willing myself to keep control in front of these brutes. Rows of darkened windows stared blankly from the tall buildings that framed the small courtyard. It was empty of carriages and horses, and lit by a single lamp that flickered next to an austere doorway. I did not recognize the place. I had never had any reason to come to this side of the Hofburg.

The two men dragged me through the door and up a set of stairs. My shoulder throbbed with pain every time they lifted me onto another step. The knee of my breeches felt wet where I had hit the stone.

We climbed another set of stairs. The officers stopped at the head of a long hallway lined with silent, closed doors. Candles in sconces on the barren walls created sporadic pools of light on the corridor floor; the rest of the lengthy passage lay in darkness. I shivered, this time from fear instead of cold.

My imagination ran wild. I could easily disappear into one of these dark rooms, never to see daylight again.

"Which one?" the taller officer asked his companion.

"Two twenty, he said," the heavy officer answered. He grunted as he grabbed me again and dragged me down the hall. My right arm throbbed. We turned a corner and continued down another long, dark passage. Just when I believed that I could no longer keep from screaming from the pain, my captors stopped before a door. One of them fumbled with the cord that bound my arms, and a moment later I was free. I groaned as I pulled my arms forward. They were both numb. The taller man rapped on the door, opened it, and pushed me in.

"The poet, sir," he said. I grabbed at the knob of the door to avoid falling. I regained my balance and looked up. The room was dark except for a single candle set on a desk directly in front of me. A man sat behind the desk, a sheaf of documents piled in front of him. He looked me up and down and nodded to the officers. "You may go," he said. The heavy one gave me a final shove and closed the door.

The man rose from the desk, crossed to the door, and turned the lock. He gestured toward a wooden chair a few feet in front of me. I fell into the chair. I leaned over to examine my trouser knee, but I could see nothing. The light was too dim. The man returned to his seat behind the desk.

"You are Lorenzo Da Ponte?" he asked.

I studied him through the candlelight. His features were sharp, his nose large and hawklike. Even in the dimness I could see that his eyes were dark and cold.

"Answer the question!" he snapped.

I had had enough. "You know who I am!" I shouted. "What is the meaning of this? Who are you? Why have I been roused from my bed and treated like a criminal? The emperor will hear about this!"

He stared at me coolly and gave a small, bemused smile. He picked up a sheet of paper from the pile on the desk. "You were ordained as a priest in 1773?" he asked.

"Who are you?" I demanded.

He studied the paper for a long moment, then put it aside and took up another one. "After your ordination, you taught at the seminary in Ceneda and moved to Venice six months later?"

I nodded, confused. How did he know all this about me? A wave of exhaustion swept over me, as if my outburst had drained the rest of my energy and anger. "Why are you asking me these questions?" I said. "Your officers accused me of murder—"

"While in Venice, you took a lover, a married woman named—" He scrutinized the document. "Angela Tiepolo?"

A cold vise closed around my heart. I had hoped I had left all that behind me thirteen years ago.

He banged his palm on the tabletop. I jumped. "Answer the question!"

"Yes," I said. "But what—"

"She gave birth to your child? A child you abandoned to an orphanage?"

I rubbed my temples as my head began to throb. After my ordination, I had been restless in my vocation, and on a trip to Venice, I had met Angela. She was the orphaned daughter of a minor aristocrat, and when she turned her dark, indolent eyes my way I had forgotten about God, my vows, my duty to my family, and the existence of her husband. She had quickly drawn me into the raucous party life of the city. We had spent our evenings at the opera or theater, and had drunk and gambled into the early morning. The days we spent in bed.

I hadn't been certain the child had been mine, but Angela's husband had left her and had disavowed the newborn. We had no money, and so had had no choice but to give the baby to the orphanage. Soon after that, my younger brother had rescued me from my life of debauchery. He had taken me to Treviso, where he had found teaching positions for both of us at the seminary there. Girolamo—my beloved brother! Lost to me forever.

I started at a soft rustling sound, the kind a rat would make, coming from somewhere behind me. I imagined myself thrown into a cell somewhere in this maze, with only rodents for company. My hands began to shake. I moved them onto my lap. I did not want this man to see my fear.

My interlocutor coughed loudly. "You taught literature at Treviso?" he asked.

I was so tired, I no longer cared who he was and why he was asking me these questions. I nodded. "Italian literature," I said softly. The job at Treviso had been a deliverance for me. I had discovered that I was a natural teacher, and I had been able to buy books and to write poetry in my spare time.

"Now—" He shuffled through a few papers and held one up to me. I squinted through the candlelight, but could not see what it said. "You were arrested for writing treasonous poetry? You were tried and convicted by the Senate in Venice?"

A bolt of fear cut through me. "That was a cooked-up charge made by my enemies!" I was startled to hear myself shout. As a teacher, I had been popular among the students, and some of the older professors had grown jealous of me. They had been determined to find a way to get rid of me.

My interrogator's voice became warm and soothing. "Tell me about it," he said.

"Part of my job was to write a long poem for my students to recite at the close of the academic year," I said. He nodded. "The tradition was that the poem must be ennobling, and must treat an important issue of the day." His cold eyes studied me intently.

"I decided to write about the famous idea of the French philosopher Rousseau—that man is happier living in a state of nature rather than under the rule of law."

"Yes, yes," he interrupted. "Tell me about the trial."

My poem had been published to critical acclaim among the intellectuals of Venice. In Treviso, however, my enemies at the seminary had seen their chance, and had denounced me for "ungodly" writings before the state education board. "I was banned from teaching," I said. "But I was never charged with treason, and I spent no time in prison!"

My heart pounded as he stared at me. I heard the rustling noise behind me again. My shoulder throbbed with pain. I watched as he returned the document to his pile and slowly tapped the papers into a neat stack, then set them to the side. He looked up at me.

"What were you doing at the Palais Gabler this morning?" he asked quietly.

"What?"

"The house of Baron Christof Gabler. You went there this morning. Why?"

I was so tired I could barely sit up in the chair. I pinched the top of my nose. "I went there on an errand for a friend," I said.

"To visit Florian Auerstein?" His icy eyes bored into me.

Florian Auerstein? Who was that? My thoughts were in a tangle. I was dizzy with fatigue. Auerstein. Oh yes, that boy in the library.

"No. I went to talk to Marianne Haiml. She is lady's maid to the baroness," I said.

"Why did you argue with the Auerstein boy?" he pressed.

I shook my head. Why was he asking me about this? "I didn't argue with him. I met him only briefly. We spoke for just a few minutes. He was acting like a fool. I may have raised my voice to him once, that's all."

"You were heard arguing loudly with him for several minutes. You threatened him."

I struggled to remember the events of the morning. Had I threatened the boy? I couldn't remember. Who had heard me? I recalled the footsteps I had heard outside the door before I left the library. Had someone been eavesdropping on me?

"No! It wasn't like that at all! He was telling me silly riddles. I was asking him about a serious matter. He wouldn't answer me. I lost my temper. I may have shouted at him. He ran out of the room. I left the house a few minutes later. That is all."

The man continued to stare at me.

"I don't understand any of this," I said. "Why am I here? Why are you asking me about him?"

"You're perfectly aware of why you are here," he said.

"No! I don't understand—"

"You are a good liar, Signor Poet." He sneered. "You are here because you killed the boy."

I gasped. "Killed—" My voice failed me.

"You pushed him out the window of the library. He broke his neck on the stones in the courtyard below."

"No! You are lying to me!"

His voice grew louder, insistent. "Why did you kill him?"

"But—I didn't—surely you cannot think—I spoke to him for only a few minutes. I told you, he ran out of the room. I didn't see him after that. I left the library, went downstairs, and let myself out of the house. I saw no one." My heart began to race with panic.

"Were you sleeping with him? Was he blackmailing you?"

"Blackmailing me? Sleeping— What do you mean?" My voice was a squeak. "I met him for the first time this morning. I swear to you. Ask Miss Haiml—" I cringed as I heard myself plead.

He gave a tight smile and leaned over the table toward me. "Come, you can confide in me," he said. His voice was gentle, quiet. "In my work, I've seen everything. I understand how you must have felt. You must have grown tired of paying him to keep quiet about your affair."

I pulled back. "What are you saying? I don't sleep with boys!" I leaped up from the chair. My bloody knee hit the edge of the desk. I cried out. "I'm telling you, you have the wrong person!"

"Did the boy know about your past? Is that why you were paying him?" He stood and moved around the desk. He pushed me back down onto the chair.

"No! My past? What about it? You are making a big mistake! The emperor—"

He leaned down and brought his face within an inch of mine. His cold eyes bored into me. I began to shake. "Tell me, Signor Abbé. Why did you have to leave Venice?"

The room started to spin. I gulped for breath, trying to control my shaking, to no avail. The rustling behind me grew louder.

"Well?" He raised his hand as if to slap me. I cringed. I closed my eyes, waiting for the blow.

"That's enough, Troger," a voice said. I opened my eyes. A man in his sixties, dressed in a formal court suit, stood next to my interrogator. Troger stepped back as the older man took the seat behind the desk.

"Signor Da Ponte," he said in a soft, cultured voice. "I apologize for my subordinate's behavior. Sometimes he gets carried away in performing his duties." The other man grunted.

"I am Anton Pergen," the older man continued. "Perhaps you have heard of me?"

I tried to answer, but still could not find my voice, so I merely gulped and nodded. Count Anton Pergen, the emperor's minister in charge of police functions. I sighed with relief as I rubbed my shoulder. He would clear up this misunderstanding, I was certain.

"You are hurt?" he asked.

"I jammed my shoulder when your men threw me into the carriage," I said, my voice returning as a whine that I cringed to hear. "I also cut my knee."

He looked over at my tormenter, who stood behind me. "This is my assistant, Georg Troger." I refused to turn and acknowledge him. "Troger, get some lamps in here. And some water for Signor Da Ponte." I heard the door open and shut behind me. I let out a long breath.

"I will only take a few moments of your time, signore, then Captain Troger will see that your injuries are attended to," Pergen said. He leaned back in the chair. "Tell me, do you enjoy living here in Vienna?"

I nodded.

"Please forgive me for eavesdropping on your conversation with Captain Troger. That poem you wrote, in Treviso, was it? The one that caused you so much trouble with the authorities? You realize, of course, that that never would have happened here in Vienna. The emperor shares the same sentiments as you and Rousseau." His voice was warm and mellifluous. I began to relax.

"Yes," I replied. "I have heard the emperor speak about the French *philosophes* many times."

"You know the emperor believes that his subjects should enjoy all of the freedoms of a modern state," Pergen continued. "People here may say or write whatever they want, even if they oppose the emperor's policies."

I nodded, thinking back to the pamphlets I had read this morning in the coffeehouse.

Troger returned. He placed a large lamp on the desk, and handed me a mug of water. My hands shook as I raised it to my lips and drank.

"We have no secret police here in Vienna," Pergen continued. "The emperor sees no need to gather information about his subjects."

Troger snorted from somewhere behind me.

"My assistant thinks the emperor is naïve," Pergen said. "He's entitled to his opinion, as is every citizen of the empire. I don't agree with him."

I yawned. When would he let me go home to my bed?

"Sometimes, though, especially when a crime occurs, we have to question people who might have some knowledge about the incident. As Captain Troger told you, Florian Auerstein has been murdered. Would you be willing to tell me about your encounter with him, so we can clear up this matter?"

"I will tell you everything I know," I said.

"Now, you said you went to the palais to see Miss Marianne Haiml, the lady's maid. Is that correct?"

"Yes, I was doing an errand for a man I know, who is her fiancé."

"What do you know about Baron Gabler?" the soft voice asked.

"Nothing. I'd never even heard of him before today."

He raised his eyebrows. "Really? You had no idea when you went to the palais that the baron is Chancellor Kaunitz's protégé?"

I drew in a sharp breath. Kaunitz, the emperor's most powerful minister, who had managed foreign policy for the last thirty years. What had I gotten myself into? "No," I said. "I knew nothing about the baron. I don't pay attention to politics. My job at the theater keeps me busy enough."

Pergen picked up a paper from the pile Troger had left, studied it for a moment, then laid it aside. He stared at me. His eyes were friendly, but I suddenly felt uncomfortable under his gaze.

"So you went to see Miss Haiml. Were you able to meet her?"

"Yes, we spoke for a few minutes."

"Where did you meet with her?"

"In the baron's library. I stayed there less than thirty minutes, I think," I added.

"I see." He looked over at the page he had set aside. "You weren't aware that the baron is being groomed to be the next ambassador to St. Petersburg?"

"I told you, sir, I knew nothing about the baron. I went to the house to see Miss Haiml. You can ask her about it."

"But surely you must have known. The young man, Florian Auerstein, must have told you all about it. After all, he was living in the house, training as an assistant to the baron. He was to accompany the baron to St. Petersburg. He must have mentioned it to you during one of your times together, no?"

"No!" My voice was tight. I was exhausted, tired of these innuendos. "I told your assistant, I had never met the boy until today!"

"Ah, I see."

"He was hiding behind the drape while I was speaking with Miss Haiml. The baroness rang for her, and I told her I could see myself out. I was looking at the baron's book collection when the boy jumped out at me."

"Why did you argue with him?"

I sighed. "He was obnoxious." I didn't want to tell him how the boy had taunted me, imitating my lisp. "He hinted that he had information regarding my errand, but he refused to tell me what it was. He was dancing around the room, shouting riddles at me." My voice grew shrill. "I'll admit I lost my head for a moment and raised my voice, but I didn't threaten him, and I didn't push him out a window! He ran out of the room, I swear to you. He was very alive then! I left the house just a few minutes later." I started to rise from my chair. "You must believe me!"

I felt Troger's hands on my shoulders, pressing me back into the chair. Pergen studied my face for several long moments. My heart began to pound. He couldn't really believe that I killed that boy, could he?

"All right, signore," he said. "I believe you."

I exhaled loudly as my entire body sagged with relief.

"But sir! We have the witness!"

Pergen held up his hand. "I know, I know. But the witness only heard Signor Da Ponte argue with the boy. We just don't know what happened after that."

"But he was seen running from the house!"

"I did no such thing—"

"Enough, Troger," Pergen said. He looked at me. "Perhaps you could help me with my problem, signore."

I nodded.

"You see, the boy's father, Prince Auerstein, is a close friend of the emperor. The boy was his only son. The prince is heartbroken at the death of his heir. He demands justice. It has fallen to me to find the boy's killer."

"Sir, I don't know what I can do to help you. I have told you everything I know, I swear to you."

"It is a tricky situation politically. This murder involves people concerned with the highest level of foreign policy. Matters are complicated for the emperor right now. You know that Frederick, the King of Prussia, opposes the emperor's plans to expand into Bavaria?"

I shook my head.

"Frederick has been angry at the emperor ever since Austria and Russia became allies," Pergen continued. "He will do whatever he can to thwart the emperor's ambitions."

I tried to stifle a yawn.

"The emperor is worried that the empress of Russia is cooling toward her alliance with him. Now is not the time for a long-drawn-out investigation of a murder committed in the home of the future ambassador to St. Petersburg. But Prince Auerstein demands that the killer of his son be caught and punished." He sighed. "The easiest solution for me would be to give you to him."

My head shot up. I jumped from my seat, my heart racing. "But I have done nothing! You just said you had no evidence against me—"

He motioned for me to sit. Troger snickered. "I know we don't have the evidence to charge you," Pergen said, "but the prince doesn't care about evidence. He wants someone to pay for the crime."

Troger's voice came from behind me. "A quick trial in secret, with only the testimony of the witness who heard you, then—" He made a choking sound.

I slumped in the chair. Pergen was examining his manicure. "You see, Da Ponte, it seems that we both have a problem." He stared down at his hands, deep in thought. "There is something we could do, though," he said, looking at me. "To clear you of suspicion, I mean."

"I'll do anything!" I cried.

"Then let me tell you a bit more about Baron Gabler. His father was a commoner who made the family fortune supplying arms in the Great War against Prussia and England. The old empress awarded him the title after the war. He became good friends with Chancellor Kaunitz, who became godfather to his son, the current baron. Kaunitz saw to the boy's education, then took him on as an assistant. When the emperor took the throne, Christof, who had by that time succeeded his father to the title, was involved in many important policy assignments—pension reform, church reform, the overhaul of the criminal code. Although he is still a young man, he is to be the next ambassador to St. Petersburg."

I closed my eyes as his voice flowed on.

"Documents have gone missing from the baron's office. We believe Frederick has planted a spy in the baron's household," Pergen said.

I sat up straight. "I'm sorry—Frederick?"

"The King of Prussia!" he snapped. He quickly regained his composure. "Please forgive me, signore. The hour is late and we are all tired. I will only take a few more minutes of your time. We suspect that the Auerstein boy unwittingly discovered the identity of the spy, and that this person murdered him."

"I don't understand," I said. "What does all this have to do with me?"

"We need to place someone in the household to help us find the spy."

I suddenly felt wide awake. My head was perfectly clear. "You want me—"

"Yes, Da Ponte, we want you—or should I say, we need you—to investigate this murder for us."

"But I am not an investigator! I know nothing of police work!"

"Exactly," Troger said from behind me. "This is not a good idea, sir. This man is a poet. What good could he possibly do?"

Pergen waved a hand in dismissal. "We don't want a police officer there. The spy would discover him too quickly. The investigator must be someone whose presence in the household no one would question. The baron would be the only one who would know why you are really there. I want you to listen, to observe what is going on around you, talk to the people you meet there, and report what you learn to us."

"But what would be my excuse for being there?" I asked.

"You have been hired to teach poetry to the baroness. You will live in the palais until the case is solved."

"But I can't! I have so much work to do. The emperor is expecting my next opera to premiere next month! I'll lose my position at the theater!" I thought I saw Pergen give a meaningful look behind me, where Troger stood.

"You'll be able to continue working. You may come and go as you please, as long as when you are at the palais, you act as my eyes and ears," Pergen said.

"Please, sir. I know nothing about investigating a murder. I don't believe I can carry this off. I don't dissemble well. What if this spy discovers me before I discover him, and kills me too?"

Troger laughed. "That's a risk you'll have to take. You'll have to have your wits about you."

The friendly expression returned to Pergen's face. "I know you can do this, Da Ponte. You come highly recommended."

"And if I refuse?"

Pergen raised both his palms upward. "If you refuse to cooperate with us, I will have no choice but to report to Prince Auerstein that we have arrested the murderer of his son."

I sank into my chair. I was trapped.

"Then you agree to help us?"

I nodded.

"Troger, tell Signor Da Ponte what you've learned thus far," Pergen said. He leaned back in the chair and closed his eyes. Troger came to the desk, riffled through the pile of papers, and pulled out a sheet. He gave me a sarcastic smile.

"The boy's body was found late this afternoon—yesterday afternoon, I mean—by Tomaso Piatti."

Piatti, the music teacher I had met.

"Piatti had spent the afternoon in his room writing music. At four o'clock, he left the palais to attend a recital at the Stephansdom. He saw the boy lying in the courtyard.

"The baron refuses to keep a guard posted at the palais, but both of the doors—the main entrance and the servants' door—are kept locked. We are confident that this was no random attack. No stranger could have entered the house. I spoke to everyone in the household, except the baron and baroness, of course. They are not involved. The baron's secretary, a man called—" He consulted his notes. "Jakob Ecker, told me the baron was at his office here in the Hofburg all afternoon. Ecker himself spent the day writing letters in the baron's study at the palais. He heard nothing.

"The baroness was ill," he continued. "Her maid, Miss Haiml, made a cosset for her and left her to sleep. Miss Haiml then went to her own room, where she spent the rest of the day mending some of the baroness's dresses."

I recalled my encounter with the charming Marianne. The poor girl must be frightened about the murder. Perhaps my presence in the house could reassure her. The thought cheered me slightly.

Troger cleared his throat. "There is an older man living in the house, a Dr. Urban Rausch. He was the baroness's guardian before she married the baron."

I raised an eyebrow. "Her guardian?" I asked.

"Yes. The baroness is the daughter of a petty merchant here in Vienna. Her parents died when she was young, leaving her as ward to their friend Dr. Rausch. He raised her well, so that she was able to marry above her station."

I made no response to the slight sneer I heard in his voice.

"The doctor was working in his room all afternoon. He is writing a treatise on . . . let me check. It is something called a pharmacopoeia, concentrating on the use of black powder to treat spasms." He looked up at me to see if I understood what he was talking about. I shrugged.

Troger reached down for another sheet of notes. "The baron's valet, Gottfried Bohm, was in the baron's chamber polishing boots. He has a daughter who lives with him in the house and works as chambermaid. Antonia."

The pale, strange girl who had shown me in. She and her father must be new to the household, arriving six months ago when Vogel left to open his shop.

"The father heard nothing. The girl was difficult to question. She was upset." He looked up from his notes, a leer on his face. "I got the impression she knew the boy very well. I could hardly get any information out of her, she was crying so hard. She did tell me she was in the cellar doing the wash all afternoon. Finally, there is a housekeeper, Rosa Hahn, who also cooks the meals."

Vogel's creditor, the stern, cold woman who had argued with Marianne while I had been there. "She was away from the house all afternoon, shopping for fabric and buttons to make a new dress. She went out alone. When she returned, Piatti had just discovered the boy's body."

"So everyone was alone all afternoon," I said.

He nodded. "No one can vouch for any other member of the household. No one heard or saw anything strange."

Pergen opened his eyes and sat up straight. He pulled out his watch. "It is now four o'clock. Troger will take you to have your injuries tended to. Someone will deliver you back to your lodgings," he said. "You should pack everything you will need and go to the palais as early as possible this morning.

The baron is expecting you. Report everything you learn to Troger."

I looked at Troger. He sniggered. "How should I contact you?" I asked him.

"Don't worry," he said. His smirk widened into an obnoxious grin. "I'll find you."

Five

By eight o'clock my knee had been bandaged, ointment had been rubbed on my injured shoulder, and a carriage had returned me to my lodgings. I went directly to my cupboard and took out my valise, trying to avoid looking at my rumpled bed. I longed to fall upon it and sleep the rest of the day, but that was impossible.

I pulled out my underclothes and my two clean shirts and shoved them into the valise. I do not have time for this, I thought, seething. It was already Thursday. I was on a tight deadline with Mozart, and had to get started on the libretto for Martín. I needed the cash those commissions would pay, but I wouldn't see a florin until the work was done. Although I lived comfortably, I had little savings, and my expenses were high. Because I was required to attend the theater almost every day, I had to own more clothing than the average man of my station. Suits, shoes, wigs, stockings, and pomade cost a small fortune.

I groaned as I pulled out my dress suit from the cupboard. It was last year's fashion, not really suitable for dinner in the house of a baron. As I folded the waistcoat, I noticed that the hem was beginning to fray. Well, it would have to do. When I was paid for *Figaro,* I would treat myself to one of those new English-style suits everyone was sporting this spring.

I walked over to the shelf where I kept my small collection of books and took down the three I never travel without: my old Dante, its pages covered with years of jottings; a petite volume of Horace; and my Petrarch, its cover worn by my almost daily consultation. I placed them in my satchel, then collected all of the papers strewn over my desk and added them to the bag.

A shiver ran down my back as I recalled Pergen's threats. I could not understand why the minister had chosen me. In my years in Vienna, I had taken care not to show any political inclinations. Did Pergen really believe that I could solve this crime? True, I am intelligent and observant, as every poet must be. I have a charming personality—I am skilled at drawing others out in conversation, particularly women. And it is true that, posing as a poetry master, an investigator could find out more from the members of the household than could a cloddish policeman like Troger. But hunting down a spy and a murderer! How had I gotten myself into this mess?

I remembered Pergen mentioning that I had been highly recommended to him. Who could have given me such an unwelcome reference? Probably that serpent Rosenberg. He and Pergen probably ran into one another every day at the

Hofburg, and if Pergen had confided his need for an investigator, Rosenberg would have jumped at an opportunity to discredit me. Distracting me from my work would sabotage *Figaro,* ruin my reputation with Mozart and the other composers in the city, and clear the way for Casti to take my job at the theater.

As I packed a few final things in my valise and closed it, I wondered who at the Palais Gabler had told Troger about my argument with Florian Auerstein. I had met only four people in the household besides the boy: the music teacher, Piatti; the chambermaid, Antonia; the housekeeper, Rosa Hahn; and Marianne Haiml. I remembered the footsteps I had heard receding in the hallway as I left the library. They had been heavy, so must have belonged to a man. But anyone in the household could have reported me. It would have been easy enough for the baroness's guardian, the valet, or the baron's secretary to casually ask one of the others my name. Had the same person who had told Troger about my argument with Auerstein also lied to him about seeing me run from the house? I shivered. It seemed I already had at least one enemy waiting for me at the palais.

I put on my old cloak and gathered my bags and stick. My eyes fell on Vogel's box. I would have to come back for it tomorrow. As I took one last look around my simple room, a stab of fear shot through me. Would I return to it in a few days, successful in my investigation, to take up my pen and resume my normal life? Or would I fail to find the killer, and spend the rest of my years rotting in an imperial prison or, worse, in an unmarked grave after a sham trial and death by hideous torture? Perhaps I would be spared that slow fate by the killer himself, who might find me before I found him. Shuddering, I locked the door behind me and dragged my bags down the stairs.

PART II

A Little Song
on the Breeze

Six

The palais courtyard was empty when I arrived, its large windows shuttered and dark. The little fountain in the corner sat silent. I hurried by the area of soiled stones where Florian Auerstein had met his death. A ragged posy of flowers lay forlornly on the spot.

The door was opened by the same girl who had greeted me the day before—Antonia Bohm, Troger had said she was named. Today her curls were tucked neatly under her cap, but her face was pale, her dark eyes red from crying. She looked like a sad child, not the self-satisfied young woman I had seen admiring herself in the mirror the day before. Troger had said that she was taking the boy's death very hard. She stared at me uncomprehendingly as I gently explained why I was there.

"You will have to speak with Miss Hahn, sir," she said. "She's gone to the market. Come back later." She started to push the heavy door closed. Come back later? My cheeks grew hot. I certainly did not intend to stand in the street until the housekeeper returned to receive me. The least the baron could have done was to alert his staff to my arrival. I took a deep breath to calm my rising anger. I was exhausted and I did not want to lose my temper in front of this poor girl. I thrust my stick in the door's path and pushed my way in.

"Could you please fetch Miss Haiml?" I asked. She stared at me blankly for a moment, then turned and ran off toward the back of the house. I pulled my bags inside. The foyer was quiet, the only sound the clock ticking on the wall to my right. I stepped over to the large mirror on my left and studied myself, pleased to see that I did not look as exhausted as I felt.

"Signore! Signor Da Ponte!" I turned to see the music master, Piatti, descending the stairs. He grasped my hand and shook it. His face was ashen, and his left eye had developed a slight tic. "I was so pleased to hear that you have taken a position here," he said. "But how strange. One day you are here to visit Marianne, the next you are the poetry master!" His laugh was bright and forced.

"It is good to see you again," I said.

His eyes narrowed as he peered at me, his face solemn. "Have you heard the news?"

I was about to nod when I remembered that I was supposed to know nothing of the murder. I shook my head.

"A young man who lived here—the baron's protégé—" His voice shook. "The boy was murdered yesterday."

"Murdered! Here in the house?"

"Yes, yesterday afternoon. He—someone pushed him out the window of the library."

I murmured words of sympathy.

"A madman must have broken into the house," Piatti continued, his voice rising. "I found him. I'll never forget the sight, never. Every time I close my eyes I see him lying there on the stones, his head in a ghastly tilt, his legs askew, like a cloth doll a child had dropped on the floor. And the blood! I—" His hands trembled violently. His eyelid jerked up and down.

I took his arm and led him to the bench under the mirror. "Come, my friend, sit. I am shocked to hear about this. How terrible for you."

"His eyes!" Piatti's voice broke. "His eyes were wide open, staring right at me!"

I grasped one of his hands, hoping to stop his trembling. "Were you close to the boy?" I asked.

"Yes. He often joined us when I gave lessons to the baroness." He looked up at me. "He was a pleasure to teach. Very bright, talented. He could write a song so quickly." He shook his head. "If his father hadn't decided long ago that the boy was destined for the diplomatic corps, I would have suggested that he go to Bologna to study music." His voice cracked as he bent over, burying his face in his hands.

"Try to calm yourself," I said gently.

He sat still for a few moments, then took a deep breath and sat up. "Yes, you are right. I must get hold of myself. The baroness will need my support. She was fond of the boy." He stood up and straightened his waistcoat, then looked around the foyer. "Where has that silly girl gotten to now? Come, I know which room you've been given. It's right next to mine." He took my valise in one hand and my satchel in the other and headed up the stairs. I snatched up my stick and followed.

"Of course, you remember the library," Piatti said as we reached the first landing. His voice grew quiet. "That is where the boy was killed." I nodded. He pointed down the hall-way. "The baron's office is down there."

We climbed another flight of stairs and stopped at a large landing with walls covered in fine pale green silk. Piatti pointed to the right. "The baroness's chamber is just here. The baron's rooms are farther down that hall." He turned to the left. "The guest rooms are on this side."

I started down the hallway. "No, no, signore," Piatti said. "We are upstairs, with the rest of the staff." He started up the next set of stairs. I frowned. The servants' quarters! Surely the baron did not intend that I— I checked my anger as I remembered Pergen's instructions. I was here as a poetry teacher, not in my capacity as theater poet. If the baron chose to house his teaching masters with the servants, I must go along. I stood on the landing for a minute to clear the em-barrassment and annoyance from my face, and followed Pi-atti up to the garret.

The landing at the top of the stairs was smaller and darker than those on the floors below, its walls painted a pale gray. Piatti led me to the left, past a small alcove fitted with a wooden bench, and opened the first door. To my surprise, the room itself was bright and airy, larger than my own lodg-ings in the Graben. A beautifully carved wooden bed, topped by a thick linen-clad mattress, shared the right-hand wall with a small fireplace. To my left was a small cupboard, ad-equate for the clothing I had brought; a washbasin; and a small desk with a wooden chair. Opposite the door was a large dormer window, under which sat a chair upholstered in fabric of the same watery shade of green I had noticed on the walls a floor below.

"The baroness enjoys decorating," Piatti said as he hoisted my valise onto the mattress and opened the latch. "Our rooms receive the castoffs." He removed a pile of clothing from the valise and carried it to the cupboard.

I hurried to intercept him. "Please, signore, there is no need. I can do that myself later," I said.

"It's no trouble," he said.

"Please, Signor Piatti." His shoulders sagged as I took the clothes from him.

"Call me Tomaso," he said.

I nodded. "And I am Lorenzo. I hope we'll have time to discuss music while I am here," I added. His eyes brightened. "But if you'll excuse me now, I'd like to settle in and organize my thoughts before I meet the baron and baroness."

"Of course, of course," he said. "I have work to do myself. I'm right next door if you need me."

I crossed the room and looked out the window. I was relieved to see that it overlooked a small formal garden, not the stony courtyard. The chair was comfortable, nicely stuffed. Between it and the bed stood a small round table with a candlestick. I had already noticed a small box of candles on the desk. For the first time since I had been awakened from my sleep by Pergen's men, I felt a glimmer of happiness. I could not afford to have such a chair in my lodgings, so I was forced to read sitting straight in my hard desk chair. Candles were expensive, so I never felt I could afford to read or work into the night. Perhaps my stay here at the palais would not be as onerous as I had expected. I could spend what spare time I had in this snug chair, reading the beloved books I had brought with me. Perhaps the baron would even allow me to borrow some of the volumes in his collection.

I leaned my head back and closed my eyes. My mouth was sour with exhaustion. My right temple throbbed, and my shoulder was filled with a dull pain. I felt as though I could sleep for a week. But I had better unpack and begin my task. The sooner I could bring Pergen and Troger some useful information, the sooner I could return to my own life.

I hung my clothes in the cupboard and turned to my satchel. I carefully removed my books and set them on the table next to the reading chair, then emptied the rest of the contents onto the desk. I decided to begin my investigation with a visit to the library. Perhaps I would get some sense of the crime there. As I left the room, I looked in the keyhole for the key. There was none. A twinge of worry crossed my mind. How could I protect myself against a murderer with no lock on the door?

The house was quiet, and I encountered no one as I went down the two flights of stairs and let myself into the library. The room was empty, still, and dark, the heavy velvet drapes drawn against the late-morning sun. No fire had been lit in the grate, and I shivered as I approached the wall of windows, whether from a real chill or from uneasiness, I could not say. I had never been at the scene of a murder before, and I struggled to keep my imagination in check as I pulled the drapes open and examined the windowsill where the boy had hidden from me just yesterday. It was about a foot and a half deep, and made a comfortable alcove from which a small-bodied boy like Florian Auerstein could eavesdrop on members of the household. I leaned over and studied the cream-colored wood of the sill, but could see no evidence of a struggle: no scuffs from the boy's shoes; no chips in the paint; and to my relief, no blood.

I climbed up onto the sill and knelt in front of the large windows. I turned the knob that held them closed. The hinges creaked loudly as the windows slowly swung outward from the center. Cool, fresh air rushed into the room. I took a deep breath and stuck my head out of the right window, forcing myself to look down at the courtyard. My empty stomach flipped as I stared down at the dark patch on the stones directly below. Piatti had said there had been a lot of blood. My head began to swim. My eyes filled with bright stars. I could hear the boy screaming as he fell through the air.

I quickly pulled my head back into the room. Blinded by the stars, I groped for the bottom of the window frame in an attempt to steady myself. I knelt on the sill until my head and vision cleared, then closed the windows and turned the knob.

I hoisted my body around and tried to sit in the position in which I had found the boy yesterday. The afternoon had been warm, and the windows had been open during my visit. Florian must have sat right where I was now, cross-legged on the sill. The murderer must have been someone he had known and trusted—he would not have sat next to a wide-open window while arguing with someone he feared. Even though the boy had been small for his age, it would have taken some strength to push him out the window. The murderer would have had to lift him a bit to clear the window frame before pushing him to his death.

I carefully pulled myself to a standing position and reached up to examine the drapery rod and the thick velvet that hung from it. I pulled on the soft drapes, first the left one, then the right, but could see no spots where the fabric had come loose from the rod, and no evidence that the boy had grabbed onto the drapes in an attempt to save himself.

As I started to lower myself to a kneeling position, my foot twisted in the left drape. I kicked at the heavy fabric and grabbed onto the window knob to steady myself. The large windows began to groan open. I kicked again at the drape, but only tangled my foot further. I clung to the latch as the right window swung out to the courtyard, taking me with it. My heart pounded as I looked down at the stones. If the knob broke I would share the boy's fate. I kicked again at the drape, then again. Pain shot through my shoulder as I struggled to keep the heavy window from dragging me farther. The pit of my stomach was empty and cold. I took a deep breath and kicked my foot again, as hard as I could. Mercifully, the fabric released me from its grasp. I jerked myself back from the window, pulled it shut, and secured the knob.

I turned around and slumped on the sill, my heart pounding. I closed my eyes and tried to regulate my breathing. After a few moments I climbed off the sill and looked around the room. Everything seemed exactly as it had been when I left here yesterday. The little Harlequin figurine stared at me from the table near the sofa. The rows of books sat silently on their shelves. I shook my head. It was clear that I would find no help with my inquiry here.

I turned to check that the windows were tightly latched and straightened the drape that had twisted around my foot. A bright patch at the bottom near the floor caught my eye. I leaned over to examine the spot. It was not a part of the drape, but a piece of ribbon caught in the velvet. I pulled it out. It was about a foot long, white, with a delicate floral pattern embroidered in gold thread—the kind of ribbon used to decorate a lady's bonnet. How long had it been lodged in the folds of the drape? To whom did it belong? Had Florian Auerstein brought it here, or had his murderer inadvertently dropped it?

"But madame—" I started as a voice came from the hallway. A moment later, the door opened.

"I must see it for myself," a warm, melodious voice said. I stuffed the ribbon into the pocket of my breeches and quickly closed the drapes.

"But madame, you shouldn't." I recognized Marianne Haiml's voice as she entered the room, followed by another woman of the same petite, slender build. "It will only upset you. Oh! It is so dark in here. Let me open the drapes." Marianne headed toward where I stood in the shadows. I cleared my throat and stepped forward.

Marianne screamed. "Who is there?" She ran to the drapes and yanked them open. Sunlight filled the room. "Signor Da Ponte? What are you doing here?"

I could not answer her, because my eyes were fixed on her

companion, who remained standing at the door. My heart twisted as I stared at her. She was dressed in white, as she had been last night. Today, her auburn hair was gathered into a thick braid. Her skin was still pale, and she looked as though she had been crying.

She crossed the room to me. "Are you the Abbé Da Ponte?" she asked, taking my hand. I could not force my lips to form words, but I was able to make my head nod. "I am so happy to meet you. I am Caroline Gabler."

Her hand felt smooth and small in mine. I stared into her eyes, which were a soft jade green. "I am looking forward to our lessons," she said.

I bowed over our clasped hands as my tongue finally untangled itself. "I am honored, Your Excellency," I managed to say. She smelled like lavender.

She continued to hold my hand as she smiled at me. "Please, you must not be so formal with me. I will be your student."

To my dismay, I found myself bowing once more. Idiot! Stop bobbing like that children's toy, that silly clown in the windup box. My cheeks grew hot with embarrassment as she gently pulled her hand away.

"Lessons?" Marianne asked, looking at me. "I don't understand."

"Yes," the baroness answered. "I haven't had time to tell you, Marianne. It all happened so quickly. My husband has wished to hire a poetry master for me for a while now. He had heard that the abbé was the best poet in the city."

My heart swelled with pride at her words.

"They were able to finalize the agreement just last night, I believe."

I turned toward Marianne. "Yes, I signed the contract while I was at the theater last night," I lied.

Her intelligent eyes gazed at me coolly. "Well, I hope this appointment will not interfere with any of your other projects, signore," she said.

"I do not expect that it will, Miss Haiml," I said.

The baroness approached the middle window and ran her fingers over the wide sill. "I cannot believe he is dead," she murmured. "He was so young—" Her voice caught. Marianne hurried to her and took her hand. I longed to do the same.

"I have heard the news," I said gently. "I am sorry to have come at such an unfortunate time." She gave me a sad smile and nodded.

"Come, madame, let me take you back to your chamber," Marianne said. "I'll make you a dish of chocolate. That will help you feel better."

The baroness gave one last sad look at the window. "Yes, I am coming," she said. She offered her hand to me again. My right arm tingled at her touch.

"I would like my first lesson tomorrow morning, Signor Abbé," she said. "Marianne will come for you."

I let go of her hand and bowed again. When I looked up, she was gone.

I stood looking after her, my mind newly invigorated despite my lack of sleep. I knew exactly which poems I would use in the lesson tomorrow. Perhaps two or three of those to start, and then—

Heavy footsteps came from the hallway. They sounded like the ones I had heard from this same room yesterday. Footsteps that belonged to the person who had lied to Troger, who had told him I had threatened Florian Auerstein, who had claimed to have seen me running from the house. Footsteps that belonged to the person who had landed me in this mess.

I strode to the door, ready to confront my enemy. I grabbed the knob and pulled open the door.

"Who the hell are you?" A short, broad-chested man in his fifties stood before me. "What are you doing in here?" he demanded.

I looked down at him and offered my hand. "I am Lorenzo Da Ponte," I said. "I have been hired by the baron to teach poetry to his wife."

"Poetry!" He snorted, ignoring my outstretched hand as he pushed by me. My eyes watered from the strong smell of French cologne. "What does she need with that nonsense? Her head is already full of fanciful sentiments."

"The baron believes his wife might enjoy the lessons," I said.

He glared at me. "I wasn't told anything about this! Caroline said nothing to me!"

"I believe the decision was made just yesterday."

He looked me up and down. "Yes, I see. Well, as a stranger to this house, you may not be aware that this is a difficult time for the baroness. There has been a murder. Someone broke into the house yesterday and killed the baron's page."

"I was saddened to hear about it," I said. "But I have just met the baroness, and she is eager to begin our lessons tomorrow."

He looked at me for a moment, speculatively. He turned on his heel, went over to one of the bookcases, and studied the titles.

"I beg your pardon, but you haven't told me your name," I said.

"I am Dr. Urban Rausch," he said without turning.

Ah, the baroness's guardian.

He pulled a book from the shelf and turned to me. "I live here as a special guest of the baroness," he said. "What did you say your name was? De Monte?"

"Da Ponte. Lorenzo Da Ponte."

"What are you, some sort of teacher at the university?" he asked.

"No, sir, I am not. I am honored to hold the position of poet to His Majesty the Emperor's Court Theater."

He waved his hand as if dismissing my title to the breeze. "I see. I'm afraid I've never heard of you. I don't frequent the theater. Where did you attend university—up north? What degree does one earn to qualify one to teach poetry?" I didn't think I imagined the sneer in his voice.

"I studied literature and poetry in my native Venice," I said through clenched teeth.

"I see." He turned back to the bookcase, replaced the book, and drew out another. I winced as he opened it widely, cracking the spine. He studied a page for a moment, then carried the volume over to the sofa, sat down, and began to read.

I stood fuming. What a pompous ass! Was I to stand here all day? I cleared my throat. He looked up with an expression of feigned surprise that I was still there. He pulled a large gold watch from his pocket and made a show of studying it, replaced it in his pocket, and waved his hand at me.

"You may go. Close the door behind you, if you will."

I stalked out, suppressing the temptation to slam the door. I stood at the stair landing for a moment to calm myself. The bombastic jackass! What degree did I have to qualify me to teach poetry! As if understanding and appreciating the true meaning of a poem could be learned through dry, technical lecturing instead of by years of reading, contemplation, and reading again.

I started up the stairs to my room, my mind brimming with questions. Could the doctor be the spy and murderer? What would be his motive? He had known the baroness since she was a child. Why would he spy for Frederick, knowing that his activities could jeopardize her husband's career?

Then again, perhaps he had grown tired of being a "special guest" of his ward, and had been offered an opportunity to make a large sum of money by spying on the baron.

As I reached the third floor and opened the door to my room, another question sprang to mind. I was sure I had recognized Rausch's footsteps as those I had heard before I had left the house yesterday. Had he been the person who had lied to Troger, claiming he saw me running from the house? Had he been acting just now, pretending he didn't know me? If he had lied to Troger, what were his motives? Why had he blamed me for the murder?

. . .

I had just begun to unbutton my waistcoat when there was a tentative knock at the door. I opened it to a thin, small, middle-aged man with a narrow face pitted with smallpox scars.

"Signor Da Ponte?" he asked in a soft voice. "I am Jakob Ecker, the baron's secretary. He would like to see you in his office."

I crossed over to the cupboard, pulled on my better waistcoat, and followed him down the stairs. As we passed the library, I noted that the door stood open and the room was empty. Dr. Rausch must not have found his reading as interesting after I had left as it had been when I had been there to ignore.

The secretary stopped at the end of the hallway and knocked on one of the wide double doors. He opened it and gestured for me to enter.

"Ecker, where is that clock Kaunitz brought me from Paris?" The deep voice came from a man seated behind a large desk across the room. His attention was fixed on a pile of documents, and he did not look up at our entrance. The secretary scurried past me.

"Let me look, sir. It is not on the table?"

"No. I saw it there yesterday, but now I can't find it. Look around, would you? Perhaps the girl mislaid it." The baron looked up from his work and stood. "You must be Da Ponte. I am Christof Gabler." He was the type of man women found handsome: strong, chiseled bones set in a wide face; long, dark hair tied back; tall, with an athletic build. He seemed to be a few years younger than me. He and his wife must make an elegant pair, I thought with a pang of envy.

I bowed.

"Is it there?" he asked impatiently, looking over to the corner of the large office, where Ecker was searching frantically through a tall cupboard. His face red with agitation, the secretary shook his head.

"We have someone with sticky fingers in this house," the baron explained as he waved me toward a chair in front of the desk. "Several things have disappeared in the last few months. Ecker, never mind, you can do that later. Bring me the letters and I'll sign them now."

The secretary scooped up a pile of papers from a smaller desk and laid them before the baron. While he signed the documents, I surveyed the room. The furnishings were lavish yet masculine. A sofa and a set of chairs in a muted blue striped fabric were grouped before the fireplace, which dominated the left wall of the room. A long sword clad in a plain scabbard, its hilt unembellished, unlike most of the swords worn by the aristocracy, hung over the mantel.

The baron handed the documents to Ecker and looked over at me. "That is the first weapon my father ever made," he said. He crossed the room in long strides and plucked the sword from the wall. Pulling off the scabbard, he presented the sword to me. "Look, it is over fifty years old, but see how sharp it is," he said. I stared at the blade, imagining it slicing into a man's neck, the blood spurting from the wound. I gulped and managed a nod, which I hoped he took as a sign of admiration.

The baron turned to Ecker. "You may go," he said as he

sheathed the sword and hung it back on the wall. "Come back in an hour and I will dictate the memorandum to Kaunitz." The secretary bowed, nodded to me, and headed toward the door. "Wait," the baron called. "Has there been a message from Esterházy?"

Ecker pursed his lips and shook his head. "Nothing yet today, sir. Shall I send over to the prince's office to see if your invitation has been waylaid?" he asked. "The dinner is tomorrow night."

The baron scowled. I heard him swear softly. "No, never mind." The secretary bowed again and left the room, shutting the doors behind him.

Gabler sprawled in his desk chair and regarded me. "Well, Da Ponte, I suppose I should be grateful to Pergen for sending you here, but in truth, I have no idea what help you will be. A poet as an investigator! What could you possibly learn? And this idea about a spy! It is ridiculous. A few documents were misplaced, that is all. No one in this house could be working for Frederick."

"I think, Your Excellency, that the count is concerned about the boy's death," I ventured.

He picked up a letter opener and began to tap it against his left palm. I noticed it was a miniature of the sword, done in silver. "That was an accident," he said. "It must have been. The boy was always jumping around. He must have been looking out the window in the library and tripped. I think Pergen has lost his mind, calling it murder."

Was I mistaken, or did I hear anxiety in his voice? "The count seemed certain that Auerstein's death is related to Prussia," I said.

He pointed the little sword at me. "Yes, I know what he thinks," he snapped. "But I can't imagine anyone here working for Frederick. It's a small household. I've known most of them for years. I'm certain of their loyalty." He threw the letter opener onto the desk. "God, I wish I had never agreed to accept that boy as a page."

"He was troublesome?"

"He was flighty, easily distracted. His work was careless. I knew there was no future for him in the diplomatic corps. I couldn't even get him to wear his livery with any pride. His father was here late yesterday, to take the body and clear out Florian's things. The boy's room was a mess, clothes and papers scattered everywhere. I was embarrassed for the prince, to have to see how his son lived."

"If, just for the sake of argument, to please Count Pergen, we assume it was murder—"

He quirked an eyebrow at me. I plowed onward. "I believe you have a new valet—Gottfried Bohm?"

Gabler laughed. "You think he is the spy? The man is stupid! Trust me, he can barely perform the duties of a valet, let alone steal state secrets." He nodded toward the door. "Ecker worked for my father. He's been my secretary since I left university."

"I met the doctor—Rausch, is it?" I asked.

"Surely you don't suspect him! He was my wife's guardian. He dotes on her. He would never do anything to embarrass me. And he is very comfortable living in my house, off my money."

"And Signor Piatti?"

"Piatti?" He snorted. "His head is full of music. I don't

think he pays any attention to politics. Besides, he's an Italian. Why would he work for Prussia?"

For the money, I thought. "I met the Auerstein boy yesterday," I said. "Although he was small, I think it would have taken some strength to push him out the window. The murderer would have had to lift him over the bottom window frame."

He rolled his eyes at me and picked up the little sword once more. I pushed on. "That would eliminate the ladies of the household from the list of suspects, I think. They all seem far too delicate to have been able to lift the boy."

"Oh, I don't know about that, Signor Abbé!" He barked with laughter. "Sometimes it is necessary to convince a woman to give in to her desires. They can be very strong when they want to play the little virgin act before they surrender to you." He gave me a knowing wink. I struggled to avoid showing my distaste on my face.

"Anyway, I think we are wasting our time, but as you say, since it would please the count and Prince Kaunitz, you should stay awhile," he said. "At least the baroness will enjoy the poetry lessons." He waved his hand in dismissal. "Let Ecker know if you need anything from me."

I stood and bowed. "Thank you, sir," I said. As I turned to go, I remembered the favor I wished to ask. "If I may, sir," I said hesitantly.

His attention was already deep into a document. "Yes?" he asked, not looking up.

"I have had the opportunity to admire your beautiful library," I said. "May I tell you what an impressive collection you have? I would be honored if you would allow me to use some of the volumes, to take to my room perhaps, to read at night." I winced at the sycophancy I heard in my voice.

"Of course," he said, still not looking up at me. "Read whatever you like. I don't even know what's there—the books came with the house when I bought it."

There was a knock on the door. "Come," the baron called.

Marianne entered the room. "Oh, pardon me, sir, I did not know anyone was here with you," she said, giving the baron a curtsy.

He looked up from his work. His eyes raked over her slim body, hungrily taking her in from head to toe. "What is it?" he asked.

She handed him a note. "The baroness asked me to deliver this, and to tell you that there will be a guest for dinner this afternoon," she said.

He opened the note and read it. Marianne looked over at me and smiled tightly. I nodded back. Her eyes widened. Her face turned white. She was staring at me, her eyes fixed on my legs.

The baron tossed the note aside. "All right, Marianne, you may tell your mistress I will be ready for dinner at three." He waved us both away. Marianne gave another curtsy, glanced at me, and headed toward the door. As I followed her, I quickly looked down and saw a small piece of white fabric hanging from the pocket of my breeches. It was the ribbon I had found in the library.

Seven

Marianne waited for me in the hall. Her face betrayed no sign of her reaction to the ribbon. It must have worked its way out of my pocket after I had left the library.

"Dinner is ready in the kitchen, signore." She whirled and headed toward the stairway.

I sighed. Dinner in the kitchen, with the staff. The baron was taking this charade too far. At least I would have a chance to learn more about the household.

The basement kitchen was large and warm. A wooden table set for six stood in front of the wide hearth. Antonia and Rosa Hahn were ladling vegetables into large bowls. My mouth watered from the aromas as I took a seat opposite Marianne. I was famished.

Jakob Ecker entered, followed by a scowling, thickset man of about sixty. Antonia's ladle clattered to the hearth as she ran to pull out the chair at the head of the table.

"Sit here, Papa," she said. "Near the fire." He grunted a greeting of sorts and sat. Antonia took the seat to his left.

I gaped. This was Antonia's father, the valet, Gottfried Bohm? He seemed much too old to be the father of a girl in her teens. I studied him. He did not look like any valet I had encountered before. His hair was unkempt and oily, his face clouded with a closed, almost surly expression. I could not imagine him as manservant and confidant to the smooth young nobleman I had just met.

Rosa placed the food on the table and took her place next to me, at the opposite head from Bohm. Marianne passed the plates as Rosa filled them with steaming carrots, potatoes, and slices of meat. My stomach growled in anticipation. The room was quiet as we all began to eat. I gazed at the large slab of overroasted pork on my plate, took up my knife and fork, and began to cut the meat into small pieces. The meat was tough, the knife dull. I sighed, longing for the dishes of home: brothy stews brimming with fish fresh from the sea; soft, cheesy polenta; risotto cooked tender to the bite. I pushed the meat to the side of my plate. I would have to make do with the carrots and potatoes. I turned my attention to making conversation.

"Signor Piatti will not be joining us?" I asked.

Rosa sniffed. "He prefers to take his meals outside the house."

"And the doctor?"

"Dr. Rausch dines with the baron and baroness," Rosa replied.

"The doctor considers himself much too fine for this

company," Marianne said. Rosa gave her a sour look. Marianne met her gaze with cool eyes.

"You will find the doctor will trumpet his connection to the baroness whenever he can, signore," Ecker said.

I smiled. "I've already experienced that."

"Madame thinks he is an old toad." Marianne giggled. "She loves to poke fun at him and his fiancée."

"The doctor is engaged to Franziska Heindl," Ecker said, turning toward me. I was glad to see him warm up to me. He could provide me much useful information if I developed a friendship with him. "You've heard of the Heindl family?"

I shook my head.

"She is the widow of a grain merchant. He died a year ago, leaving her his fortune. Dr. Rausch is her physician, and as he treated her for her grief, he found his way into her heart." Ecker's eyes twinkled.

"And her purse," Marianne added.

"That's enough," Rosa said sharply. "There will be no gossip at my table." She turned to me, her face red. "Please ignore them, signore," she said. Her voice was high-pitched. "I am certain the baroness is happy to have her guardian here with her at this difficult time."

The company returned its attention to the dinner. I sawed at the meat, finally succeeding in cutting it into smaller pieces. As I finished the potatoes and began to discreetly hide the bits of meat under the remaining carrots, I wondered how to go about getting information from the staff. I decided to use the housekeeper's last remark as my opening. I put down my utensils and turned to her.

"The boy's death must be very difficult for both the baroness and the baron," I said. I heard a sharp intake of breath from the end of the table, where Antonia sat with her father. I looked around. "And for all of you," I added.

"A murder!" Ecker said. "It is nerve-racking. The idea that a madman could gain entry to this house and kill that boy in the middle of an afternoon, while we were all going about our daily routines. What if he strikes again?"

I looked down the table at Antonia. Her face was pale, and her hands trembled as she lifted her fork to her mouth. Her dour-faced father concentrated on his plate.

"That's nonsense," Rosa said. "The front door and servants' door are always kept locked. No one can just walk into this house. The murderer must have been someone Florian knew from the outside, someone he invited into the house himself."

Antonia dropped her fork.

I looked across at Marianne, who was staring at me, her face thoughtful.

"What was the boy like?" I asked.

Rosa pursed her lips. "He was a troublemaker."

"You must understand, signore," Ecker said. "Florian was young, very immature. One of my duties was to give him a basic education about our work here, so the baron would not have to waste his valuable time. He was an inconsistent student, one day completely absorbed, asking dozens of questions of me, the next day lazy and flighty, hiding when I sought him out."

Antonia gasped.

"He poked around everything," Ecker continued. He

turned to Bohm. "Didn't you find him going through the baron's private cupboard?"

The valet grunted.

Antonia's fork fell to the table. "Stop it!" she shrieked. She rose from her seat, knocking over the chair. "You are horrible! None of you really knew him! He was a gentle boy. He loved me! He was going to marry me!" She burst into tears.

The staff stared at her, mouths agape.

"Don't be ridiculous, Antonia," Rosa said. "The boy was not going to marry you. He was the son of a prince. If he did tell you he loved you, it was just to use you."

The girl turned to her, eyes ablaze. "What do you know about it, you dried-up old witch! He promised me he would take care of me. He told me I would have beautiful things, like before—"

She stopped as her father rose from his seat.

Bohm's slap was quick and loud. Antonia screamed. Her hands flew to her cheek. She stared at her father, her eyes wide with shock. Marianne jumped from her chair and ran to her, cradling the girl in her arms. Bohm gave a grunt, looked around the table, and stalked out of the room.

Marianne drew Antonia to her feet. "I'll take her to her room," she said. The rest of us sat quietly as she led the weeping girl away, then turned our attention back to our plates. The food had grown cold.

"Forgive me, madame," I said to Rosa. "I should not have brought up the subject of the murder. I had no idea she would react so violently."

She smiled tightly at me. "Yes, she is a foolish girl, full

of fanciful dreams. Sometimes I think there is something wrong with her. She makes up such stories. And that pig of a father."

We sat silently for a few minutes. I pushed the meat around on my plate, then gave up and put my utensils down, cursing the day a year and half earlier when I had trusted that scoundrel Doriguti with my health. I had recently had a tooth pulled, and a painful tumor had formed on the spot. The court surgeon had advised me to have it lanced, but I had been squeamish about sharp instruments and had delayed having the procedure performed. Doriguti was also a surgeon. He was passionately in love with the daughter of my landlord. Unfortunately, the girl had eyes only for me. Doriguti had told me that surgery was unnecessary. He had given me a liquor to dab on the growth a few times a day for two weeks. The tumor had disappeared after a few days, but Doriguti had urged me to keep using the liquor for the full two weeks. By the next week, I had lost sixteen of my teeth. The serpent had given me aqua fortis, an acid used in cleaning and engraving. If the maid who washed my clothing had not recognized the bottle, I would be dead. As it was, I had just now begun to recover my appetite after the damage the poison had caused to my innards. But now I had only stumps where before I had teeth. If dinner at the Palais Gabler was always going to be roasted meat, I would have to join Piatti and eat outside the house.

The long silence had grown uncomfortable. I racked my brain for something to say. "Did you enjoy your Easter?" I asked the housekeeper.

She sniffed. "To be truthful, I enjoyed the service much more before the emperor made all these silly new rules," she said. "I miss seeing the statues and pictures decorated, and the glorious music. And I always enjoyed the processions." As part of his church reforms, the emperor had shortened the service and banned some of the more elaborate, medieval rituals.

"I don't know why he has to meddle in everything," Rosa continued. "Every time it storms, I hide down here in the basement, since the emperor stopped the bell-ringing." For hundreds of years, the churches of Vienna had rung their bells during thunderstorms, for it was believed that the bells warded off lightning strikes. The emperor had banned the practice, citing the American Franklin's discovery that lightning was actually electricity. Now lightning conductors, not superstitious bell-ringing, protected Vienna from thunderstorms.

"The church is none of the emperor's business!" Rosa said.

"Shh!" Ecker hissed. "Be careful what you say!"

"I have a right to my opinions!" she snapped. She rose and began to clear the table.

I turned to Ecker. "The baron told me you have worked for him for a long time," I said.

He reached for the pitcher in the middle of the table and poured water into his mug. "Yes, I worked for his father before he died."

"You must have done a lot of traveling with the two of them," I said.

"There has been some travel, yes," he said. "It's one of the advantages of the job. I enjoy seeing the world, getting out of Vienna. I'm looking forward to going to St. Petersburg when the baron assumes the ambassadorship."

"Were you born here?" I asked.

He looked at me closely, his eyes narrowing. "Why do you ask?"

"You seem to have an accent of some sort. It's a hobby of mine to identify accents," I lied. "There are so many different ones here in Vienna."

"No, I was born here," he said, his voice cold.

"Did you ever get to my native Venice in your travels?"

"No, I'm afraid I haven't been there." He pushed his plate away.

"You must have traveled all over the empire with the baron," I said. "I'd like to see more of it myself—Hungary, Bavaria, even up north. Have you been to any of the northern principalities?"

His face reddened. He stood and looked down at me. "Are you interrogating me, Signor Da Ponte?" he asked.

I held up my hands. "No, no. Forgive me, I am just curious about people. I meant no harm."

"If you are to stay in this house, signore," he said softly, "you should mind your own business!" He left the room.

I sat and sipped my mug of water, watching as Rosa cleared the table and stacked the dishes. I considered the various theories of the murder I had heard. I did not agree with Ecker that a madman had entered the house and killed Florian Auerstein. But perhaps someone from the outside had come to visit Florian on the day of the murder. I should ask Troger if he knew if anyone besides me had come to the house that day. I shuddered at the thought of seeing him again.

One thing was certain. The members of the staff were worried, and afraid. For it must be as obvious to them as it was to me that a third theory of the murder remained unvoiced. If a madman had not been able to enter the house, and no one had visited Florian on the day of his death, then the conclusion was unavoidable. Florian's murderer lived at the Palais Gabler.

I stopped by my lodgings to pick up Vogel's box, intending to bring it back with me to the palais later, then walked past the Stephansdom and turned into the Schulerstrasse. Ahead of me, several doors down, a finely dressed aristocratic couple climbed out of a carriage in front of the cheery yellow façade of the city's best hotel. I turned into the inner courtyard of number 846 and climbed the stairs, admiring the handsome curlicued iron railings and stuccoed walls of the court. I stopped at the nearest door at the top of the first flight of stairs. My knock was answered by a maid, and as I entered the apartment and handed over my cloak and stick, Constanze Mozart came out to greet me.

"Lorenzo! It is good to see you again. Wolfgang will be right out."

I shifted Vogel's box to one arm and bowed to kiss Constanze's hand. Her large, almond-shaped eyes lit up as she laughed and pulled her hand out of my grasp.

"You are well?" I asked.

"I feel as fat as a sausage!" she answered. "This is my third pregnancy, but I'd forgotten how bad the swelling is at this stage. I can't get my feet into any of my good slippers."

"You look beautiful. Aglow, like the Madonna," I said.

"Such nice words! Enough! Enough!" She waved me off, laughing. A moment later, a small brown terrier, chased by a chubby toddler, darted into the vestibule and tangled itself up in Constanze's skirts. Wolfgang Mozart followed. He grabbed the child and swung him into his arms just in time to save the poor dog from a painful squeeze.

"No, no, Carl, don't torture Gauckerl," he said. "Lorenzo! Welcome!" He shifted the child in his arms and offered me his hand. The boy, laughing, pulled at his father's hair. "No, not Papa's hair! Don't muss Papa's beautiful hair!" Mozart cried as he tried to loose his son's grasp. The child laughed and gurgled as he tried to grab more of the light, fine hair on the composer's head. As I watched them, I felt a brief stab of regret as I remembered the dark night when I had left a tiny, warm bundle at the hidden window of the Ospedale della Pietà in Venice.

Constanze reached for her son. "You two go in. I'll bring some wine."

We moved into Mozart's study, a large room with tall windows overlooking the Schulerstrasse. A fine pianoforte held pride of place in the near corner. A large table surrounded by armchairs sat in the middle of the room, and served as the composer's desk. On the far right wall, a large birdcage sat next to a manuscript cabinet. I put Vogel's box on the desk and walked over to the cage, clicking my tongue.

A starling, resting on the perch within, raised its head and ruffled its feathers.

"Don't wake him up," Mozart warned. "He likes to show off his voice and he always sings off-key."

I placed my satchel on the floor and settled onto the long sofa in front of the windows. I ran my fingers over the rich damask cushion. Mozart was a renowned keyboard artist, in demand all over the city for private concerts. He and Constanze could easily afford this expensive apartment, with its high-quality furniture and lush fabrics.

"It's quiet here today," I said. Usually when I was here, the house was full of people and noise: Mozart's students practicing on the pianoforte; singers rehearsing arias composed by him; friends made on his many journeys visiting as houseguests.

"Yes," Mozart said. "I had a student this morning, and the guest room is empty right now."

I stood as Constanze entered, carrying a tray of glasses and a bottle of white wine. Mozart opened the bottle and poured two glasses. Constanze carried a glass to me and settled next to me on the sofa. I sipped. The wine's slight sweetness played over my tongue. "Rhine wine?" I asked.

Mozart nodded. "We had friends from Mannheim staying last week."

I took another sip, savoring it. I love wine, but it was hard to get anything but Hungarian Tokay in Vienna these days. To boost business in the wine-producing regions of his domain, the emperor had recently ordered that only wine produced in the empire be sold in the city. Most of the affordable wine came from large producers in Hungary.

Only wealthy noblemen had the contacts and money to import wine from the farther reaches of the empire, or to flout the directive and obtain French or Italian wines.

"What's in the box?" Mozart asked.

"Some things that belong to a friend of mine," I said. "Do you know Vogel, the barber?"

Mozart nodded.

"I went to have a shave Tuesday and found the shop closed. It seems Vogel has a large debt he cannot pay. While I was there, the constables took him off to prison."

"The poor man," Constanze murmured.

"He was distraught, but not only because of the prison sentence. His mother died last week. On her deathbed, she revealed that he was not her natural son."

"He never knew, all these years?" Mozart asked. "Why, he must be my age, or older."

"After his adoptive mother died, he found this box hidden in her cupboard. He believed the contents were valuable and that they might have belonged to his birth mother. He decided to try to find her."

Constanze raised her brow. "He thinks she was an aristocrat, with money that would help him pay off the debt?" she asked.

I nodded. "Since he is to spend the next year in prison, I took pity on him and offered to help him find his real parents."

Mozart rubbed his hands together. "A mystery! Can we see?" I nodded, and he pulled the lid off the box. Constanze joined him at the desk, and together they removed the muff, the ring, and the grammar book. Mozart studied the ring a moment and handed it to his wife. "What do you think?"

She rubbed the stone and turned the ring around in her fingers, eyeing it carefully. "Glass," she pronounced. Mozart picked up the book and riffled through the pages. "I had a copy of this grammar when I was a boy," he said. "You could buy one anywhere in Salzburg."

"I know," I said. "I just had an appraiser look at everything. He told me none of these things have any value." I looked at Constanze, who was holding the muff, slowly rubbing her fingers against its fur. "My expert did not know what kind of fur that is," I said, "but he was certain it was not white fox or ermine."

She laughed. "It's cat hair! A worthless piece."

Mozart took it from her and winked at me. "That's my girl, Lorenzo," he teased. "She can pick out a cheap imitation a mile away!" He ducked as Constanze slapped him playfully. Her face grew serious.

"The poor barber," she said. "He pinned all of his hopes on this box. What will you do next, Lorenzo? Do you have any other clues?"

"Yes, we need a packet of mysterious letters, preferably written in code," Mozart said, his eyes gleaming. "Perhaps we can trace Vogel's lineage back to the Habsburgs!"

Constanze swatted at him again. She turned back to me. "These things look like trinkets that a young, naïve girl might think were valuable. Perhaps they were given to her by some rich older man who was trying to seduce her."

"I had the same thought," I said.

"But how to find that man?" she continued. "Truly, Lorenzo, the task seems impossible. There is nothing to be learned from these things."

"I know," I said. "I am going to have to visit Vogel in prison and break the bad news. I hope that if I talk to him awhile, he might remember something he heard or saw when he was younger, something that could help me figure out my next step."

"Don't spend too much time on this, Lorenzo," Mozart warned. "Remember, we premiere in three weeks." He sat down at the worktable.

I winced. "I remember," I said. I hesitated, wondering if I should tell him about my predicament with Pergen. I had been warned to keep my investigation a secret, but didn't Mozart have a right to know about any possible impacts it might have on our project?

"What is it, Lorenzo?" Constanze asked.

I looked at the two of them. Constanze stood behind Mozart, her hand on his shoulder. He reached up and placed his hand over hers. I shook my head. "Nothing," I said. "I'm tired, that's all."

"I'll leave you to your work," Constanze said. I rose and kissed her hand again. As she closed the double doors behind her, I retrieved my satchel, carried it over to the table, and sat down opposite Mozart. I pulled out some papers.

"What did you come up with for the end of the third act?" he asked. He picked up Vogel's ring and began to fiddle with it.

The opera takes place on the wedding day of two servants of the lecherous Count Almaviva of Seville: his valet,

Figaro; and his wife's maid, Susanna. The two servants join forces with their mistress to prevent the count from exercising his feudal privilege of droit du seigneur, the right of a lord to be the first to bed a female servant on her wedding night. At the end of the third act, the two servants are finally married. During the festivities, the bride passes a note to the count, proposing a tryst in the garden. Unbeknownst to both the count and Figaro, the rendezvous is actually a plan concocted by Susanna and the countess to catch the count being unfaithful to his wife and to end his womanizing once and for all.

"I wrote some verses for a duet between Susanna and the count," I said. "Susanna will sing about her true intentions as she passes him the note—"

"I've been thinking about a pantomime," Mozart said as he lightly tossed Vogel's ring from hand to hand. "How about this: the orchestra will play as the characters mime the wedding ceremony. Wait—let's begin with a song praising the count, maybe from two of the peasant girls. You can write something short and quick. Then the ceremony. Susanna will find a way to give the note to the count. No words, just music. After that, general dancing. Maybe a fandango."

"No poetry?" I snatched the ring mid-toss and placed it and the muff into the box.

"No poetry, no arias. I think this idea will make for better theater. I'll write some dance music, the peasants will dance to it while the wedding is going on. The singers will mime the ceremony. After the dance, we can have the count and Figaro comment on it all. But nothing fancy."

My face must have shown my reaction to this plan, for

he laughed. "Don't look so disappointed, my friend," he said. "Let the music and action shine here. No need to clutter things up with words."

I opened my mouth to speak.

"I know, I know," Mozart said. "You're going to tell me that the poetry is as important as the music."

It was a long-standing friendly argument between the two of us.

"Well, it is true," I said. "The poetry is the door to the music, it's an integral part of the opera. If it is not necessary, why not set your music to a pharmacist's recipe collection, or a bookseller's catalog, or even this?" I held up Vogel's grammar.

"My music would be sublime even set to those," Mozart said. We both laughed. "No, I like the pantomime idea, with the dances. Let's try it. Your poetry will enhance every other part of the opera." He began to scribble on a piece of paper. I pulled the rejected duet toward me and, taking up a pen, began to edit it. We worked for a while, our pens scratching over the papers, the silence interrupted only by Mozart's occasional humming of a few bars of music.

I heard the bells at the Stephansdom chime the hour. I put down my pen and looked over at my friend, who was engrossed in his work. I leaned back in the chair and closed my eyes. Fatigue seeped through my bones. My mind retraced the events of the last two days, starting with my run-in with Casti and Rosenberg, then Salieri's mysterious remarks, and finally the hours I had spent with Pergen and Troger. I hadn't been able to tell Mozart and Constanze about the Auerstein murder. I was certain that Rosenberg was behind my predicament, that he had recommended me to Pergen in order to distract me from work on the opera. I did not want Rosenberg and Casti's conspiracy against me to harm my young friends. I sighed. I had to concentrate on my work. I had to find Florian Auerstein's killer. For if I was able to solve the murder for Pergen, and *Figaro* was a success, my enemies would be quieted once and for all.

Eight

The library in the Palais Gabler seemed less gloomy the next morning, its windows wide open to admit the breezes of the warm day, the heavy drapes pulled back to let in the sunlight. I sat at a small table, my notes spread before me.

"I apologize, Signor Da Ponte," the baroness said. "I had hoped that by today this room would seem less haunted." She shivered and pulled her lacy white shawl around her shoulders. "Although now that I am here, I can see that it will be some time before we can use it again without thinking of poor Florian."

Marianne rose from her place on the sofa beside her mistress and gathered her sewing. "Shall we move, madame? Perhaps the salon would be better?" I stood.

"No, it's all right, Marianne, we are settled here. We don't want to waste Signor Da Ponte's time." She turned to me. "Please, signore, why don't you begin? I am sure that once I hear the poems you have chosen, I will forget my cares."

"Very well, madame." I sat and took up a sheet. "If you will allow me, I shall read the first verse of this poem in its original Italian, and then translate it for you. That way you will be able to hear the rhythm of the work the way the poet intended." I looked up to see her velvet eyes regarding me. My heart started to beat faster and my hands suddenly felt clammy, like those of a schoolboy facing his first recitation. "This is a sonnet by Francesco Petrarch, written in the fourteenth century." Her eyes met mine again as she gently nodded for me to proceed. I took a breath and cleared my throat.

Amor m'à posto come segno a strale,
come al sol neve, come cera al foco,
et come nebbia al vento; et son già roco,
donna, mercé chiamando, et voi non cale.

I looked up to see the baroness leaning back into the cushions of the sofa, her eyes closed, her hands clasped as if in prayer.

"Such a beautiful language," she murmured.

"So many vowels!" Marianne said as she took a small pair of scissors from her mending basket and snipped a long thread. "What does it mean?"

"It translates to this," I said.

Love has placed me as a target for his arrow,
like snow in sun, like wax in fire,
like mist in wind; and I am already hoarse,
calling for mercy, lady, and you do not care.

Marianne frowned. She opened her mouth to speak. The baroness touched her shoulder, hushing her. "Please read us another verse, signore."

I cleared my throat again and continued.

From your eyes came the mortal blow,
against which neither time nor place can help me;
from you alone—and you take this lightly—
come forth the sun and fire and wind that makes me so.

"The poet is in love," the baroness said. Her eyes met mine and held them. The pit of my stomach felt strangely hollow.

"Yes, madame, he is. This sonnet is one of a large collection Petrarch wrote about his love for a lady named Laura. He first saw her in a church in Provence when he was twenty-three. He spent the rest of his life writing about his love for her, continuing even after her death, twenty-five years later."

"Were they married?" Marianne asked.

"No, Miss Haiml. We don't know for certain, but most scholars believe that Petrarch never even spoke once to the lady in all those years."

"He spent his whole life writing about a woman he never spoke to?" Marianne laughed. "That's ridiculous!" She looked at her mistress. "Can you imagine that, madame? The poor man spent his life besotted with a woman he didn't even know!"

The baroness smiled.

"I imagine there were plenty of women around him who longed for his attention," Marianne continued. "Men! Such fools!" She rolled her eyes.

My heart sank as the baroness tittered along with her.

I cleared my throat. The baroness stopped laughing, gave Marianne a little slap on the arm, and sat up straight. "I am sorry, signore," she said. "Please continue."

I turned to Marianne. "You see, Miss Haiml, no one knows whether Laura was a real woman in Petrarch's life, or an ideal woman he created for the purpose of his poetry." She frowned. "The poems are not really about Laura, they are about Petrarch himself. He describes the changing feelings of a lover, an arc of development from physical to divine passion." Marianne's face was blank, but I forged ahead with my explanation. "Many students of Petrarch believe that Laura is a symbol; that the poems, instead of being about a man's love for a woman, are really about the poet's love of fame, and his struggle to live a virtuous life without striving for human glory."

I looked over at the baroness, who was nodding at my words. "It is thought that Petrarch chose the name Laura to call to mind the laurel, which was the tree whose leaves were used to crown the poet laureate of Rome. That was the highest honor awarded to a poet during Petrarch's lifetime."

"Are there more verses, signore?" the baroness asked.

"Yes, two more, madame."

My thoughts of you are the arrows, your face the sun,
and desire the fire; with all these weapons
love pricks me, dazzles me, and destroys me;

My voice began to shake.

and the angelic song and the words,
with the sweet spirit from which I cannot myself defend,
are the breeze before which my life flees.

"The poor man," the baroness said. "He is passionately in love with her, and she doesn't even seem to know." She rose from the sofa and came to me. My heart leaped into my throat as I stood. "If she did exist, she was a cruel woman," she added. She took my hand. "Thank you, Signor Da Ponte," she said softly. "That was beautiful."

I leaned toward her. My lips moved involuntarily toward hers. I caught myself, swallowed, and gave a sterile bow. "He is my favorite poet," I said. She squeezed my hand. I stood stupidly, my heart in my throat, as she took her place on the sofa.

Marianne shook her head. "The words are beautiful, yes," she said, "but I can't get over how silly the poet was! To waste your life on someone who doesn't know you are alive? Or who might not even be a real person?" She laughed, and returned her attention to her mending.

"What else have you brought us?" the baroness asked.

I hesitated, then drew another sheet of paper from my pile. "I have another poem here, madame, one that I wrote myself." She smiled. "Of course, I am no Petrarch," I added.

"I would love to hear it, signore."

Had I imagined it, or did her cheeks color slightly as she looked at me this time? "This is another poem about love, from a different perspective," I said. I stood and read.

I don't know anymore what I am, what I do,
one moment I'm on fire, the next I'm freezing,
every woman I see makes me redden,
every woman I see makes me throb.

Just the mention of "love" and of "pleasure"
unsettles me and stirs my heart,
and I am compelled to speak of love
by a desire that I cannot explain.

I speak of love while waking,
I speak of love while dreaming,
to the waters, to the shadows, to the mountains,
to the flowers, to the grasses, to the fountains,
to the echo, to the air, and to the winds,
which carry away with them
the sound of my futile words.

And if I have no one to hear me,
I speak of love to myself!

As I finished, the two women burst into applause.

"Bravo, Signor Da Ponte," Marianne said. "Now that is a poem I can understand!"

I turned to the smiling baroness.

"That was charming, signore. Thank you for sharing it with us."

I flushed with pleasure and bowed.

"Is that for the new opera you are writing?" the baroness

asked. She knew of my opera! She must have asked some-one, probably Piatti, her music teacher, about me.

"Yes, madame," I replied. "It will premiere in three weeks. As a matter of fact, we will be rehearsing this piece tomorrow morning."

"Who is the character who sings the poem?" she asked.

"A teenage boy, madame, who is discovering women and love for the first time. As you can tell from the poem, he is in love with the idea of love. He—" I broke off. The women were silent. Marianne bowed her head and busied herself with the work on her lap. Tears filled the baroness's green eyes. She reached over and took Marianne's hand.

I looked at them, confused. My shoulders sagged as I realized what I had done. What a dolt I was! Why had I chosen that poem? I rose and went over to the sofa. "My apologies, madame," I said. "It was thoughtless of me to say such things. I did not mean to upset you."

She shook her head. "No, signore, you must not apologize. I know you intended no harm." She looked around her. "It is just this room . . ." Her voice trailed off.

"Shall I read another Petrarch poem?" I asked, though I knew that the pleasant mood had been irreparably broken.

"No, I think that is enough for today," she said, standing. Marianne gathered her sewing and the two women made their way to the door. I followed, murmuring apologies. Marianne went out into the hallway. The baroness stopped at the door and turned to me. She placed a finger on my lips to quiet me. Her delicate touch shot a lightning bolt through my body. I gazed at her, hating the knowledge that I was the cause of the sorrow on her face.

"Thank you so much, signore," she said. "The poems were beautiful." Her hand dropped to her side. Her eyes traveled around the room, as though searching for something, then came to rest on my miserable self again. She stood silently for a moment, as if she were wrestling with a decision, then spoke. "Perhaps—"

"Madame?"

"Perhaps on Sunday you could come to my chamber for the lesson. We will be more comfortable there."

My heart began to pound. My mouth was dry, and I could not force my lips to form words. I nodded dumbly.

"Come at one o'clock," she said. She left, closing the door gently behind her.

Come to her chamber! I smiled. A lady entertained only her most intimate friends in her private chamber. I floated over to the table and gathered my papers, left the library, and bounded up the stairs to my room, humming the tune Mozart had set to my poem.

I spent about twenty minutes working on the pantomime scene Mozart and I had discussed yesterday, then threw my pen down. I was too excited to work after my encounter with the baroness. I made a mental note to copy out a few more Petrarch poems for our meeting on Sunday.

My eyes fell on Vogel's box, which I had put next to the cupboard when I returned yesterday. I went over and carried it back to the desk. I took the muff out and turned it idly in my hands. I would have to go to the debtor's prison, I knew, but I was reluctant to tell my barber that I had reached a dead end in the investigation so soon. I didn't really believe that he would remember something from his past that would help us, as I had told the Mozarts.

The fur on the muff, although cheap, was silky and soft. I put my hands inside it. What woman had worn it last? What were her circumstances? If she was indeed Vogel's birth mother, had she wept when she placed her treasures in this box and gave her child away? I wished the muff could tell me.

As I withdrew my hands, the fingers of my right hand brushed against a rough patch in the lining. I turned the muff inside out. The fabric lining was sewn in tight, small stitches all around both edges, but as I peered at it, I could see an area about an inch wide that was sealed with broader stitching. I pressed my fingers around the area of the stitching. There seemed to be something buried inside the stuffing under the lining. I hurried to the cupboard and rooted through my valise, where I kept a small mending kit. I carried the kit back to the desk and withdrew a small pair of scissors.

A sharp rap sounded at the door. I put down the tool and went to the door.

"May I come in?" Urban Rausch asked, pushing me into the room. I shrugged, and gestured to the reading chair in the corner.

"I prefer to stand, if you don't mind," he said. "This won't take long."

"How can I help you, Doctor?"

"I demand to know the true reason that you are in this house," he said.

I raised my eyebrows. "I am here to teach poetry to the baroness, Doctor," I said. "That is all."

"Come now, don't take me for a fool! I'd heard not a word from my ward or her husband about plans to bring on another tutor, then that boy is killed in this house, and the next day you arrive."

"An unfortunate coincidence, sir," I murmured.

He stepped closer to me and drew up his chest so we were eye to eye. "I ask you again. Will you tell me your purpose here? Are you working with the police?"

My heart began to race. Had I been so obvious, that he was able to find me out so quickly? I laughed. "Me, working with the police? I am a simple poet, sir. The police would have to be very desperate if they believed I could help them with a murder investigation!"

"Yes, I suppose you are right," he said. "But you must admit, your arrival is suspicious."

"I think it is just an unfortunate coincidence," I repeated.

"Dammit, I am worried about Caroline, Da Ponte. I feel that she is burdened by something she will not share with me."

"I have only met the baroness twice, sir, I wouldn't know anything about that. A murder in one's household is a trying matter. Perhaps she is just grieving for the boy."

"Perhaps." He began to pace around the room. "I know she was fond of Auerstein. And she is probably worried about the family's reputation. The heir to one of the princes of the empire murdered here! The baron's career could be threatened."

"I know nothing about politics, Doctor," I said. "If you are concerned about your ward, I suggest you speak to her."

He stopped by my desk and looked curiously at the muff.

I crossed the room and shuffled my papers into a pile, put the muff back into the box, and replaced the lid. He looked at me, speculation in his eyes.

There was another knock at the open door. Rosa Hahn stood there. I beckoned her to enter.

"I'm sorry to interrupt, signore, I thought you might need more of these," she said, handing me a box of fresh candles. She did not acknowledge Rausch, who had moved over to the window and stood looking out on the garden below.

"Thank you, Miss Hahn," I said. I placed the box on the desk.

"Is there anything else you need?"

"No, I am fine," I said. She glanced over at Rausch and nodded at me. She turned to leave. As I began to turn back to Rausch, I saw Rosa pause. Out of the corner of my eye, I could see her staring toward the window. The look of hatred on her face sent cold down my spine. A moment later, the door closed.

Rausch left a few moments later. I hurried over to the desk and removed the muff from the box. I took up the scissors and gently snipped one of the large threads, then pulled it from the lining. I pulled out several more stitches and stuck my finger into the gap I had created. There was definitely something hidden inside, something smooth and cool. I grabbed onto it and teased it out of the muff.

I turned the object in my fingers. It was an oval bronze medallion about an inch and a half long, half as wide. The obverse side showed a robed woman standing on a pedestal, her arms stretched in front of her in a gesture of either blessing or supplication. On the reverse side were a simple cross and two small letters, a *K* and an *S*. A suspension ring was attached to the crest of the oval, but whatever chain or ribbon had been threaded through it had long ago disappeared.

What was a religious medallion doing in Vogel's muff? Had his birth mother hidden it there? Why? A rush of excitement seized me as I turned the medallion around in my fingers. Perhaps I had not reached the end of my investigation for my barber after all. After dinner I could—

I started as a gentle tap broke me out of my thoughts. I put the medallion down on the desk and quickly stuffed the muff back into the box. "Yes?" I called.

"Sir, may I clean your fireplace?" a small voice asked.

I opened the door to Antonia Bohm. She curtsied, then carried her pail, brush, and pan over to the fireplace. As she knelt and began to work, I noticed that she was still pale, and looked as if she had been crying again. I turned back to the desk and pulled out the scene I had been working on. For a few minutes we both worked without speaking. I jotted down a few ideas for the scene to the rhythmic scratching of Antonia's brush as she swept up the ashes. I wanted to ask her about Florian Auerstein, but was afraid that she might react violently again.

Finally the soft noises stopped. I looked up to see her standing a few feet from me. She was gazing at the desk, clutching the fireplace poker absently. I watched as her eyes explored the desk's surface, looking first at my papers, then at the box of candles, next at the medallion, then at Vogel's box. She blushed when she saw me regarding her. She opened her mouth to speak, but quickly closed it.

"Did you want to ask me something, Antonia?" I asked gently. I remembered what Rosa Hahn had said, that the girl was not quite right in the head. I guessed that like any child, she was wondering what was in the box.

She started. "Oh! No, no, sir. It is just—do you need anything else?"

"No, thank you," I said. She gave a quick curtsy, but did not turn to leave. I decided to take a chance on questioning her.

"Antonia, tell me about Florian. What was he like?"

"He wasn't like they all say, sir. Not at all. If he caused trouble for anyone, it was because he was bored. He was smart. And very handsome." She blushed.

"Did you spend a lot of time with him?"

"Yes. He used to come into the library when I was cleaning. He liked to kiss me." She blushed. "He told me I was beautiful. No one has ever said such sweet things to me. He told me all about his home. He lived in a grand palace, sir, with many servants. Not like here. He missed it very much." Her eyes filled with tears. "Just like I miss my old home. And he was a good listener. It was nice to have someone to talk to, someone my own age. Everyone here is so old." She wiped her eyes on her sleeve. "Marianne is the youngest of them, and she's much older than me."

"You and Florian were friends," I said.

"Oh, more than friends, sir. We were going to be married."

"He promised to marry you? When was this?"

"A week or so ago, sir. We were in the library. He promised he would take care of me—that I would not be a chambermaid here forever."

"Did he ever confide in you?" I asked.

"What do you mean, sir?"

"Well, did he ever tell you anything and ask you not to repeat it? Any secrets?"

She blushed again. "He told me many such things, sir."

"I don't mean love talk, Antonia. I mean something else—something about someone else in the house. Was there anything like that?"

She chewed on her lip. "I don't know what you mean, sir." She began to play with a lock of hair that had escaped from her cap. "He had plans—"

"He had something planned? What was it?" My voice was harsh and insistent. "You must tell me."

She began to cry softly. "I cannot, sir. I promised."

"Florian is dead, Antonia. You owe him no promises anymore."

She buried her face in her hands and wept. "I don't know. I don't know. He told me he would take care of me. What will I do now?"

I cursed myself for pressing her. If Auerstein had discovered the identity of the spy in the household, this simple, innocent girl would have been the last person he would have confided in. I reached over and took her hand. "Don't cry, Antonia. Everything will be fine. You will marry someday, I am sure. Why, any lackey or shopkeeper's son would be honored to have you as his bride."

She snatched her hand away from mine. Her face contorted

in rage. She lifted the poker above her head. "You fool!" she hissed. "How dare you say such things to me?" My heart pounding, I shrank back and raised my hands to protect myself.

"A lackey's wife? I was to be the next Princess Auerstein!" Her eyes narrowed. "If you want to help me, signore," she spat, "find the person who killed Florian—who murdered him so that we could not marry!" The poker fell to the floor next to me as she ran from the room.

Nine

An hour later I sat at a table in a catering shop next to the Am Hof church, sipping a spoonful of warm soup. After Antonia's outburst, I had sat at the desk for a few minutes, wondering how I would ever untangle the passions and animosities of the Gabler household's residents. I had pushed my work aside, pocketed the medallion, and headed down the stairs. At least there was something I could do to advance my investigation for Vogel. I had met Tomaso Piatti in the foyer of the palais, and he had invited me to dinner. I had quickly accepted, hoping to get the music tutor's impressions of the household members.

We sat at the end of a long table in one of the private rooms at the shop. The food was a bit more expensive here than in the larger public rooms, but we had agreed that we wanted a bit of quiet for conversation. At this, the prime midday dinner hour, the public rooms were filled with the lackeys of the various noble houses, all shouting back and forth at one another in some sort of competition about whose employer kept the finest carriage.

"It's a strange coincidence," Piatti was saying. He paused as the waiter approached and offered platters of stewed beef and potatoes. Finally, something I could eat! We loaded our plates high with the food. I was starving and began to eat with gusto.

"You came to the palais on Wednesday, and the next day you are hired to teach the baroness," Piatti continued. His plate sat untouched. "Were you there on Wednesday to speak to the baron about the job?"

I had treated myself to a glass of wine. I took a sip and nodded toward his plate. "Eat, my friend, it will get cold." As he took up his fork, I bit into a piece of meat and studied him. His face was pale, his eyes creased with worry. The death of the page had shaken him, I could see. "Yes, I know it seems odd," I said. "I came on Wednesday to speak to Miss Haiml. I know her fiancé."

"But how did the baron hear of you?" Piatti persisted. He picked at his dinner.

"I was introduced to him at the opera that night," I lied. "He told me he was considering hiring a poet to give lessons to his wife, and we agreed on the contract then and there."

Piatti sopped his roll in gravy and chewed it thoughtfully. "You must admit, it is peculiar," he said.

I laughed. "True, but stranger things have happened to me, I assure you." I wanted to get him off the matter of my presence in the palais and steer him toward talking about the murder. I lowered my voice and put on a serious expression. "I had no idea I was coming the day after a murder."

"Yes, it is an unfortunate time for all of us." He sighed. "The baroness is upset about the boy's death. She's canceled our lessons for a few days. She wants to be alone in the mornings."

My heart jumped at this news. She had put off Piatti to find time for me! A warmth spread through me as I momentarily contemplated our next meeting. I forced my attention back to Piatti. "Tell me about the boy," I said.

He hesitated, looked around him, and leaned in toward me. "I don't like to speak ill of the dead—"

I gave a conspiratorial nod.

"But to tell the truth, the boy was a nuisance. It was impossible to get a serious word out of him. He eavesdropped on conversations and spied on everyone. I think he even peeped at the ladies through the keyholes sometimes."

I raised my eyebrows.

"He ridiculed everyone who worked in the house—and even Rausch! Just last week I heard him call the doctor a pompous quack—to his face!"

"What did Rausch do?"

"He was so angry I thought he was going to strangle the boy, but he managed to get a hold of himself and walk away." Piatti shook his head. "To say that to a man who trained at one of the finest medical schools in the north. I don't think I could have controlled myself if he had said that to me!"

I took another forkful of the flavorful stew.

"Florian did a nasty imitation of Bohm, the valet—walking behind him, aping that lumbering gait Bohm has, with his hair messed up and shirttails out. Of course Bohm was angry, but what could he do? He is just a valet after all."

"I had dinner with him yesterday. He seems a strange choice to serve the baron," I said.

Piatti nodded. "I know! Such a boor, and so unkempt. I don't know why the baron hired him. Vogel left suddenly to open his shop, and the baron was desperate, I suppose. Bohm turned up a few days later with that strange daughter of his, and got the job." He pulled out his watch. "Good, I have a few more minutes. Not that Florian was the most virtuous member of the household, mind you," he said.

"How do you mean?"

"He was so sloppy! Of course, he was always clean, but his shirts always hung loose, and his hair was never neatly tied. And his work—the lessons he turned in to me were a mess, inkblots all over the place, his handwriting a scrawl." His face saddened. "He was a talented musician, though. I think I mentioned that the other day."

"You did," I said.

"Anyway, Bohm was very angry at Florian." Piatti hesitated.

"What is it?" I asked.

"Oh, I probably read too much into the incident. I shouldn't say," he said. He took a sip of water.

I lowered my voice. "You can trust me, my friend."

"Well—a few days ago, I was about to go into the library when I overheard voices," he said.

I nodded encouragingly.

"It was Bohm and Florian. They were arguing. I don't know what about exactly. But I think I heard—mind you, I wasn't eavesdropping; they were yelling at one another; I couldn't help but hear—"

I sighed inwardly and nodded again.

"I heard Bohm tell Florian that if he didn't stop, he, Bohm, would kill him."

"Stop what?"

"I don't know. I didn't hear that part, just the end. I heard Bohm's footsteps near the door, so I turned and hurried down the hall. I didn't hear anything else."

"Did you tell the police?" I asked.

He shook his head vehemently. "No, no, I don't want to become involved. I'm not a citizen here. Besides, I may have just imagined that they were arguing. I only heard that small part." He looked at me. "Please, Lorenzo, don't tell anyone."

"All right," I said.

Piatti signaled to the waiter for the check. "But enough of all these people," he said. "I invited you to dinner because I wanted to hear about your opera. What are you writing now?"

"I'm finishing the finale—the long ensemble piece—for the second act," I said.

"That must be difficult to write, no? Finales are so long, and so important to an opera."

"Yes, it is a challenge," I said. "You know, my words have to show off Mozart's genius, and that of each singer. I must use every speed of singing: slow, moderate, fast, superfast, extra superfast."

He laughed.

"Every singer must be included. Solos, duets, trios, quartets, quintets. If there are a hundred singers, I am required to have them all sing together at some point. And my carefully crafted plot is thrown to the wind while all this virtuosity is on display!"

The waiter brought the check.

"Of course, if the finale turns out to be a muddle, if the soprano's voice cracks, if the tenor cannot reach his note, it will all be my fault!" I winked at him.

"I'm sure it will be brilliant," Piatti said. "No, no, this is my treat." He threw some coins on the table. "I'd love to look at your writing sometime, if you wouldn't mind. I enjoyed your last opera immensely. I'd like to see how you put things together."

"Of course. Come by my room and I'll give you something."

We gathered our belongings and went out into the Am Hof. A trapezoidal area that had been the jousting grounds of the Dukes of Austria in the thirteenth century, the plaza was not a fashionable gathering place like the Graben or the Michaelerplatz. It was used for more-practical pursuits. Market stalls dotted its expanse. Its east side was dominated by the snowy white façade of the baroque Carmelite church, while the west side contained a series of buildings that had at one time housed the city's arsenal but now stored equipment for fighting fires. At the center of the plaza stood a tall monument dedicated to the Virgin Mary, who, legend has it, helped the Viennese repel the Swedes during the wars of the last century. The good lady stood on top of a column of black marble, its plinth defended by cherubs clad in battle armor.

"Which way are you headed?" Piatti asked.

"To the Stephansdom," I said. Ahead of us, a motley group of about twenty men and women, all dressed in coarse jackets and wearing paper dunce caps on their heads, were sweeping the stones. These were the city's felons, chained together and forced to suffer public humiliation.

Piatti elbowed me in the side. "Look, there's that ass Count Harzy." He laughed, pointing at a tall, elderly man in the middle of the chain. "He's come down in the world, eh? No fancy palace for him anymore!" As part of his criminal law reforms, the emperor had insisted that all criminals serve on the chain gang, no matter into which class of society they had been born. I felt a twinge of sympathy for the count, who stumbled as he tried to keep pace with the chain as it moved along the periphery of the plaza. I wondered what crime he had committed.

Piatti had stopped laughing. "Do you know the musician Klein?" he asked quietly.

I nodded. Klein was a violinist in the court orchestra.

"There he is."

I looked at the man who brought up the rear of the chain. It was indeed Klein. I had heard that he had been arrested for forging a bill of sale for several valuable musical instruments. As I stared at him, his eyes lifted from the ground and met mine. I gave him a small, encouraging smile, but he quickly looked away, his face full of shame.

"Well, my friend, I go this way," Piatti said as we reached the Bognergasse. I shook his hand, thanked him for the dinner, and promised to come to his room for a glass of wine one evening. He headed in the direction of the Palais

Gabler, and I turned the opposite way. I quickly looked back over my shoulder. The chain gang had begun another miserable peregrination around the plaza.

I shivered as I watched Klein shuffling along. If I could not solve Florian Auerstein's murder, my fate would be much worse than Klein's. Despite the emperor's liberal philosophies and love of reform, the punishment for murder was still death.

Ten

I turned left onto the Tuchlauben and cut across to the Stephansplatz. The great church loomed above the plaza. I tucked my head into my chest and hurried into a building across from the north tower. I trudged up four flights of stairs, turned down a small corridor, and knocked on the door at its end.

"Come," a voice called.

I pushed open the door. "Alois?"

"Lorenzo!" A gray-haired priest stood and slowly came from behind a large desk to greet me. He felt insubstantial in my embrace, as if age were reducing him to mere bones; his skin felt like parchment, easily torn.

"How good to see you. To what do I owe the pleasure? Do you have a new book for me?"

"No, not today, my friend," I said. "I need a favor, something with which I think only you can help me." I pulled the medallion out of my cloak pocket and handed it to him. "Could you possibly identify this for me?"

"Let me see, let me see," he said, waving me to a seat near the desk. He returned to his chair and pushed aside the large volume he had been reading. His hands trembled slightly as he put on a pair of spectacles. As he examined the medallion, I closed my eyes and breathed in the smell of the place— the must of the hundreds of old books piled everywhere in the small room accented with the sharp scent of the peppermint drops Alois loved.

"Where did you get this?" he asked.

I told him about Vogel and the box, how I had just about given up tracing Vogel's birth mother when I had found the medallion hidden in the lining of the muff.

"Well, I don't think this will lead you to his mother," Alois said, his lined face crinkling into a smile.

"What do you mean? Do you recognize it?"

"Yes, it's the medal that was given to the nuns at the Sisters of the Blessed Virgin convent."

"It belonged to a nun?"

"Yes, it was their custom to give each novice one when she began her residency at the convent. These initials on the back, they are probably those of one of the nuns."

"Is the convent here? In Vienna?" I asked, scratching my cheek.

"It was, but no longer." Alois turned the medallion in his hand and sighed. "It was just a few blocks from here, over near the Jesuit church and the university. It was closed a few years ago, under the emperor's reforms, when he cut the number of religious by two-thirds. I believe the building is apartments now. I'm sorry, Lorenzo, that doesn't really help you, does it?" he asked, leaning over the desk to pat my hand.

"I was hoping that the medallion belonged to Vogel's mother, that we would be able to trace her somehow. But now I don't see how that is possible."

"Well, the sisters did take in unwed pregnant girls, I believe," Alois said. "They ran a small hospital. Perhaps one of the nuns gave it to your friend's mother. Although I think that highly unlikely. A sister would have treasured it, kept it near her heart all the time."

I sat for a moment, my head in a muddle. The medallion had belonged to a nun? How did it get into Vogel's birth mother's muff? Alois had grown quiet. I looked over at him. His eyes were closed, his breathing steady.

"So many sisters and brothers cast out," he murmured.

I gave a small cough.

He opened his eyes. "Forgive me, Lorenzo, an old man's mind starts to wander." He handed the medallion back to me. "You may want to talk to Rupert Maulbertsch. He's in the Treasury Ministry now, but he was involved in the dissolution of the religious houses. He might still have information about what happened to the nuns from the convent." He leaned back in his chair. "Now tell me, how are you?" he asked. "Are you teaching?"

I shook my head. "No, I am writing another libretto."

"I've been meaning to get in touch with you. There's an opening for a priest out in Gumpendorf. The church is small, but the salary is decent. We need modern thinkers like you in these churches."

I shook my head. "You know I no longer practice as a priest," I said.

"I know, but I have to keep trying. The archbishop is opposed to reform from within the church. Our only hope is to place young priests such as yourself in the smaller churches, to educate the people, to get them used to liberal ideas."

I remembered Rosa Hahn's complaint that the emperor had banned bell-ringing as a precaution against lightning strikes. "I am not suited for the priesthood," I said gently. "I only took orders to be able to get an education, to study poetry." When I was fifteen, my father had remarried, and our family had come under the protection of the local monsignor. He enrolled me in the local seminary, where I found a young teacher who showed me the beauty of Italian poetry. I had spent many happy hours studying the words of Dante, Ariosto, and Tasso, copying their verses, memorizing their stanzas, dissecting their most graceful phrases in order to comprehend the genius behind them. I had even been inspired to write poetry myself, at first haltingly, worrying over each word, then later with more confidence.

All that changed a year later, however, when our patron died suddenly. My family fell back into poverty, and the seminary informed my father that if I were to continue with my studies there, I must train for the priesthood. I was appalled. Even at such a young age as sixteen, I knew myself well enough to recognize that I was ill-suited for that profession. But by that time, my stepmother had embarked upon a lifetime of pregnancy, and I was no longer welcome in my father's household.

"But to waste yourself on writing for the theater!" Alois

said. "At least think about teaching again, at one of the seminaries here."

I shook my head again, but said nothing. We sat quietly for a few moments.

"You know," Alois said, "I believe the abbess of that convent is still here in the city. What was her name? Elsa—no, Elisabeth. I met her once. A lovely woman."

"How would I find her?" I asked.

He shrugged. "I will ask around for you." His eyes wandered to the book he had been reading when I arrived, and I sensed that he wanted to return to it. I stood to leave.

"Aha, wait, I think I remember something that could help you! There is a man, a cobbler who repairs the shoes for all of us here at the cathedral. I remember him saying a few years ago that his wife's aunt was moving in with them, that she had been the abbess of a small convent that had been closed. She had nowhere else to go, he said. That might be the Abbess Elisabeth. You might go over there, Lorenzo, and talk to her. She is old, like me, but she might remember something. Who knows?"

"I don't have any other leads," I said. "Where is this cobbler's shop?"

"On the Schultergasse, over near the Hoher Market," Alois said. "His name is Bernhard. Gunter Bernhard, I think. I don't know his wife's name."

I thanked him, and tucked the medallion back into my cloak pocket. He rose and took my hand in his. "It was good to see you, my friend. Come again soon. It's been a while since we spent the day drinking and discussing poetry. I have a nice bottle of Tokay tucked away in my cabinet."

A twinge of guilt played in my chest. Alois must be lonely, spending most of his time in this small room with his books, his time come and gone, while the young, ambitious priests ran the cathedral.

"I will," I promised. "Thank you for your help, Alois."

"I'll save that bottle for you, Lorenzo," he said. "Good luck with your search."

I walked out into the corridor. As I pulled the door shut, I looked back with fondness at his gray head, already bent over his volume.

Eleven

The next morning I rose early and walked over to the theater. This was our first rehearsal with full cast and orchestra in the performance hall, and when I arrived, the singers were on the stage, standing in clumps. The two married couples, the Bussanis and the Mandinis, chatted animatedly, while the prima donna, Nancy Storace, held court at the other end of the stage, attended by the handsome young bass Benucci (whom it was rumored she had taken as her latest lover), and the pubescent soprano, Anna Gottlieb. The second soprano, Luisa Laschi, stood in the wings, nervously testing her scales. Members of the orchestra chatted as they tuned their instruments, while Thorwart, the fretful assistant theater manager, supervised the lighting of the candelabras closest to the stage.

"Ah, good, Lorenzo, you're here," Mozart said. "I want to start with the pantomime scene. Would you mind explaining it to the singers while I speak to the orchestra?" I pulled my copy of the libretto out of my satchel and climbed to the stage. "Everyone, gather round, please," I shouted. "We have a new scene to rehearse." Nancy Storace led her acolytes over to where I stood. Luisa Laschi joined us after a moment, followed by the young, wild-haired Irish tenor, Michael Kelly.

I looked over to the corner, where the two married couples still stood chatting. "Signor and Signora Bussani? Signor and Signora Mandini? Your attention, please?" Dorotea Bussani, the soprano who sang the role of the love-struck boy in the opera, glanced at me out of the corner of her eye. She said something I could not hear, and the others laughed. I strode over to them. "Ladies, gentlemen," I said. "We are about to begin. If you please?"

Stefano and Maria Mandini walked over to the other singers, but the Bussanis lingered. I turned back to them. "Everyone is in this scene, signore and signora. Would you please join us?" Dorotea tittered and her husband gave me a dark scowl, but they finally followed me.

"We've changed the wedding scene," I explained. "Instead of a brief dance followed by two arias, we've decided to make the entire scene a pantomime. Two peasant girls will sing a song in praise of the count; then the orchestra will play while you go through the wedding ceremony; and then you, Miss Storace, will silently hand Signor Mandini the note that invites him to a tryst in the garden later. Everyone will dance—"

"What? I do not sing? There is no aria?" Nancy Storace asked.

Stefano Mandini began to grumble. "I thought I was to have an aria here, Signor Da Ponte," he objected. "Or at least a duet with Miss Storace."

"You expect me to dance?" his stout wife asked. "I am not a dancer." Luisa Laschi nodded in agreement.

"Please let me finish," I said.

"Are you telling me that two girls from the chorus will sing in this scene and I will not?" Storace stepped toward me, her hands on her hips.

"An opera scene with no singing?" Dorotea Bussani shook her head. "I've never heard of such a thing." Her husband nodded grimly.

"The nine of us will dance around the stage?" Michael Kelly chimed in. "That will look ridiculous, Da Ponte."

"We will get some ballet dancers to do the complicated choreography. You all just have to move around a bit. Everyone, please, please—let us just run through it, see how it comes out." They grumbled as I arranged them on their marks. Mozart sat at the pianoforte, lifted his hand to the orchestra, and the rehearsal began.

We worked on the scene for about an hour, and when Mozart was finally satisfied with it, we took a short break. I ran down to my office to organize some work to bring back to the palais later. As I was shoving the pages into my satchel, there was a knock at the door. My eyes lit up when I saw my visitor.

"Vicente, how are you?" I asked Martín.

"Good, good," he said. "Do you have a moment?"

"What can I do for you, my friend?" I asked, even though I already knew what he wanted.

He hesitated. "Lorenzo, I know you are still busy with

Mozart," he said. "But I am wondering—have you made any progress on *A Rare Thing*?" I flushed with guilt. I had promised him last week to sketch an outline, but then I had been dragged to Pergen's office.

"I'm sorry, Vicente," I said. "I've done a little bit, but I haven't had a lot of time this week. I'll get you the outline and the first few scenes by the end of next week, all right?" He nodded. We exchanged a few pleasantries and he left.

When I returned to the theater hall, Mozart approached. "I'm trying to get everyone together for the sextet. These singers! No one will sit still." He sat down at the pianoforte and called to the baritone Mandini. "Signor Mandini, where has your wife gone? And where are my two Francescos? Signor Benucci, Signor Bussani? Ah, good. We are waiting for the prima donna, but where is Kelly?"

The young man appeared from behind us. "H-h-here I am, m-m-maestro," he said. He looked over at me and winked.

"I see you are already in character, Mr. Kelly," Mozart said. The sextet was part of a trial scene, and Kelly had the role of the judge. In his play, Beaumarchais had added a comic note by making the judge a stutterer, and I, knowing that Kelly had a gift for mimicry, had borrowed the device for my libretto.

I took a seat a few rows back in the parterre and watched as Mozart, playing the accompaniment on the pianoforte, led the six singers through the recited portion of the scene. Everyone laughed when Kelly began to stutter. Nancy Storace slipped onto the stage and stood a few feet away from the rest of the group. Mozart raised his hand and the orchestra began to play. First a verse from Maria Mandini, then one from the young bass, Francesco Benucci. The other Francesco, Bussani, followed, and then Kelly joined in, weaving his phrases with those of the baritone, Mandini.

"Stop, stop, stop," Mozart cried, waving his hands above his head. The orchestra ground to a halt as the composer stood and approached the stage. "Mr. Kelly—what are you doing?" he asked.

The tenor came forward. "I'm sorry, maestro, what do you mean?" he asked, his brow furrowed.

"You are stuttering!" Mozart said.

"Of c-course I am, m-m-maestro. I play the Stuttering Judge! It's right here, in the libretto!"

"Yes, I know," Mozart said. "But that is for the recitatives. You are stuttering while you are singing."

"I know, maestro. Doesn't it sound good?" He grinned. "I've been practicing my stutter song a lot. I think it adds to the comedy. Don't you like it?"

Mozart looked over at me, a wry smile on his face. I rolled my eyes.

"You are magnificent in the recited parts, Mr. Kelly," he said patiently. "But I would prefer that you not stutter during the sextet. It interferes with the timing of the music." He sat back down at the pianoforte and shuffled through his score.

Kelly remained at the front of the stage. "Maestro, I know it is presumptuous of me to disagree, but I assure you I have thought this through. I'm only trying to produce the effect of stuttering. I'm sure it will not interfere with the other singers' parts."

Mozart shook his head.

"And just think about it for a minute," the young tenor continued. "Why should someone stutter in conversation and not stutter when he sings? It makes no sense!"

"Mr. Kelly—"

Kelly persisted. "Do I undergo some sort of miraculous cure when I tune up my singing instrument?" He cocked his head at Mozart. The other singers laughed.

Mozart smiled. "Let me think about it, Mr. Kelly. But for today, please just sing the lines without the stutter."

Kelly looked as though he had more to say, but Nancy Storace stepped up and pulled him back into the group. "We are wasting time," she said.

"All right, everyone, let's begin again, at the beginning of the sextet," Mozart said. *"Riconosci in questo amplesso."* He hummed the musical phrase. The orchestra began to play. I sat back in my seat. Thorwart approached and leaned over me. "Don't stay too long, Signor Da Ponte," the assistant theater manager said. "Miss Storace must rest her voice. And these candles cost money." I nodded and watched as he scurried out the side door. I leaned back, took a deep breath, and relaxed, listening as the singers wove my words and Mozart's music into a glorious fabric.

The rehearsal lasted until one o'clock. I ate a quick dinner in a nearby shop, and returned to my office to sketch some scenes for Martín. At around four, I headed to the Palais Gabler, happy to have spent a day in my old life without worrying about the murder investigation or my promise to Vogel. As I entered the courtyard, the baroness was alighting from a carriage. My heart turned over as she stood before the door, waiting for me.

"Signor Da Ponte!" she said. "Are you coming from your rehearsal?"

I bowed. How beautiful she looked standing there in the fading light, wrapped in a rich evergreen cloak with gold trim, her hair caught up under a chic feathered cap. I followed her into the foyer.

"I wanted to thank you again for the lesson yesterday," she said. "It cheered me considerably."

"It was my pleasure, madame," I said. As I helped her with her cloak, I glanced to the side, and saw our happy faces reflected in the mirror—her cheeks colored from her ride in the park, my own face warm with the pleasure of being so close to her. I inhaled the lavender scent of her hair. As I handed her the cloak, our hands met. Did I imagine that she left her fingers touching mine just a moment longer than accident allowed?

"I am looking forward to tomorrow afternoon," she said. "Please, I would like to hear more of the Petrarch. I cannot stop thinking about that story."

"I would be delighted, madame," I said. The clock sounded the hour.

"Oh, I didn't realize it was this late," she said. "Please excuse me, Signor Da Ponte. Christof and I have a supper to attend and I must change my clothes."

I bowed again.

"Until tomorrow, then?" she asked, smiling.

I stood there, once again tongue-tied like a schoolboy. She turned and ran lightly up the stairs.

. . .

I spent a happy few hours reading in my room and preparing the lesson for the next day, then retired to my bed. I fell asleep right away, and did not dream of the torments of my past. I did not know how many hours I had slept when my ears perked and my eyes snapped open. The room was dark, the house quiet. As I began to drift back to sleep, I heard it. A slight sound, a scraping noise. I was wide awake now, alert to the noise. Another scrape. A bump. Where was it coming from?

I sat up, straining to hear. My heart began to pound as I heard it again. Bump. Bump. It was coming from the hallway. My mind raced. I had been uneasy when I found no lock on the door, but had slept unaccosted for several nights, secure in the belief that no one in the palais knew my real mission here. What was that slight click? The doorknob? My eyes had by now grown accustomed to the darkness, and I held my breath, concentrating all of my senses on the door, my heart sick with fear.

Was that another click?

Go open the door.

I sat frozen, my mind racing. I pictured my body found the next morning sprawled on my bed, my life smothered out of me by the spy in our midst; or perhaps Ecker's madman lurked outside my door, waiting to kick it down and, with otherworldly strength, grab me and hurl me out the window.

If you are going to be murdered, at least put up a fight.

I strained to hear over the pounding of my heart. Nothing.

Enough.

I swung my legs onto the floor and rushed to the door. I turned the knob and flung the door open, ready to confront my would-be assailant. "Who is—"

No one. The hallway was empty. I took a few steps out of my room and stood quietly, listening intently. Nothing. And no time for anyone who had been there to make an escape. I shook my head. I had probably just heard the breeze blowing through the tall window that stood open at the end of the hall.

You fool. You and your imagination, running wild.

Nevertheless, before I returned to my bed I moved the desk chair under the doorknob, and I did not regain my happy sleep that night.

Twelve

On Sunday mornings, all of Vienna goes to church. The streets are crowded with the carriages of the wealthy: the horses in their finest plumage; the lackeys wearing their most lavish uniforms. The aristocracy frequents the four inner-city churches: the Stephansdom, seat of the archbishop of Vienna; the newly consecrated Italian church; the old Carmelite church on the Am Hof; and the elegant St. Michael's, closest to the Hofburg. The rest of the population attends the smaller neighborhood churches.

I spent the morning in my room at the palais, outlining the libretto for Martín. When I heard the rumbling of carriages returning from the churches, I took my cloak and stick and headed toward the Graben.

Once I reached St. Peter's Church, I continued down the Tuchlauben toward the Hoher Market, then turned into the Schultergasse. My destination was on the right side of the street, at the end. I peered in the window, and saw I was in luck. I knocked on the door. The proprietor sat hunched over a table, deep in concentration. He looked up and scowled. I knocked again. He put aside his work and came to the door.

"We're closed today, sir," he said. "Can you return tomorrow?" He started to close the door. I put my stick in to block it.

"Are you Gunter Bernhard?" I asked.

He nodded.

"I'd like to speak to you for a moment, please."

"I'm not allowed to sell anything or take in work on Sundays, sir," he said.

"I'm not a customer," I said. Suspicion filled his hard, small eyes as he looked me over. "Don't worry, there's no trouble. I'm wondering if you could help with a personal matter," I added.

He sighed and opened the door, gesturing me inside. The shop was dim, and cluttered with shoes, boots, and scraps of leather. He returned to his worktable and sat. "I'd like to keep working while you talk, sir." He picked up a last onto which was tied a smooth leather sole. "My wife will be waiting with my dinner." He began to work a stitching awl into the leather.

"Actually, this is about your wife. I think it is she I really need to talk to."

He looked up with a surprised expression. "Therese? What could you possible want with Therese?"

I saw no chair or bench on which to sit, so I leaned against a counter near the front window. "I was told that she has an aunt, the Abbess Elisabeth, of the Sisters of the Blessed Virgin convent."

Although his head was bent over his work, I thought I heard a sharp intake of breath when I said the abbess's name. But he said nothing, just continued to twist the awl into the leather. "I'm trying to find someone for a friend of mine. I was told the abbess might be able to help me."

He laughed sharply. "Well, sir, you are right. You'd better speak to my wife about her aunt. But I don't think you'll find what you're looking for here," he said, looking up at me. "Go around the corner. Second floor." He returned to his work.

I thanked him and went into the street. A few steps took me to the door of the lodgings. I climbed up two flights of stairs and knocked on the only door on the landing.

"It's unlocked," a light, silvery voice called. I opened the door. A plump woman of about thirty was regarding herself in a cheap mirror that hung by a nail just inside the door. A frilly white cap sat on her blond curls, which surrounded a pretty round face.

"Oh, pardon me, sir, I thought you were my husband," she said. She glanced at her reflection in the mirror and pulled off the cap, patting her hair back into place.

I gave a slight bow. She blushed. "My name is Lorenzo Da Ponte, madame," I said. "Your husband sent me up to speak with you."

She smiled and pointed me toward a small sofa in the center of the simple, neat room. Its fabric was worn, but the cushions were well stuffed. I leaned back into them. The aroma of baking bread wafted over me, and I remembered the meager roll I had taken from the palais kitchen for breakfast. She placed the cap on her head again and looked in the mirror. "I just can't tell if this cap sits properly on my head. What do you think?"

"It frames your face very well, madame," I said.

"Do you really think so? I made it myself. I'm just not sure—"

"It looks lovely on you," I said.

She blushed and turned toward me with sparkling eyes. "Tell me, what can I do for you, sir?"

"I am looking for your aunt, the Abbess Elisabeth."

Her hands dropped to her sides. "Oh dear. Auntie?"

I nodded. "Is your aunt available? I will only take a few moments of her time."

"What is this about, sir?"

I sighed inwardly. I did not wish to explain things twice, first to this woman and again to her aunt.

She looked at me expectantly.

"I am doing a favor for a friend of mine, madame," I began. "He has recently learned that he is adopted. He is trying to trace his birth mother." She frowned. "I've found a medallion that I think belonged to the woman. An expert at the Stephansdom sent me here. He told me it belonged to a nun at your aunt's convent, the Sisters of the Blessed Virgin."

Her hand went to her throat.

"I was hoping your aunt might recognize the initials on the medallion, and tell me something about its owner."

Tears filled her eyes. "Oh, sir, I am sorry. You have come here for nothing. My aunt can be of no help to you."

"I understand she is very old. Is it her memory? Perhaps if I talked to her—gently, of course—I could learn something."

She shook her head.

"Please, your aunt is my friend's only hope of finding his mother."

She drew a kerchief from her apron pocket and dabbed her eyes. "Oh, sir, I feel terrible for your poor friend. To grow up not knowing your mother—I can't imagine that. But there is nothing here for him. My aunt has been dead for a year now."

My heart softened as I looked at Therese. Tears were streaming down her cheeks. "I'm sorry for your loss," I said gently. "Your aunt must have been an extraordinary woman."

"She was," Therese said. "She worked so hard to become the abbess, but she still had time for a young niece whenever I needed her advice. My mother died when I was in my teens, you see. Aunt Elisabeth was like a second mother to me." She smiled softly. "I remember visiting her in the convent. I wanted to become a nun, just like her, but she would have no part of it. *Find a good man to love, Therese*, she would tell me."

I thought of the grim, taciturn man working in the shop below.

"She loved that convent," Therese mused. "I remember when the emperor ordered it to be closed. Those poor old nuns, who had spent their whole lives inside those walls. They were given a small pension and sent out to make their way in a world they knew nothing about. Even Auntie, who was a woman of the world—she had to be, to fight with the church officials for everything the convent needed—even she had nowhere to go."

I nodded sympathetically.

Her voice grew steely. "Gunter did not want her here. He said it would cost him too much to support her. But I insisted. How could I turn her away?"

I nodded again.

"He never gave her a chance. He always treated her like a burden. And after all that, she was only here for a year before she fell ill. She stopped eating and sleeping, and lost weight. It took her another year to die."

"The wasting disease?" I asked.

"That's what the doctor said, sir. But if you'll forgive me for saying so, I blame the emperor for her death. When he closed the convent, he took away her reason for living. My aunt died of a broken heart."

As I cut across the Judenplatz on my way back to the Palais Gabler, my thoughts were in a whirl. I had hoped the Abbess Elisabeth would know the name of the woman who had owned the medallion. I was puzzled by its presence in the muff. Alois Bayer had said the medallions were given to the novices at the convent. Had one of these girls been tempted by the gifts of a man, strayed from her vocation, and become pregnant? Why had she put the medallion in the muff?

I started as my arm was grabbed from behind.

"Where have you been, Signor Poet?" Troger's cold, dark eyes stared at me.

I pulled his hand off my sleeve. "I can't talk now, Troger. I have an appointment."

He took my elbow. "You'll talk to me when I want you

to. Now." Pain shot through my forearm as he pinched his fingers together, hard. "What were you doing at the cobbler's shop?"

"Are you following me?"

"I am watching you. What were you doing there? What do that cobbler and his wife have to do with the Auerstein murder?"

I tried to pull my elbow away from his grasp. He tightened the pinch. "Nothing. I was doing an errand for a friend, that is all. Now let me go. I have an appointment with Baroness Gabler."

"Ah, the beautiful baroness. Enjoying the benefits of the palais, are you, Da Ponte?"

"Don't offend the lady, Troger," I said.

"What have you learned? Have you discovered the spy?"

"No, not yet."

"What have you been doing all these days, besides romancing the baron's wife?"

"I've been listening, observing—just as the count instructed. You know I'm not an investigator! I've had to feel my way around. I don't know how to discover the things you policemen can get from people."

"You'd better learn fast, hadn't you? You have nothing for me?"

I shook my head.

"You're wasting time, Da Ponte. The prince wants the murderer of his son. Count Pergen is getting pressure from Kaunitz and the emperor." He shook his head. "I told him this plan would never work," he muttered.

I recalled Rosa Hahn's theory that the murderer had been

invited into the palais by Florian Auerstein himself. "I do have a question for you. On the day of the murder, did anyone visit the house? Perhaps a friend of the Auerstein boy?"

His smile was cold and sarcastic. He released my arm and gave me a push. I stumbled and bumped into the wall. "No, Da Ponte. No one else. Just you."

I rushed back to the palais and went to my room. As I pulled off my cloak, the medallion fell from the pocket. I leaned over and picked it off the floor, put it on the desk, and put on my better waistcoat. I grabbed my Petrarch and my notes and hurried down to the baroness's chamber.

The room was bright and airy, its walls covered in the same watery green silk I had seen around the house. The baroness sat at a large dressing table opposite the door. She still wore her dressing gown, a frothy white robe that set off her auburn tresses. She smiled at me through the mirror and indicated a settee a few feet behind her chair. I settled myself on the peach-colored velvet, and inhaled the sweet, fresh scent of her lavender perfume.

She picked up a brush and ran it through her hair. Our eyes met in the mirror. She smiled. I shuffled my papers, wondering whether I should begin. "Are we waiting for Miss Haiml?" I asked.

She shook her head. "No, she is out doing some errands. It is just me today." My heart began to pound as I watched the brush move rhythmically through her long curls. "Have you brought me another of the Petrarch poems?" she prompted.

"Yes, madame. Are you ready to hear it?"

She nodded.

My hands trembled as I lifted the sheet of paper. What was wrong with me? I had romanced many women in my thirty-seven years. With this one, I felt like a callow youth. I read the poem.

> *Sometimes, lady, blushing with shame that I have*
> *still not spoken of your beauty in my rhymes,*
> *I turn to the time I first saw you;*
> *there will never be another who pleases me.*

My voice rose to a squeak at the end of the verse. I cleared my throat.

> *But I find a weight not for my arms,*
> *a work not to be polished by my file,*
> *and my talent, judging its lack of strength,*
> *freezes in all its attempts.*

I stopped and looked at her. The brush had stopped its movement. Our eyes met in the glass.

"Please, continue, signore," she said.

"Madame, perhaps, if I might be so bold as to ask—"

"Yes, signore?"

"I would be honored if you would call me by my Christian name, Lorenzo."

She smiled. "All right, if it pleases you, I will be glad to. Lorenzo."

My heart leapt to my throat to hear my name swirled in her delicate mouth.

"Please, go on with the poem, Lorenzo," she said.

I cleared my throat again.

Many times already have my lips opened to speak
but my voice remains in my chest—
for what sound could ever soar so high?

Many times have I begun to write verses,
but the pen and the hand and my intellect
remain defeated in the first assault.

We sat silently for a moment. I rubbed my fingers over the soft velvet of the settee. The baroness sighed. "The poor man," she said softly. "He seems so unhappy, even though he is in love with this Laura."

"He is a poet, madame, who cannot find words beautiful enough to describe the object of his longing," I said. I held her gaze in the mirror. "That is frustrating for any poet."

"I find his story tragic, Lorenzo. To pine for someone for so long, to never speak the words of love. That feels terrible, I am sure. Why did he never try to speak to her?"

"She is a symbol, madame. Of the unattainable."

"But he should have tried," she cried. She threw down the brush. "Perhaps she was in love with him also. Perhaps she was unhappy in her marriage." She began to weep. I cast my papers aside and stood as she turned to face me. My heart wrenched at the sight of tears on her cheeks. I crossed to her and took her hand.

"Oh, forgive me, Lorenzo. I am a silly woman. I don't know why I am crying." She shivered. "It is this murder. It has affected me more than I would like everyone to know."

I knelt down beside her chair. My heart pounded as I lifted her hand to my lips and kissed it. "Madame, may I say—"

She did not pull her hand away.

"May I tell you that you have my undying affection and loyalty. I am your servant, madame. I would do anything for you."

"Oh, Lorenzo, I don't know—"

"Please, madame. Caroline. I see your sorrow. Your husband—"

She placed her finger on my lips. "Lorenzo—"

"You are a beautiful woman. You deserve to be desired, loved, adored."

She looked down at our hands, which were clasped on her lap. "I don't know if I can trust you," she said in a small voice.

"Caroline. My loyalties are only to you. I am not the sort of man who spreads gossip around the city. You must believe that anything you ask of me will remain between the two of us." I gazed into her tear-streaked face. She frowned, then was thoughtful, making her decision. She looked into my eyes, smiled gently, and nodded. I clasped her hand again, and leaned over to kiss her lips.

To my surprise, she dropped my hand and rose from her seat, gently pushing me away. She crossed the room to the fireplace and took a small silver box from the mantel. She opened the box and pulled out a letter, folded small, then returned to the dressing table. I stood, puzzled, as she opened up an ornate jewel case and pulled out a long, thin golden pin. She pushed the pin through the top right corner of the note, fastened it, and handed the packet to me.

"Would you deliver this message for me, Lorenzo?" she asked. I looked down at her neat handwriting. My eyes widened as I read the name of the addressee. My heart sank to my feet.

"Please give it directly to the man to whom it is addressed, no other," she said. "And Lorenzo?" I nodded miserably.

"Tell him to send the pin back with you if he agrees to meet me."

Thirteen

It took another few minutes for me to escape the room. I stood in the hallway, wondering what to do next. My head throbbed from the noxious scent of lavender. My arms hung heavily by my side, and I could not find the energy to propel my cumbrous legs up the stairs to my room. The small billet-doux weighed heavy in my hand, the golden pin attached neatly to the corner, a gleaming invitation that should have been mine. As I shoved the letter into my pocket, I felt a sharp sting. I pulled out my hand. A droplet of blood wept from my finger, where the infernal pin had stabbed me. I poked around my pockets with my other hand, found my handkerchief, and wrapped it around the wound.

The chiming of two o'clock by the small clock at the end of the hall brought me out of my stupor. I decided to go to the kitchen for dinner, to see if I could find out anything new from the household staff. If all that was served was tough roast, all the better. The sour taste in my mouth had dulled any appetite I might have had an hour before.

When I arrived, all was quiet in the large kitchen. The table was set for dinner, and I could smell meat cooking. The room was empty except for Gottfried Bohm, who sat in a chair by the fire, a long quill and a short, sharp knife in his hand.

"A valet, cutting pens?" I asked. "Where did you learn to do that?"

"In my last job," he said.

"Where was that?"

He did not answer.

"Have you always worked as a valet?" I asked.

He grunted.

"Here in Vienna?"

He looked up at me. "Do you always stick your nose into other people's business, Signor Da Ponte?" he asked.

I raised my hands. "Sorry, I'm just trying to make conversation." I decided to try another tack. "Everyone seems so jumpy in the house since I arrived—since the murder."

"I don't know what you're talking about."

"The ladies especially seem very upset."

"I wouldn't know anything about how they feel."

"But your own daughter—I know she was fond of the boy."

He stiffened. "She has foolish ideas. She is here to do her job, not mix with her betters."

I plowed ahead. "It's natural for a girl her age to have romantic fancies. And of course all the ladies are shaken. A young, handsome, innocent boy like that, thrown to his death—"

He snorted. "You don't know what you're talking about. He got what he deserved."

"What do you mean? He deserved to die? What had he done?"

He put down the quill and stuck the knife in his pocket, then took a brush from beside the hearth and swept the scrapings into the fire. He rose and smiled at me grimly. "Tell Miss Hahn I'll be dining out this afternoon."

I stared after him. What was the source of his enmity toward Florian Auerstein? Had his daughter been telling the truth all along, that the boy had promised to marry her? Had her sullen father seen through the boy's promises, and threatened to kill Auerstein to protect his daughter's honor? But what about Pergen's belief that Florian had been killed by the spy? The baron had told me that Bohm was too uneducated to be a spy, and I hadn't seen anything to convince me otherwise.

My conjectures were interrupted by the entrance of the staff, and a few moments later, I sat at the table, again pushing small bits of tough meat around my plate. There were five of us: Ecker; the three ladies, Rosa Hahn, Antonia, and Marianne; and myself. Once again Piatti had chosen to dine out. The company was quiet, everyone lost in his or her own thoughts. I struggled to push my despondency over Caroline to the side so that I might think clearly about the murder.

Troger had said I was the only visitor admitted to the palais that day, so the murderer/spy must be a member of the household. Everyone had been alone that afternoon, with no one else to vouch that he or she had not confronted Florian in the library. I looked over at Ecker. His pockmarked face was pale, his expression drawn. He had been defensive when I had asked whether he had ever traveled to the north, where the King of Prussia ruled. But why would he spy for Frederick? He had worked for the baron for years, and for the first baron before that. Had something happened to turn his loyalties?

I thought about the pompous doctor, Rausch. He had studied medicine at a northern university. It was possible that as a student, he had developed an admiration for Frederick, as many youths had at the time, and thus had welcomed an invitation to spy on his ward's husband for the Prussian king. I shook my head. Although I disliked the man, it was obvious that he cared deeply for Caroline. He had seemed worried that the scandal of Auerstein's death might affect the baron's standing in Vienna, and thus hurt his ward, whom he had raised from childhood. I also wasn't naïve enough to believe that his concern was only for Caroline. His engagement to the wealthy widow might be threatened by the murder scandal.

The idea of Piatti being the spy seemed far-fetched, also. As far as I knew, Vienna was the farthest he had traveled from his native Bologna, and he seemed to take deep pride in his position as music master in the household. The position must pay well, so he would not have needed the money the Prussian king paid. I hadn't heard him speak of politics, so what could possibly be his motive for stealing secrets from the baron?

Antonia hiccupped. I turned to regard her. Once again, her eyes were swollen from crying. Her plate remained untouched. I recalled her fancies, her claims that Florian was going to marry her. He had promised to take care of her, she had told me. It was obvious that she had been in love with the boy, which made her the least likely candidate to be the murderer. I had not considered that a woman could have the strength to commit this crime until the scene in my room with Antonia, her anger as she raised the fireplace poker over her head. Was it possible that they had quarreled that day in the library, and she had grabbed the poker there, and threatened Florian with it? Perhaps he had dashed her dreams, made clear to her that he would not marry her. I closed my eyes and pictured him sitting on the windowsill, trying to defend himself as she raised the poker to strike him. Could he have fallen out the window trying to protect himself? If that was the case, then what about the spy? Who was it? Certainly not this flighty girl, who seemed most of the time to reside in a dreamworld.

I could not say the same for Rosa Hahn. The housekeeper sat at the head of the table, helping herself to another serving of potatoes. She sensed me regarding her, and lifted her eyebrows to ask if I wanted the bowl passed. I smiled and shook my head. I remembered the conversation she, Ecker, and I had had after Antonia had collapsed at dinner. She had made clear her dislike of the emperor's religious reforms, and so might have been receptive to an offer by Frederick's agents to spy on the baron. What better person to have access to all parts of a house than the housekeeper? And where had she gotten the large amount of money to loan to

Vogel? But could she have murdered Florian Auerstein? Although she was slender, she must be strong, lifting heavy pots and piles of laundry all day. She certainly possessed the coolness of mind to commit murder, I was certain. But who had reported to Troger that I had argued with Auerstein and run from the house? The footsteps I had heard in the hallway had been heavy, a man's.

Finally, my eyes fell on Marianne. Caroline's maid had been cool toward me since she had seen the ribbon hanging out of my pocket. She had recognized it, I was sure. But whose was it? Her own? The boy's? I had no idea if it even was a clue. It could have been sitting in the drape for months, its loss long forgotten by its owner.

I sighed. I was getting nowhere. I had so many questions, but had no idea how to seek their answers. My hand brushed over my pocket, and I felt Caroline's missive within. I recalled her face as she had given it to me, her cheeks flushed with excitement and anticipation. Misery flooded my heart. I was suddenly wearier than I had ever felt: tired of this investigation, tired of Vogel and his box, tired of this house and all of its inhabitants. I was certain that I would not solve the murder, and for the moment, I no longer cared.

Fourteen

Caroline's cursed message was burning a hole in my pocket, so after dinner I put on my best coat and glumly set out to deliver it to its recipient. My destination was not far, just a few blocks, near the old Minorite church. The emperor had closed the Minorite order two years before, and had given the building to the Italian community of Vienna. The church was a stubby yet charming Gothic heap with an unadorned, fortresslike roof and a tower that had been truncated by a Turkish cannonball a century ago and never repaired. The church plaza was surrounded by the mansions of some of the wealthiest nobles in the city. I stopped in front of the largest, the Palais Starhemberg. Its owner had been the late empress's minister in Brussels, and it was now owned by a senior advisor to the emperor. The palace occupied an entire block, competing with the medieval church for God's attention. I shook my head. How I hated these bulky rectangular boxes that the aristocracy had built all over the city. I missed the delicate, multicolored *palazzi* of Venice, which hugged the curves of the canals and seemed to float on the water.

My knock on the monumental front door was answered by a lackey, and after replying to a long list of questions about who I was and what I wanted, I was ushered into a grand foyer and left to wait while he fetched the addressee of Caroline's letter. I looked around me. Unlike Mozart, Martín, and even Casti, I rarely see the insides of these grand houses, for the theater poet is not invited to an aristocrat's soirées, even when he has written the poetry for the arias that are performed at recitals held there. The room was dominated by a sweeping staircase of white stone, each baluster a miniature Corinthian column, its capital overlaid with gold. The newel posts were massive, squat pillars of deeply veined red granite, upon which sat lofty, overwrought candelabras. A large but ordinary statue of Minerva sat in a niche at the top of the first flight.

A man in his mid-twenties came down the stairway, followed by the lackey. "I am Matthias Starhemberg. You wished to see me?"

I bowed and took the letter out of my pocket. "I have a message for you, Your Excellency," I said. I lowered my voice, for the lackey hovered in the background, his ears straining with curiosity. "From the Baroness Gabler."

"From Caroline! Give it to me!" He snatched the message from my hand, removed the pin, and hurriedly unfolded the paper. While he read, I studied my rival. This was not the heir of the family, but a younger son. He was taller than me, dark-haired, slim yet muscular. His face, while not classically handsome, was striking: doelike brown eyes set over a slender nose; thin lips, which spread into a smile as he read the note. A stab of jealousy shot through me.

When he looked up from his reading, he seemed puzzled to see me still standing there. "Ah, the pin! You are waiting for the return message." He passed the devilish object to me. I slipped it into my pocket, bowed, and turned to leave.

"Wait!" he cried. I turned back. He pressed a coin into my palm.

My cheeks burned. I handed it back to him. "I beg your pardon, Your Excellency, but I am not the baroness's servant. I am a friend of hers," I said.

His eyebrows rose. "Oh, I see. Well—take this anyway. For your trouble." He pressed the coin back into my hand, turned, and bounded up the stairway, whistling.

I hurried into the street, my cheeks still hot. I looked down at my coat. How shabby it looked. I desperately needed a new one. Perhaps after I received the fee for *Figaro,* after the premiere, I would go over to Adam's tailor shop and order a whole new suit. Satin, maybe, or velvet.

By the time I reached the Herrengasse my dismay had turned to anger. How could Caroline have humiliated me like this? She must have sensed how I felt about her. How could I have misjudged her so badly? She was just like the rest, attracted to men with money and looks, the superficial sort. What kind of lover could that inexperienced young man be? As I fingered the pin in my pocket, I longed to just drop it on the ground, to let the horses' hooves bury it in the mud, and to tell her that, sadly, there had been no return message.

The street was crowded and noisy this time of day. I moved close to the building on my right as a gilded carriage drawn by four horses rushed by. As I continued down the street I saw Ecker, the baron's secretary, walking a few yards ahead of me. I did not relish returning to the palais just yet, so I decided to follow him.

The Michaelerplatz was more crowded than the street. Pedestrians milled about. Cabs stopped to discharge passengers outside the court office buildings. Guards on horseback patrolled the grand arch that led to the Hofburg courtyard. I stepped around a group of chatting courtiers. Ahead of me, Ecker consulted his pocket watch, then quickened his stride.

I bumped into something. A child began to wail. "Sir! Mind where you are going, please!" A stout woman pulled the small boy to her skirts. I quickly dug a coin out of my pocket and handed it to the child.

I looked across the plaza. Where was Ecker? Ah, there, heading toward St. Michael's Church.

"Make way!" A large cart laden with wine barrels trundled by, blocking my view of the church's entrance. I darted to the right and craned my neck to find Ecker in the throng. Damn! He was nowhere to be seen. I sighed. I just was not cut out to be an investigator.

As I was about to turn back in the direction of the palais, the little secretary appeared at the very edge of the crowd, pushing his way through a group of laughing merchants. I hurried to follow him.

"Da Ponte!" a voice called. I tried to keep my shoulders from sagging. I recognized the voice. It was one I could not possibly ignore. I stopped and watched as Ecker hurried out of the plaza and headed down the street past the Spanish Riding School stables.

. . .

I turned and dropped to my knees before a nondescript man in his forties, of average height and weight, his countenance engaging only because of his lively, cornflower-blue eyes. He was dressed in a simple brown coat and breeches, such as a merchant might wear to survey his warehouse. I took his hands in mine and kissed them.

"Get up, Da Ponte, get up," the emperor said, pulling me to my feet. "Why do you Italians always insist on kissing my hands? You know I hate that."

I blushed. "My apologies, Your Majesty," I said. "I was surprised to hear you call me, and my emotions got the better of me." I looked past the emperor. A single servant stood a few feet behind him, watching us, but beyond that, as was his preference, there were none of the trappings of his great office: no gilded carriage, no retinue of fawning nobles, no satin-clad lackeys.

"Apology accepted," he said. "I'm glad I ran into you. Tell me, how goes the opera?"

"Very well, sir. Mozart and I are putting the finishing touches on it, and we are in rehearsals, as you probably have heard." The emperor was a passionate opera fan, and consulted with Rosenberg about many of the details of his theater's operation. I will never forget that it was he who hired me, a poet who had never written a libretto; he who had overruled the theater director when my first opera with Salieri failed; he who had given me a second chance.

The emperor dug into his coat pocket and brought out two chocolate drops. He popped one into his mouth. "How are you finding working with Mozart?"

I eyed the other chocolate drop. My stomach growled a bit, reminding me that I had only picked at my dinner. "I'm enjoying it very much, sir. Of course, I've had to write many more ensemble pieces than in the usual comic opera, but we both are pleased with our work. It will not be the shortest opera ever performed in your theater, but I think you will find it one of the best."

He laughed. "Good. But I hope you haven't cut all the bite out of the play. We will still tweak the noses of my princes, eh? Now, what's next for you? Something for the Spaniard, Martín, correct?" He bit into the second chocolate.

"Yes, Your Majesty. Another comedy."

"Good, I'm glad you are busy." He clapped me on the shoulder.

I hesitated and bit my lip, debating whether I should confide my predicament with Pergen to him.

He peered into my face. "What is it, Da Ponte? Some problem with the Spaniard? Is he difficult to work with?"

"Oh no, Your Majesty. Nothing like that. He is my good friend, we work well together. It is just—"

"Just what? Tell me, man!"

"I haven't had much time to work on the opera for Martín. There have been certain distractions. I—I have found myself in a difficult situation."

He looked at me, his eyes full of concern. The words tumbled from my mouth. "Oh, Your Majesty. I have been framed for murder." To my horror, I began to weep. "I innocently went to a noble house and spoke with a boy. He was murdered that same afternoon. Now the police have forced me to investigate for them, to live in the house to find the murderer. They told me I came highly recommended to them, probably by my enemies at the theater, I believe. They have threatened that I will hang for the crime if I cannot solve it. I am filled with fear, sir. I cannot sleep, I cannot eat, I cannot work."

He pulled his handkerchief from his pocket and handed it to me. "Come, Da Ponte, stop blubbering." I wiped my eyes. "This is the Auerstein boy's murder, I presume?"

I nodded.

He sighed. "I shall have to speak with Pergen. He's gone too far."

My heart leaped with joy. I chided myself—I should have gone to the emperor as soon as Pergen released me. I should have known that he would help me.

"Threatening you with hanging. That is a bit heavy-handed. I told him that I wanted simply to get you into the Gabler house. He needn't have frightened you so."

I stared at him. "I don't understand, Your Majesty," I said slowly. "*You* wanted me in the house?"

"Yes. Pergen came to me six months ago, telling me that he suspected Frederick had placed a spy in the Gabler house, asking for an increase in his budget so he could hire someone to go undercover. I was occupied with the Dutch treaty, so I put him off. When the boy was murdered, I realized it was the perfect time to put someone in there. I wanted someone intelligent and observant, someone I could trust, to find out what was going on. I immediately thought of you."

"But Your Majesty, I have no experience. I am no police professional."

"That is just what Pergen argued. No, Da Ponte, you are the one I want in that house."

I swallowed and nodded at him.

He leaned closer to me and lowered his voice. "I need you to do this for me, Lorenzo," he said. "The security of my throne depends on you."

"I am humbled by your confidence in me, Your Majesty," I said.

"Well then. I look forward to hearing the opera. Try to get some work done for Martín."

"I will, Your Majesty."

He turned and walked away, followed by the manservant. I watched as he made his way through the plaza, stopping now and then to give a coin to a child or to converse easily with a passerby. A moment later, he disappeared under the arch that led to the Hofburg courtyard.

I turned and walked down the street that hugged the side of the Hofburg, my thoughts in such a whirl that I barely noticed the gate through which the police had taken me that fateful night. So Pergen's threats had been hollow, just meant to frighten me. I trusted the emperor. I knew he would look after me. I clutched my stick tightly and hurried toward the Palais Gabler, my sense of purpose renewed. My Caesar needed *me* to solve this case. I vowed to do it for him.

I reached the Minoritenplatz and walked past the long cloister that clung to the left side of the old church. The afternoon had grown late, and the interior of the covered archway was dark with shadows as I passed by.

"Signor Da Ponte? Is that you?"

I stopped and looked around the plaza. It had emptied since I had been here earlier.

"Signor Poet?" The voice came from inside the cloister.

"Yes, who is there?" I asked. I walked through one of the tall arches into the shadows. A hand grabbed my arm. My stick clattered to the ground.

"Who is there?" I cried. My arms were pulled behind me. Pain shot through my injured shoulder. "What do you want?" My knees shook as I waited to feel grubby hands groping my clothing, searching for the small purse in which I carried my coins.

A sharp object pressed into my back. A guttural voice sounded in my ear. "You are sticking your nose where it does not belong, signore." I retched at the smell of rotten meat on his breath. "Stop it, or you will be sorry."

"Who are you?" I shouted.

My assailant twisted my arms tightly against my back. I winced with pain.

"Be quiet!" he hissed. "You know what I am talking about. Mind your own business." He grunted. "Don't tempt me. I've always wanted to kill a Jew."

I twisted and struggled to release myself from his grasp. "You have the wrong person! I am a priest." He laughed and threw me to the ground. I lay hugging the cool stones, my heart pounding wildly in my chest, listening to his footsteps recede.

I lay still for a few minutes, until my heartbeat had slowed, then pulled myself up gingerly. My shoulder throbbed and

I had a large scrape on my hand, but otherwise I was un-
hurt. I picked up my stick and hobbled down the street toward the Palais Gabler, my mind filled with worry. My
attacker's accent had been northern. Had the spy discovered
my true purpose at the palais and sent him to frighten me
off the case? Why had my assailant called me a Jew?

The palais was dim and quiet. The baron and baroness
must be out at some soirée, the others out or in their rooms.
I sighed as I trudged up the stairs. The day seemed intermi-
nable. I was exhausted. As I reached the first-floor landing,
the library beckoned. One of the baron's fine volumes of
poetry, the comfort of the stuffed chair in my room—an
evening of reading was what I needed. Work could wait until tomorrow.

As I stopped before the library door and began to turn
the knob, I heard a noise: high, sharp, a grunt, perhaps of
frustration. I looked down the hall. The baron's office door
stood ajar. A dim light emanated from the room.

I quietly placed my stick on the floor and crept down the
hallway, hugging the wall. The noise sounded again. I stopped
about a foot from the doorway, and listened. I heard a shuffling sound, as if someone were searching through papers. I
inched closer to the door. Did I dare stick my head into the
opening? I slowly moved forward.

Another sound, this time a drawer opening and closing.
I pulled my head back. My pulse began to race. I moved forward again, craning my head around the door frame. A tickle
caught in my throat. I fought back the urge to cough.

The sharp grunt sounded again. I glanced into the room.
It was dark, except for a single candle sitting on the baron's

desk. Even in the dim light, I recognized the figure that leaned over the desk, systematically searching through the piles of paper that covered its surface. I drew my head back and quietly crept back to the landing.

I hurried up to my room, my reading project forgotten. I removed my coat, lit a candle, and sat in the reading chair, puzzled. Rosa Hahn, the spy? True, I had briefly considered her, wondering where she had gotten the money to lend to Vogel, remembering her disdain for the emperor's religious reforms. But had she murdered Florian Auerstein? Who was the man who had just threatened me? Had she sent him? Or did she merely work for a larger organization? My mind was in a muddle. I took the candle over to the writing table and sat down, pulling a blank sheet of paper toward me. I needed to write down some thoughts, clear my head. As I pushed Vogel's box to the side, I noticed its lid was ajar. Seeing it reminded me that I should put the medallion in my satchel. I rooted through the box. Hadn't I put the medallion back? When had I last had it? Yes, after Troger had accosted me in the Am Hof, I had come up here, in a hurry to get to Caroline. I had taken the medallion out of my pocket and placed it on the desk. Perhaps the girl had put it somewhere for safe-keeping.

It was not on the table by the chair, or on the bed. I went over to the cupboard and searched through the pockets of my clothes. I pulled out my valise and opened it. Empty. Damn, where was it? I returned to the desk, took the muff, ring, and book out of the box, and turned it upside down. No medallion. I grabbed the large pile of work on the desk and looked through it. My Petrarch. Notes from the last lesson with Caroline. A few sheets of paper with my scribbled outline of the libretto for Martín. No medallion. Some drafts of the pantomime scene for *Figaro*. A small notebook, tied with a ribbon. I paused. Where had I gotten that? I threw it aside. An old receipt for silk stockings. No medallion. I slammed my palm on the desk. Why hadn't I taken the time to put it away before I went to Caroline?

My eyes fell on the notebook. I never use such little ones. As I picked it up, a memory came to me. I carried the notebook over to the chair, untied the ribbon, and began to read.

PART III

The Ungrateful Heart

Fifteen

Monday morning was bright and chilly. I wrapped my cloak tightly about me as I walked over to the Hofburg. The large courtyard of the old castle, which housed the imperial departments, was filled with bureaucrats hurrying toward their offices. The sun gleamed off the rows of windows lining the long quadrangle.

I entered the door at the center of the southwest wing and stopped to ask directions of the passersby in the long corridors—most of them clerks scurrying from door to door, carrying piles of documents to and fro between offices. After a few wrong turns, I finally stumbled upon my destination.

The room, well lit by the sun streaming through leaded windows along its rear wall, was as large as the parterre of the theater, its expanse partitioned only by a waist-high wooden wall that ran the entire width of the room about eight feet from the doorway. Behind the wall were arrayed ten rows of six desks apiece. Each desk was occupied by a young man in a dark suit. Some were bent over their labor, while others conversed with their neighbors.

I approached a large desk on my right, where a middle-aged clerk was sorting a large stack of papers. I cleared my throat to get his attention. He did not look up from his task. I crossed my arms. He continued to riffle through the pile. I coughed. No response. He came to the end of the stack, pushed some wayward sheets into place, and rapped the bundle against the desk.

"Excuse me, I am looking for—"

"Just one moment," he said, his eyes fixed on the papers. He licked his index finger and began to flip through the pages once more. I exhaled loudly. His fingers moved through the sheaf of documents. When he was halfway through the pile, he paused and peered at a page. "Humph."

My pulse quickened. "I just need a moment of your time—"

His eyes did not leave the document. After another moment, he sighed, put down the papers, reached over, and took up another packet.

"I am looking for—"

"Just another moment," he said. He began to read the top page of the new bundle. My cheeks grew hot. I wanted to reach over, grab him by the neck, and choke the pittance of information I required out of his officious little mouth. I took a deep breath to calm my temper and looked around the room. Many of the young men had left their desks. Some flitted through large doors at either side of the office, others had congregated around a few of the farthermost desks and, as

THE UNGRATEFUL HEART   ✢   199

evidenced by the laughter coming from the area, seemed to be sharing the latest gossip and jokes.

After what seemed to be another five minutes of study of the same document, the clerk finally looked up at me. "Who is it you wish to see?" he asked.

"Rupert Maulbertsch."

"Do you have an appointment?"

"No. You can tell him Alois Bayer referred me to him."

The clerk sniffed. "I'm afraid without an appointment—"

I leaned across the desk, hovering over him. To my satisfaction, he shrank back a little. "Would you please tell Mr. Maulbertsch that Lorenzo Da Ponte, the theater poet, would like to see him on an important matter?"

He stood. "I'll check for you, but I can't guarantee that he'll have time for you."

"Thank you," I muttered through clenched teeth. I watched as he ambled down a long corridor. The twit! Next time I'll use the emperor's name. I rubbed my left temple.

A few moments later, a tall, lanky man came down the passage toward me. "Signor Da Ponte?" he asked. "I am Rupert Maulbertsch." I shook his hand. His bright blue eyes protruded from a perfectly egg-shaped head, on which a wig was perched askew. "You are a friend of Alois's? How can I help you?" He gestured down the corridor. "Come, let us talk in my office."

He ushered me into a small, low-ceilinged room lined with tall cabinets on all four walls. The sole window was blocked by the height of the furniture. A large desk, on which sat a solitary lamp and a large volume bound in dark sheepskin, took up most of the remaining space in the dim office.

Maulbertsch indicated a chair and took a seat behind the desk. "How is Alois?" he asked. "I owe him a visit."

"He is well, busy with his books, as usual," I said. "He recommended that I speak to you about an investigation I am conducting."

He raised an eyebrow.

"I am trying to help a friend find his birth mother," I said. I explained about the muff and the medallion. "Alois identified it as one given to the novices of the convent of the Sisters of the Blessed Virgin. He said you might know how to trace the medallion's owner."

"Oh yes, the sisters. I remember that convent well. Small, only about ten sisters left at the time of the dissolution, I think. Most of them were elderly." He sighed. "It was a difficult process, dissolving that convent. I remember the old abbess, she was very upset that we decided to shut them down. But it was necessary. The emperor was determined to close all the monastic houses that served no purpose to society. Those nuns spent most of their time in contemplation. That did nothing to help the people of the empire."

"I understand that they ran a hospital for young women who had gone astray," I said.

"A minor activity, I assure you. Many years ago, they were known for their nursing, but that declined as the nuns grew older. And the emperor had just built the new hospital, which would have taken over the maternity ward anyway. The sisters were given a choice, but they did not want to teach in the schools or work in the new hospital as nurses. We needed to sell their building and treasury to fund the emperor's new public health programs. Those nuns wanted the emperor to forgo that money so they could live out their lives in that old convent." He shook his head. "I'm sure they are all better off wherever they landed, these years later."

"The Abbess Elisabeth is dead," I murmured.

"Is she? Oh, that is too bad. Well, she was quite old, as I recall. Now, tell me about this medallion. May I see it?"

I shook my head, but did not offer the information that I had lost it. I described it.

"The initials 'K.S.,' you say?" He thought for a moment. "If the medallion belonged to one of the nuns or novices, we should be able to match those initials with the records we took from the convent." He looked around the room at the cabinets. "That might narrow your search a bit."

Excitement rushed through me. "That would be of great help. Do you have those records here?"

"Most of them were kept by the junior minister who ran the dissolution project, but I have a few of them here. I'll look around for you. It may take a few days, though." He paused. "Do you believe that the owner of this medallion is your friend's birth mother?" he asked.

"She must be," I said. "Why else would the medallion be in the muff?"

"A novice or nun who had to leave the convent because of pregnancy would be quite a scandal," he mused. "It would be useful to speak to one of the former nuns. Give me time to look for the records."

I thanked him and told him how to contact me. As I opened the door to leave, he called to me.

"You might want to go over to the Deaf School. I just

remembered—one of the nuns who belonged to the convent, the cellarer, works over there now. She was a bit younger than the other women. When the convent was closed, she found a job at the school. She does all the purchasing for the kitchens over there. What is her name? Josepha. Yes, that's it. Josepha Hassler. Tell her I sent you."

I walked back into the busy Michaelerplatz. As I passed the theater, I saw Mozart, astride a gray horse, approaching from the Kohlmarkt. Although the beast was only about five feet tall, the small composer appeared to be hanging on to the reins for dear life.

"You don't look all that comfortable up there, Wolfgang," I said. "When did you get the horse?"

"Just yesterday. My doctor's been nagging me to get more exercise. The Spanish Riding School was selling this fellow. It seems he marches to his own tune, not that of their choreographer. This is our first outing."

The handsome animal flicked its tail at some imagined pest and regarded me with soulful, dark eyes.

"Have you found anything about your barber's parents?" Mozart asked.

"I have a few avenues to investigate," I said. He fiddled absently with the reins as I told him about finding the medallion and my visits to Alois Bayer and Maulbertsch.

"The mystery gets deeper and deeper," he said. He pulled up on the reins. The horse started. Mozart grabbed onto the long gray neck.

"Don't wriggle around so much while you're on that creature," I said.

He laughed. "Yes. It wouldn't help my doctor's reputation if his prescription for exercise ended in my death by a broken neck."

I rubbed the horse's shoulder. "What's his name?" I asked.

"I haven't decided yet. Carl wants to call him 'Horse' but I think we can do better than that, can't we, boy?" He rubbed the horse's long head. "So far I only have ideas about who to name his ass after." We laughed.

Mozart climbed off the horse. "Oh, that reminds me," he said as he tethered the animal to a nearby post. "Rosenberg wants to see you. I was here yesterday working with Miss Laschi and he came looking for you."

A pang of anxiety stabbed me. "What do you think he wants?"

"Probably nothing important. Just to have his fingers in the pot, I'd say, so when our opera is the hit of the season he can take credit for it." He opened the theater door. "Are you coming in?"

I hesitated. Should I see if Rosenberg was in his office now? The bell of St. Michael's chimed the hour. No. I'd better wait until tomorrow. I was due in Caroline's chamber in a half hour to give another lesson—and to deliver her lover's message.

"No, I have an appointment," I said.

Mozart nodded. "Let me know what Rosenberg wants," he said. He went inside.

The horse gave me another sad look. "What do you have to worry about?" I asked him. He flicked his tail. I sighed, and with a heavy heart, trudged down the Herrengasse toward the palais.

. . .

Back in my room, I gathered my papers and tucked the pin into my pocket. As I approached Caroline's chamber, I heard her voice through the door.

"You must do it, you must!" Her voice was loud, angry.

"Caroline, you have no right to tell me to do this," Urban Rausch said.

"Of course I have the right! This is my house!"

"Caroline—"

"I know everything now! You must confess!"

"You know I cannot—how can you ask me to do this, after all I've done for you, all I've given you?"

"If you do not, I will tell—"

"Please, Caroline," Rausch pleaded. "I cannot. You know I cannot. What will happen to me?"

I pressed my ear to the door, but Caroline had lowered her voice, and I could not make out her reply. Someone coughed behind me. I jumped, and turned to see Bohm standing at the end of the hallway, a sly grin on his face. My cheeks grew hot. I rapped sharply on the door. It flew open. Rausch, his face purple with rage, stormed out.

"Get out of my way!" he yelled, pushing me aside. I stumbled, then righted myself, gagging at the wind of cologne that followed the doctor down the hall.

I looked into the room. Caroline sat in a chair by the fireplace, her posture stiff and erect, her face white. I tapped on the door.

"Oh, Lorenzo, come in. I didn't hear you." She smiled tightly. "Please close the door."

I crossed the room and sat in the other chair. "Are you all right, Caroline?" I asked.

She waved her hand. "Yes, I am fine. Just a disagreement with my guardian, that is all." She looked closely at me. "Did you deliver my message, Lorenzo?"

I nodded miserably.

"And?"

I reached into my pocket and handed her the pin. I hated the smile that came to her face. Jealousy surged through me. Why could she not smile like that for me? I cursed the day I had agreed to help Vogel find his mother. Had I walked away from the closed-up shop, I never would have met this bewitching woman, never would have felt this misery.

She rose and slipped the pin into her jewel box, then crossed over to the window. "Now, what poems have you for me today? Any more from Petrarch, about his mysterious love?"

I took up my notes and shuffled through the poems I had copied out, settling upon the last one I had chosen. My throat was dry as I read to her.

Love has locked me in a lovely, cruel embrace
that kills me unjustly; and if I protest
he doubles my suffering; thus it is better
that I die in loving silence, as I would.

For her eyes could burn the Rhine however much frozen,
and shatter his every rugged rock;
her haughtiness is so equal to her beauty
that to please others seems to displease her.

I looked over at her. She stood staring out the window, a contented smile on her face, her eyes far away. My heart wrenched. I took up my reading.

I cannot with my wit wear down
the lovely diamond of her hard heart;
the rest of her is a marble that moves and breathes;

But neither can she, with all her contempt,
and with all her darkened looks,
take away my hopes and my sweet sighs.

She stood silently for several long moments. I cast my papers aside and rubbed my forehead. She came and stood over me.

"Do you judge me, Lorenzo?" she asked softly.

"Madame, I have no right to judge anyone," I said. Oh, how I wished I could stand up from my chair, leave this wretched room, this miserable house!

"You don't understand what it is like to be a woman, Lorenzo," she said, her voice tightening. "You spend your youth waiting to be chosen. You do everything you can to please your husband. You watch while he chases after every young woman he sees."

"Madame—"

"You have to put up with that! You have to put up with everything!" She paced the room now, her hands balled into fists.

"Caroline, I—"

"You are humiliated, day after day!" Her voice rose to a shriek. "Your husband brings a young man into your house and you must do everything to keep the boy happy, because if you do not, your husband's career could be ruined. So you put up with him, you let him paw you, fondle you, you cannot stop him as he tries to go further—"

I stared at her, my mouth wide open, my heart pounding.

"Would you deny me a few moments of happiness?"

A knock sounded at the door. "Madame, are you all right?" Marianne called. Caroline froze. She did not look at me as she took a deep breath and smoothed her skirt.

"Come in, Marianne," she called.

"Are you ready for me to do your hair?" the maid asked as she entered. "Oh, Signor Da Ponte! I'm sorry, madame. I thought you were alone."

"It's fine, Marianne. Signor Da Ponte was just leaving." She sat down at the dressing table and began to undo her hair.

I gathered my papers and fled.

My heart was still pounding as I entered my room and shut the door. I went over to the desk, pulled the little notebook from the pile, and sat in the reading chair. Slowly, I turned the pages. It was a diary of sorts. The first few pages were carefully lined with staves, where Florian had jotted down snatches of music. I remembered Piatti telling me he had been a gifted composer. About ten pages of this, then journal-like entries, each dated and written in a neat, small hand:

Attended opera with K., singing good, plot boring;
Walked in Prater, saw C.G. there;
Lesson today, the passacaglia;
Letter from P., he wishes I were home;
Argument with R.H.;
Received 20 florins from C.G.;
J.'s name day;
Saw U.R. coming out of pawnshop?;
Received 30 florins from C.G.;
Ask A. about G.B.'s past?

The entries went on for several pages, the dates covering the last six months.

My heart was numb. A scene came to my mind. The library, its windows open to the sunny, warm day. A rapacious boy pulls a slight woman toward him, onto the window seat. She tries to pull away, but he taunts her with what he knows. He quickly unties the laces of her bodice and, despite her protests, fondles her breast with one hand, while pulling her skirt up with the other. She tries to push him away. He squeezes her breast, hard. At that moment, the rage she has kept buried for years rushes to the surface. She shoves him off her. He tumbles through the open window to his death on the rocks below. His victim's hands shake as she ties up her bodice. She takes a deep breath, tucks a loose auburn strand behind her ear, and walks to the door.

Ice spread through my heart as I tucked the book away in my cloak pocket for safekeeping. I did not know if I could find the will to give it to Troger.

Sixteen

The old city hospital covered two large blocks between the Hofburg and the Karntner gate in the city wall. Founded in the Middle Ages as a small infirmary attached to a church, the institution had grown in both size and utility, encompassing a hospital for the city's poor, an orphanage, and a modern medical clinic, until it was closed three years ago. The emperor opened his new general hospital in the northwest suburb right outside the city. The medical patients had been transferred to the new facility; the orphans had moved to new space less than a mile away on the Rennweg; and the large, empty buildings were in the process of being converted to apartments. Everyone benefited: the sick and the orphans now enjoyed the healthier open spaces of the suburbs; residents of the suburbs who wanted to move into town would soon have apartments available; and the city's builders were making a hefty profit.

The emperor had given the oldest part of the complex,

formerly occupied by the orphanage, to Deaf School, a school founded by his mother. It was there that I headed the next morning, Tuesday, to find the ex-nun Maulbertsch had mentioned. Despite my worries about Florian Auerstein's diary, I allowed myself a scintilla of excitement about my progress on Vogel's matter. Surely between this visit and Maulbertsch's efforts to find the convent records, I was nearing the solution to the mystery of the medallion and its owner.

I passed under an arched doorway and entered a small foyer. A young man was seated at a desk. When he saw me, he rose, and greeted me with a smile and a nod.

"Good morning, I am looking for Josepha Hassler," I said. He nodded again and pointed me toward a bench along the wall. As he hurried down a corridor, I took a seat and looked around. The room's low, vaulted ceiling gave it a coziness, and although there was no furniture besides the desk, a small chair, and the bench on which I sat, the room did not feel sparse. The walls appeared to have been recently whitewashed, and I could smell the pine soap with which the ancient stone floor had been scrubbed clean. A tapestry woven of gaily colored wool hung behind the reception desk, offering a warmer welcome to the deaf students than I imagined had ever been extended to the building's previous occupants, Vienna's poor orphans.

A moment later, the young man returned, accompanied by a tall, thin-faced woman with keen gray eyes and skin as smooth as porcelain. My heart sank as I rose. She seemed to be about my own age, too young to have resided at the Sisters of the Blessed Virgin convent when Vogel had been born, thirty years before. She glanced at me, turned to the young man, and began to gesture at him frantically. He nodded at her and responded with his own gestures, moving his fingers wildly. When he finally returned to his chair behind the desk, she turned to me and, seeing my astonished expression, smiled.

"I gather this is your first visit to a deaf school, sir," she said.

I nodded.

"Heinrich is a student here. We were conversing using the signing method developed by the Abbé de l'Epée in France."

"The boy is deaf? But how did he understand me when I asked for you?"

"We train all of our students to study lip movements. While Heinrich would have had trouble following you if you had made a long speech, he was easily able to recognize my name and assumed you wished to see me." She smiled again as I shook my head in amazement. "Now, how can I help you? Are you here to learn about the school?"

"No, madame, I am here to see you in particular," I said. I introduced myself and explained about my investigation for Vogel and my discovery of the medallion. Her smile turned to a frown as I finished my story.

"I'm sorry, signore. It still saddens me to think about the sisters. I lived at the convent for twenty years. My life was turned upside down when the emperor closed it."

"You seem to have made a new life for yourself here, Sister," I said.

Her look was sharp. "You must call me Miss Hassler. I am no longer a nun. The emperor saw to that." She took a deep breath. "Yes, you are right. I was able to land on my feet. Because I was the cellarer for the convent, I had good business experience. But many of the nuns, especially the older ones, had nowhere to go. I often wonder what happened to them."

I decided to spare her the sad fate of the Abbess Elisabeth. "Do you remember anything about such a medallion?" I asked.

"Oh yes, sir. One was given to every novice upon entry to the convent. I have mine tucked away somewhere, if you would like to see it."

I shook my head. "Do the initials 'K.S.' mean anything to you? Was there a nun in the convent with those initials?"

She thought for a few moments. "No, no one comes to mind. But I did not join the convent until ten years after the year your friend was born. I'm sorry I cannot be of more help to you, signore. Now, if you'll excuse me, I have work to do."

"Please, madame. If you could answer one more question. I apologize if it sounds fantastical to you."

She raised her eyebrow.

"Do you remember any stories you might have heard while you lived at the convent—about a novice, or even a nun, discovered to be with child years before you arrived?"

She laughed. "No, signore. And I'm sure I would have heard about it if such a thing had ever occurred. Nuns love gossip just as much as other women!" Her expression grew thoughtful. "I don't see how it could have happened. The Abbess Elisabeth kept a sharp eye on all the younger sisters. It's more likely your friend's mother was a patient at the convent's hospital. It was a very busy place in its time. Rich or poor, married or unmarried, they all came to us. The abbess placed many babies in adoptive families." She looked at me sadly. "I am sorry, signore, but I don't think your chances of finding your friend's mother are good."

"Perhaps you are right," I said softly. I thanked her for her time and watched as she strode purposefully down the corridor. The young man at the desk had his head buried in a book, so I turned and left the building. Another dead end! I had felt sure that Vogel's mother had been a novice or a nun at the convent. Why else would the medallion have been hidden in the muff? Yet Josepha Hassler seemed sure that she would have heard about any scandal befalling one of her fellow nuns. I plodded back to the Hofburg, the optimism of the morning dissipated. My hopes of finding Vogel's mother lay solely with Maulbertsch now.

I stopped by the theater to see if Rosenberg was in his office. "He's out hunting with the emperor," the secretary told me. "He's due back this evening. You might catch him at the theater tonight."

Tonight was the premiere of an opera I had written with Righini, one of the more mediocre composers in the city. I hadn't wanted to work with him, but Salieri had insisted. I did not hold out high hopes for the success of the opera, but I always enjoyed premiere nights, when I was entitled to sit in the special box reserved for the composer and the librettist. And although I knew better, I vainly hoped the Viennese public could see past the inferior music and enjoy my poetry.

"I'd better make an appointment," I told the secretary. "I might miss him tonight."

He consulted his book. "Tomorrow, three o'clock."

"Did he mention why he wanted to see me?" I asked.

"Not that I recall. Wait, let me see if I made a note." He studied the book. "Oh yes, he wants you to bring your copy of the libretto." He looked at me apologetically. "That's all I know."

I thanked him and left. What did Rosenberg want with the libretto? Were he and Casti up to some trick? As I walked down the Herrengasse, my mind was so deep in thoughts about my two enemies that I did not even notice when I passed the turnoff to the Starhemberg Palace, where I had delivered Caroline's message two days ago.

I let myself into the palais and trudged up the stairs to the top floor. When I was just a few feet from my room, I stopped short. The door was ajar. I hadn't left it that way this morning, I was sure. Since the medallion had disappeared I had taken care to put my things away and leave the door closed.

Heavy footsteps came from my room. I strained to listen. I heard the cupboard doors open and close, then a loud rustling of papers. I pushed the door open. "What—"

The intruder gasped. "Oh! Lorenzo! It is only you! You gave me such a fright!" Piatti said, as several sheets of my libretto scattered to the floor.

"Tomaso? What are you doing?" I asked.

His face turned red. He laughed quickly. "Oh, my friend, you've caught me out," he said. He kneeled and gathered the papers he had dropped.

"What are you doing in my room?"

He rose and placed the papers on the desk. "I had a free moment, and I wanted to look at your libretto. Remember, you told me I could see it the other day? I knocked, but you were not in."

"So you just walked in and went through my things, without my permission?"

He held up his hands. "Please, please, Lorenzo. I saw your papers lying on the desk. I hoped perhaps I could read them here. Please forgive me." His left eye twitched.

I took the pile from the desk and shuffled through them, putting them back in order.

"Your libretto is very good, my friend," he said. "If Mozart's music is half as good as your poetry, the opera will be a great hit, I am sure."

I remained silent as I finished organizing the pages.

"Lorenzo? Please forgive me. I never meant to anger you." His voice took on a pleading tone. "Please. Our friendship means so much to me. I have no one here in the house with whom I can discuss music, literature, art—"

I held up my hand to silence him. His upper lip glistened with sweat. "Yes, Tomaso. You are forgiven." I took the first few pages from the pile. "Here, take this. It is the first act of the opera."

"But—is this your only copy?"

"No, that is a draft." I took off my cloak and placed it in the cupboard. "Now, if you'll excuse me, Tomaso. I have a bit of work to do." I tried to make my voice gruff.

He bowed slightly. "Very good, my friend. I apologize again."

I pulled out the desk chair and sat. He remained standing near the door, clutching my pages. I looked over at him. "Anything else, Tomaso?" I asked.

"You seem distressed, Lorenzo," he said. "Is there anything wrong—besides my innocent trespass, that is?"

I shook my head. "No, just a few personal problems. Nothing I care to talk about right now."

"A lady?"

I could not help myself. I nodded.

"She is lovely?"

I nodded again.

"She does not return your love?"

I shook my head. "She uses me for her own purposes, Tomaso. That is all there is to our relationship."

He smiled sympathetically. "Ah, Lorenzo. I understand," he said softly. He nodded. "All beautiful women are like that." He gave a small bow and closed the door behind him.

My stomach growled as I turned my attention to the work before me. I scribbled idly for a few moments on a page of the draft, then threw down my pen and went down to the kitchen. The large room was empty except for Marianne, who sat in the chair by the fire, bent over some mending, a large basket at her feet. I cleared my throat.

She jumped. The sewing fell to the floor. "Oh, Signor Da Ponte! I did not hear you come in."

"I'm sorry, Miss Haiml. I didn't mean to startle you. I was working and grew hungry."

She pointed over to the table. "Just cold meats today, signore. Miss Hahn has the day off."

I groaned inwardly as I looked over at the platters. More tough roasts for my miserable teeth. Why could the housekeeper never make anything meltingly tender? As I turned back toward Marianne, I saw her quickly stuff something into her sewing basket.

"Signore, have you learned anything to help Johann?" she asked. "If you don't mind my saying so, you don't seem to be spending much time finding his mother. We both are counting on you."

I sighed at her disapproval. I pulled out a chair from the table, dragged it toward her, and sat down.

"I know it doesn't look as if I'm making progress," I said. "But I assure you I've been following a lot of leads."

She arched her brow.

"I took the things in the box to a pawnbroker," I told her. "Unfortunately, he believes they are of no real value, merely trinkets a woman of lesser means might treasure."

Her face fell. "Oh no," she whispered.

"Don't give up hope yet," I said. I explained how I had found the medallion sewn into the lining of the muff.

"A religious medallion? How strange." She frowned.

"I showed it to a friend of mine at the Stephansdom. He recognized it immediately. It belonged to a nun or novice at a convent called the Sisters of the Blessed Virgin. The convent was closed a few years ago, when the emperor dissolved the religious houses. I spoke to a bureaucrat who was involved in those reforms. He's promised to search for any records he might have kept, to see if we can identify the medallion's owner."

"But why would Johann's birth mother have a nun's medallion?" Marianne's face paled. "Oh no. You don't think his mother was a nun?"

"It's a possibility, strange as it sounds."

"Poor Johann. He was so sure his parents were rich," she said softly. "May I see the medallion, signore?"

My cheeks grew warm as I shook my head. "I've misplaced it. I left it on the desk in my room the other day, and I can't find it anywhere."

"The thief!" Marianne said. "Everyone in the house has lost something. Johann gave me a beautiful hairpin on my name day. Someone took it out of the drawer in my cupboard."

I sighed. "I think I should go talk to Johann. Maybe he can remember if his adoptive mother ever mentioned anything about a convent." Marianne had returned to her work, stitching white ribbons to a bonnet decorated with gold thread.

"I am going there tomorrow morning," she said, as she drew out a small pair of scissors and clipped the thread. "Why don't you come along?"

A bell on the wall shrilled. "Oh, that's the baroness. Good, I finished her bonnet just in time," Marianne said. "I'll leave you to your dinner, signore. Shall we meet in the foyer tomorrow at ten?"

I nodded. She pushed her sewing basket aside and left the kitchen. When I had counted her footsteps on the stairs, I leaned over and rustled through the basket, shoving aside a tangle of colored scraps and threads. My heart grew heavy as I pulled out what I had suspected I would find underneath: a single white silk ribbon, embroidered with gold thread in a pattern of delicate flowers.

Seventeen

I sat for a while in the lonely kitchen, morosely picking at cold tubers that had had the flavor boiled out of them, then I scraped and rinsed my plate, climbed up to my room, and attempted to work. I fought to keep my thoughts from turning to Caroline, to my unwelcome suspicions. The record of payments in Florian Auerstein's notebook; Marianne's attempt to hide the partner to the ribbon I had found in the library drapes, obviously torn at some point from Caroline's bonnet; Caroline's own confession that the boy had forced himself upon her—I did not want to follow these indicators to their logical conclusion.

The afternoon dragged on, and I accomplished little writing. At sunset, I pulled on my finest evening suit, a blue satin I save for special occasions, trying to ignore the fraying at the coat sleeves. I sighed, remembering Salieri's beautiful green wool suit. Perhaps when I received the payment for *Figaro*—I shook my head. I had already spent that money threefold in my mind. I would just have to take the coat to a tailor to see if the fabric could be rewoven.

The crowds in the streets on this warm spring night slowed my progress toward the theater, and so it was just a few minutes before the performance was to start when I joined Righini and his bovine wife in the box. I looked around the large hall. Mozart and Martín sat together down on the main floor, deep in conversation. Rosenberg and Casti were directly across from me in the emperor's box, and they rose with the rest of the audience as my Caesar entered and took his seat. The conductor raised his hand and the performance began. The opera was a comedy about an eccentric, pompous philosopher who continually finds himself in amorous difficulties. The tenor Kelly had the lead as the philosopher. As the orchestra labored over Righini's overture, my attention returned to the emperor's box. Casti whispered in Rosenberg's ear. I knew that he and the count would spend the evening denigrating my work to the emperor.

Loud guffaws all around me startled me from my contemplation of my enemies. The overture had ended and Kelly had made his entrance, clad in a shabby old blue satin suit with tears in the coat that were visible even from my seat high above the stage. He waved an ornate walking stick in the air, put it behind him, leaned on it, and began to sing. The audience howled as he sang his lines in the same Venetian dialect that I speak, his words accented by a strong lisp. He picked up the stick and strolled across the stage with a strange gait, mugging for the audience all the way.

My cheeks grew hot. My heart began to pound. Some of the people on the floor pointed up at me, showing their neighbors where I sat. Righini and his wife tittered. I could feel every eye in the theater upon me. I forced myself to look across at the emperor's box. Casti was elbowing Rosenberg in the ribs, while the count laughed heartily. To my greatest dismay, the emperor himself was laughing as hard as everyone else at Kelly's joke. But then his eyes met mine. He stopped laughing and gave me a nod. That small sign of encouragement fortified me. I quickly stood, smiled broadly, bowed to the audience and then to Kelly, and sat back in my seat. To my relief, that satisfied the crowd, and they turned their attention back to Kelly.

When the performance ended, it was all I could do to get away from the theater. Everyone I met slapped me on the back and imitated my lisp as they praised me for being a good sport. I heard Mozart call me, but I ignored him and hurried out the door into the night.

My stomach churned as I stood in the shadows, watching people leave the theater and climb into carriages, heading toward suppers in the fine palaces. I would be the subject of much amusement this evening, I supposed. When the crowds had cleared, I decided to treat myself before I returned to the Palais Gabler. I walked down the Kohlmarkt and turned into the Graben. I passed my lodging house and stopped a few doors down, at my favorite delicatessen, Amicis. The owner was a Neapolitan who ran a small trattoria in the shop's back room, open only to special customers. There he served delicacies from all over Italy: the hard cheese of Parma, anchovies from the Adriatic, olives from the islands. A small light burned in the window of the closed shop, a signal that the back room was open. I knocked on the door, and in a minute, Gaetano peered out at me and opened the door.

"Signor Abbé, welcome." He smiled at me and ushered me into the dark shop. "You have just come from the theater?"

"Yes, one of my works was performed tonight," I said. He took my cloak and stick and gestured me toward the back room. "You are not too busy tonight, I hope?" I was not in the mood to face another crowd.

"No, signore. Just a few gentlemen. Go on through. I have a new shipment of oysters. I'll bring you some."

I walked into the small dining room. Only one of the six tables was occupied, by fellow Italians, tourists perhaps. I nodded at them and took a seat at the table farthest from them. Gaetano hurried toward me and placed a large plate of raw oysters in front of me. "Prosecco?" he asked.

"Yes," I said. I was due for some luxury, I told myself as I watched him pour the glass. "Would you like something else, Signor Abbé?" he asked. "I have some good prosciutto tonight."

I shook my head. "This will be fine, Gaetano," I said.

"*Buon appetito,* signore," he murmured, and left me. I took a sip of the sparkling wine, relaxing as the bubbles tickled my nose and throat. I sucked an oyster from its shell. The cold, slimy mass slid past my injured teeth and down my throat. If I closed my eyes and tried hard enough, I could conjure up the characteristic brininess of the bivalves. Gaetano had to import them all the way from Trieste, so by the time they reached Vienna, they were already stale. A longing for

Venice welled up in my breast. The seafood there was plucked right out of the lagoon, or came in on day boats from the Adriatic. I doubted I would ever taste a really fresh oyster again in my life.

I sucked a few more of the oysters and sipped my wine. The men at the table across the room conversed in low tones. The humiliation of the evening began to subside.

As Gaetano poured me another glass of wine, a loud banging sounded at the door of the shop. "Excuse me, signore," he said and hurried out of the dining room. Several loud voices greeted him in fractured Italian. A minute later, Michael Kelly and two friends entered the room.

"Da Ponte!" The tenor slapped me on the back. "Good to see you, my friend. No hard feelings about tonight, eh?" He waved for Gaetano. "Champagne and oysters for all of us. More oysters, Signor Abbé? My treat."

"No, thank you, Mr. Kelly," I said in the haughtiest voice I could muster. "I've had enough." I stood and signaled to Gaetano for the check.

Kelly grabbed at the small slip of paper. "Let me get this," he said.

I pulled the check from his hand. "No, Mr. Kelly," I said. My voice shook. "I am quite capable of paying my own bill." He shrugged and laughed, then turned back to his friends.

I dug in my pocket for a few coins and handed them to Gaetano. "But signore, your food, your wine, you are not finished—"

"I no longer like the company, Gaetano," I said. "I'll come back another time." He ushered me through the shop, his face apologetic. I took my cloak and stick, shook his hand,

and opened the door. I heard the tenor and his friends roaring with laughter in the back room. I closed the door behind me and tromped across the Graben, back to the palais.

Damn Kelly. I hoped he choked on an oyster shell.

Eighteen

By midmorning the next day I had already breakfasted in the Kohlmarkt; hailed a hackney cab back to the Palais Gabler; assisted Marianne in packing the vehicle with panniers filled with clothing, linens, and food for her imprisoned fiancé; and directed the driver toward the suburb immediately northwest of the city walls.

I tried to stifle a yawn as the horses clopped past the emperor's sprawling new hospital complex, said to hold five thousand patients, each with his own bed. I had tossed and turned all night, my emotions ranging from anger at Kelly to discouragement about my search for Vogel's mother to despair over my realization that I could not ignore the evidence that indicated that Caroline had murdered Florian Auerstein.

Marianne shared my mood. She had greeted me with none of her usual liveliness, and now she sat staring out the window of the cab, lost in her thoughts.

Once past the hospital, the cab turned down a short street

and pulled up at a simple, long building with a steeply pitched roof. A row of small leaded windows lined the face of each of its three floors. I climbed down and turned to help Marianne, but she had already descended and was pulling the panniers out. I paid the driver, asked him to return in an hour, and helped Marianne carry the load through the arched entrance into the foyer.

The guard seated at the desk greeted Marianne and called to a small boy, who loaded himself with most of our bundles and started up a stairway on our right. Marianne, the guard, and I followed him up one flight, then down a long corridor lined with doors. Many of these stood open, revealing large light-filled rooms. Small groups of men sat about on beds or at tables. The effect was that of a large dormitory, clean and bright.

The guard stopped at an open door at the end of the corridor and waited patiently while I dug coins out of my pocket to tip him and the boy. When I entered the room, Marianne already stood in the center, her arms around Vogel, who was trying to return her embrace while holding a sharp razor in one hand. A portly, bald man sat in a chair nearby, his face half covered with foamy soap. Two other men sat on one of the beds, in line for the barber's services. Across the room, another three prisoners sat at a small table, playing cards.

"Signor Abbé!" Vogel put down the razor and reached over Marianne's head to shake my hand. "Thank you for coming."

"You seem to be coping very well, Johann," I said.

He laughed. "Yes, it's not too bad. The guards let me earn a little money." He whispered to Marianne. She let go of him and sat on one of the empty beds. Vogel gave his customer's face a few flicks with the razor and wiped the soap off. The man wiggled off the chair, handed the barber a few coins, bowed to Marianne and to me, and left. Vogel looked at the two men waiting on the bed. "Could you come back in an hour, gentlemen?" They nodded and shuffled out of the room.

"Sit, sit, signore," Vogel said, gesturing me toward the bed where Marianne sat. "I'm sorry, the chairs are all taken." I sat down on the hard little bed. Vogel pulled over the customer's chair close to Marianne, turned it around, and sat down, leaning on the back. Marianne reached for his hand. "Marianne told me you are working at the palais," he said.

I nodded.

"I am glad you are there to keep an eye on her for me. I don't like the idea of her staying in a house where there's been a murder."

"I told you, I can take care of myself," she replied. Her words were not angry. Her mood had lifted as soon as she had embraced her fiancé.

Vogel squeezed her hand. "Have you learned anything about my parents?" he asked eagerly.

I related everything: what I had learned about the items in the box from the pawnbroker; my finding of the medallion; the leads I had received from Alois Bayer and the bureaucrat Maulbertsch; and my disappointment at not being able to learn anything about the owner of the medallion.

"But there is still hope," Vogel said. "This Maulbertsch fellow might find the convent records."

"Perhaps," I said. "Did your adoptive mother ever mention

anything about that convent? About anyone with the initials 'K.S.'?"

He shook his head. "No, I can't remember anything like that. To tell the truth, she was not very religious. Of course, she made me go to church, but we never talked much about it at home."

I sighed. "I don't want you to get your hopes up," I said. "I told you at the beginning that this might be an impossible task."

"I know, signore. But hope is all I have right now."

"I will keep trying, then."

A guard poked his head in the door. "Visiting hours are over," he said.

I rose from the bed. "I'll wait for you outside," I told Marianne. Vogel pumped my hand.

"Thank you, Signor Abbé," he said. "Once you get me out of here, I promise you free shaves for life."

"I will do my best," I said. I stepped into the corridor. When I turned around, I saw Vogel and Marianne deep in an embrace. A pang of longing stabbed me. As I watched, Marianne pulled herself away and drew a small purse from her pocket. "Here are my wages," she said. "Have the guard bring you dinner from outside."

Vogel's face reddened. Tears filled his eyes. "No, love, I cannot take your money. I am fine, don't worry about me." She pushed the purse at him. He took it, threw it on the bed, and enveloped her in his arms. They clung to each other, whispering.

I looked away. The guard gestured to me. "We must go, Miss Haiml," I said. She nodded, pulled out her handkerchief, and gently dabbed Vogel's eyes. He took it from her, then let her go. As she passed before me into the corridor, I saw him sit down on the bed, clutching the handkerchief, his normally cheerful countenance a picture of forlornness.

Marianne was quiet on the ride back to the city, staring out the window of the carriage, chewing on her lip. As the cab rumbled toward the Palais Gabler, I reached over and squeezed her hand. "He'll be all right," I said.

She turned to me, tears in her eyes. "Do you really think so, Signor Abbé?" She balled her fists. "He has so much pride. That's what I fear. You must have seen how he didn't want to take my money. But I can't stand the idea of him eating the slop they serve in that place. I'm afraid that if he has to spend a whole year in there, it will wear him down."

"He'll be fine, whatever happens," I replied. "Why, he's already started a business in prison! He knows how to land on his feet." My words brought a small smile to her face. "And I give you my pledge that I will do everything in my power to get him out of there. Johann is right. We will find the convent's records. If I have to spend days going through them looking for this 'K.S.,' I will. In return, I expect to be invited to dance at your wedding!"

Her smile widened. "Oh, Signor Abbé, please forgive me. If I haven't seemed welcoming to you, or grateful for helping us, it is because I've been wrapped up in my own problems."

"There's no need for apologies." I looked at her closely. "But if I may, Miss Haiml—Marianne?"

She nodded.

"Is there something else bothering you, besides Johann's imprisonment?"

She lowered her eyes and shook her head.

"My dear, is it the murder? You must be frightened. I know I don't sleep well myself in that house. And Johann is afraid for your safety."

She turned her attention to the scene outside the window. The cab had passed by the Scottish church just inside the city wall. We would reach the palais in a few moments. "He has no need to worry about me," she murmured.

Icy fingers gripped my heart. My suspicions were confirmed. The two women trusted one another—the mistress knew that her servant would not reveal her as the murderer of Florian Auerstein, and the lady's maid knew that her mistress would not harm her because of her knowledge. I hated Caroline for involving this innocent girl in her crime. I grabbed Marianne's arm and turned her toward me. "Do you know something about the murder?" I asked.

She shook her head. "I know nothing."

"I know you are torn, Marianne, but your loyalty is misplaced. You must look after your own interests, yours and Johann's. You cannot go on protecting a killer."

The cab turned into the courtyard of the palais and pulled up at the front door. Marianne pulled away from me and descended onto the stones. As she ran toward the door, it opened. "Oh, Marianne, good morning!" Tomaso Piatti said. He looked over to where I stood paying the driver. "An outing on the Prater?" he asked.

"Don't be ridiculous, sir," Marianne snapped. "I have no

time for rides around the park. Signor Da Ponte kindly took me out to visit Johann."

Piatti frowned. "Oh, forgive me, I forgot all about him. How is he doing?" He nodded at me as I joined them at the door.

"As well as can be expected, sir. Please excuse me. The baroness must need me." She turned to enter the house.

"Wait, Marianne," I said, grasping her by the elbow. I leaned in and murmured, "Think about what I said. You must go to the police."

She shook loose from my grasp. "I will think about it, signore. Thank you again for coming with me." She turned and fled into the house.

"What was that all about?" Piatti asked.

"Just some problems with Vogel." I shrugged.

"I thought I heard you mention the police."

My mind moved quickly. "Vogel is running a little barbershop in the prison. He has some clients who refuse to pay him."

The music teacher laughed. "Well, what can he expect? He is in debtor's prison, for God's sake!"

I shook my head and laughed too. "I know, I know." I moved toward the door.

"Do you have time for dinner, Lorenzo? I've read the portions of the libretto you gave me. I'd love to discuss them with you."

I made a show of pulling out my watch. "Perhaps tomorrow, Tomaso. I have an important appointment at the theater this afternoon." We said our good-byes. I hurried into the house and up the stairs to my room.

A message addressed to me sat on the desk. I quickly broke the seal and unfolded the paper. It was from Maulbertsch.

I have found something of interest. Come Thursday morning.

I washed the dust from my face and pulled on my best coat. On the way to the theater, I stopped and had a quick dinner. I worked a bit in my office until three, then went up to see Rosenberg. His secretary was apologetic: the count had gone out on a personal errand; he was due back at any moment; no, the theater poet should not return later; if he would just take a seat—

I sat for fifty minutes before the corridor door opened and the count entered, followed by a boy carrying a large crate. "Oh, Da Ponte, come in," he said to me. I followed him into his office. Three times the size of my own windowless precinct in the theater basement, the room was dominated by a large mahogany desk set next to a row of tall windows overlooking the Michaelerplatz. On the left wall, a large painting of an elaborate hunt scene hung over an ornate marble mantelpiece. The blazing fire warmed the entire room, a feat that I could not attribute to the wheezy stove that purported to heat my own workspace.

"Put that down there," Rosenberg told the boy, pointing to a small table to my right. "Can you get it out of the box? Quickly, we don't have much time!"

The boy opened the crate and slowly lifted out its contents. "Careful, careful!" Rosenberg bustled over to the table to supervise. "Da Ponte, come have a look. I've been after Deym to sell me one of these for years."

Rosenberg's prize was a large gold clock. He waved the boy away. "You may go. Take the crate, if you would." The boy waited a moment, then realizing that the highest nobility did not deign to tip, seized the crate and left.

Rosenberg consulted his pocket watch and began to wind the clock. "We just have a minute," he said.

The clock stood about two feet high, its base just as wide. Along the base were several openings covered in fine grill-work. The clock face was made of mother-of-pearl, and sat atop the base, surrounded by small golden nymphs who pointed delicately toward the timepiece. I opened my mouth to ask what made the clock so special.

Rosenberg held up his hand to hush me. The clock hand hit the hour, and instead of sounding a chime or a gong, began to play a breezy tune.

"Haydn," Rosenberg said.

We stood while the machine went through its little song. It sounded as if an orchestra of tiny cherubs was playing flutes inside of the clock.

"There's a small flute organ built inside the barrel," Rosenberg explained. "That's why they are so rare and expensive. Deym collects them for his gallery. It took me a long time to convince him to sell one to me."

"It's charming, Excellency," I said.

"Yes, I'll enjoy having it. Oh, by the way, let me congratulate you on the premiere last night."

"Thank you, Excellency." I rarely heard praise from the count.

He looked at me slyly. "Yes, it was quite the hit. Kelly was brilliant. His imitation of you was perfect."

I clenched my teeth. Silly of me to think that this man would offer me genuine praise.

"Now, about your opera with Mozart—I've had some disturbing news about it."

"Really, Excellency? What kind of news?" My heart began to beat faster.

"I've been told your libretto contains a ballet. Is this true?"

"Yes, Excellency. It does. At the end of the third act, during the wedding scene, Mozart and I decided to insert a pantomime. All of the characters dance while the maid hands the note to her lascivious master. Mozart has written a wonderful fandango to accompany the scene."

He frowned. "But Da Ponte, how could you write such a scene?"

"I don't understand—"

"You of all people, the theater poet—you should have known better!"

My pulse raced. "I'm sorry, Excellency. I don't understand. What is it that I should have known?"

"The emperor does not wish to have ballets performed in his operas. He hates that French style. I believe I made that clear to you last year, when His Majesty informed me of his desires."

I shook my head. "I do not remember—"

"That is why there are no dancers in the opera company!"

My cheeks were hot. "But, Excellency, our ballet is not in the French style. It is not dancing for dancing's sake, there is a dramatic purpose to it. It is a wedding celebration. People always dance at weddings. And the scene is very short, just a few minutes long."

He sighed. "I see. Yes. I see your point."

I let out a deep breath.

"Did you bring the libretto? Let me see the scene."

I flipped through the pages of my libretto, pulled out the relevant sheet, and handed it to him. "Here, Excellency, this is the scene. You can see how short it is, just a few spoken lines. Mozart's music is brief, also. It is a charming scene. I believe you'll agree when you see the dress rehearsal on Saturday."

He studied the page, then walked over to the fireplace. "Yes, I see," he said. He threw the paper onto the blazing fire.

"Excellency, what are you doing?" I cried.

My heart was pounding, and I knew my face was turning purple. He gave me a small, satisfied smile. "That will be all, Signor Poet," he said, waving me toward the door. "Tell Mozart to cut the music from his score."

Nineteen

My stomach was still churning an hour later as I sat in the library at the Palais Gabler, idly flipping through the baron's copy of Dante's *Inferno*. That philistine Rosenberg! Although I had initially been skeptical when Mozart had proposed the pantomime, I had come to see that he was right, the scene did enhance the dramatic pace of the opera. I had lied to the count when I said I did not remember that the emperor did not want ballets in his operas. He himself had told me how tiresome he found the long dances that broke up the action in the French operas, many of which had nothing to do with the plot of the opera. But I also knew that my Caesar was open to new ideas, and I suspected that he would appreciate what Mozart and I had done once he had seen it.

I looked over to the windows. Dusk was falling. Casti's fingers were all over this, I was certain. We had dress rehearsal in less than seventy-two hours. It would be difficult to rewrite the scene, set it to music, and coach the singers and orchestra in the new material before then. Rosenberg would run to the emperor, complaining that due to my negligence, the opera could not possibly be ready for the scheduled opening.

I crossed over to the fireplace and stoked the fire. Who had told Rosenberg that Mozart and I had put a ballet in the scene? Had it been Thorwart, the jittery assistant theater manager? He had never seemed close to Rosenberg. I thought back to the last rehearsal, to the singers' complaints about the new scene. I remembered the Mandinis and Bussanis laughing at me behind my back, and Francesco Bussani's dark scowls. The bass and his wife were part of Casti's clique.

I felt a headache coming on. Why did they all hate me so? Why could I not work in peace, write my operas, enjoy some success? I was tired of all the intrigues. I wanted to go home to Venice. The little Harlequin figurine gazed at me sympathetically. I shook my head. Enough self-pity, I told myself. I could hold my own with the backstabbers if I had to. But I did not relish telling Mozart about Rosenberg's decree.

I turned my attention to the book. I had read the first two cantos when the door opened. "Oh, Da Ponte, I didn't know anyone was here," Baron Gabler said. He wore a satin dressing gown, his long hair loose. One hand held a half-full bottle of brandy, the other a glass.

I jumped to my feet and bowed. "I was just enjoying your collection, Excellency," I said. I closed the Dante and returned it to its place on the shelf. "I'll leave you alone."

He waved the bottle at me. "No, stay. Have a drink with me." He motioned toward the cabinet on the far side of the room. "There are glasses in there."

I nodded my thanks and got a glass. His hands shook as he poured the brandy. He sprawled on the sofa.

"It's French, not that Hungarian swill," he said. "One of the advantages of knowing Prince Kaunitz."

I took a sip. The amber liquid trickled down my throat, its warmth bringing its usual false sense of well-being.

"How is your investigation?" he asked. His voice was slurred. "Have you learned anything?"

"Not much, I'm afraid, sir. I've observed every member of the household, and have a lot of questions, but it's difficult to get them to confide in me."

He laughed. "I expected as much! I knew this was a bad idea. If there is a spy in this house—and mind you, I don't really believe it—it would take a professional to root him out. The emperor just wants to save money, that's all. He thinks that using men such as you will get the job done at a lower cost than creating a special police force." He shook his head.

"But the murder—"

"I told you before, that must have been an accident. The boy was dancing around, he tripped and fell." He swirled the brandy in his glass. "This whole mess is a plot to discredit me," he muttered.

We sat silently for a moment—I sipped the brandy, he stared into his glass. He reached over and grabbed the bottle, sloshed more liquid into the glass, and slammed the bottle down on the table. "Damn, you don't know how lucky you are, Da Ponte!"

I raised my eyebrows.

"You don't have to bow and scrape to these arrogant old families every day in order to keep everything you've earned," he said.

I opened my mouth to correct his misconceptions about the job of theater poet, then shut it.

"Esterházy! That old ass! He's so high-and-mighty. I can advise the emperor, I am talented enough to be named the next ambassador to the Court of St. Petersburg, but I am not good enough to step inside his damned palace! My father made the arms that let us win the war, that protected that asshole's lands, but I am not considered noble enough to warrant a dinner invitation!"

I nodded sympathetically.

The baron stared into his brandy snifter. "It's all her fault," he muttered. I sat up straight.

"Have you ever been married, Da Ponte?"

"No, Excellency. I have not had the good fortune," I said. "I am a priest—"

He laughed. "That's a nice excuse to keep them from expecting marriage," he said. He raised his eyebrows. "There have been plenty of women willing to distract you from the church, I'll bet."

I said nothing.

"You are smart. Just love them and leave them." He shook his head. "I should never have married Caroline. She's common. She does nothing to help my career. I'd be welcomed everywhere if it weren't for her."

Bile rose in my throat as I recalled Caroline's tale of having to withstand the Auerstein boy's advances. "A beautiful woman like the baroness could only be an asset to you, sir," I said tightly.

"So she's seduced you too," he said, his voice mocking.

My pulse began to race. Could he read my feelings on my face?

"When I think of her when we first met—she was like a bitch in heat. We spent hours in bed."

My cheeks grew hot. I wished I could get up and walk out the door.

"But then I made the mistake of marrying her. Now it is all about love, love, love. True, she goes along with anything I want, but damn, can't a man want a little variety in his life? I want the excitement of the chase. You disapprove?"

"I'm in no position to judge you, Excellency," I said coldly.

"So I find my excitement elsewhere. Now she is locking her door against me!"

I stood. "Please, sir, I don't want to hear this."

"Why not? We are just two men talking." He peered at me. "What is it? You know something. Has she confided in you? Has she taken a lover? Or have you had her yourself?"

My hands shook as I placed my glass on the table. "You do a great disservice to your wife, sir," I said. "You are drunk, so I will ignore that last remark." I turned to go.

He grabbed my arm. "Sit down! I haven't dismissed you!"

I pulled my arm away, but sat.

"Tell me what you know. Does she have a lover? Who is it?"

I hoped he could not hear my heart pounding in my chest. "I know nothing, sir. The baroness and I merely discuss poetry when we are together. She does not consider me a confidant."

"You think I have no right to be suspicious of her?"

I said nothing.

"Listen, Da Ponte. You tell my wife to be careful. If she does anything to jeopardize my career, I'll kill her."

I raised my hands in a defensive gesture. "Sir, I know nothing—"

A loud knock sounded at the door. Bohm entered.

"There you are, sir," he said gruffly. "It is time to dress for the theater." I watched as the valet took the glass from the baron's hand, pulled him from the sofa, and put his shoulder under the deadweight of the drunken man.

The baron shook him away. "I'm fine!"

Bohm nodded. A brief look of satisfaction crossed his face. "Yes, sir. Come, it is time to dress." He led the baron out the door.

I exhaled and looked down at my trembling hands. Did the baron sense that I was attracted to his wife? I chided myself for letting him draw me into the argument. Why hadn't I just kept my mouth shut, let him rant?

And Caroline herself—she had guessed my feelings for her, I was sure. I had believed she returned them. Instead she had humiliated me by using me as her errand boy, asking me to take the note to her lover. After finding the notebook, I had begun to suspect that she had murdered Florian Auerstein. Why had I leaped so vigorously to her defense?

My hands had stopped shaking. I sighed, and buried my face in them. The answer to my question was clear. I could not help myself. Despite what she had done to me, I still loved her.

Twenty

The skies were threatening rain when I arrived at Maulbertsch's office early Thursday morning. The bureaucrat was
in the large anteroom, consulting with a colleague.

"Good, you came promptly," he said as he ushered me into
his office. "Did you have a chance to speak to the Hassler
woman?"

I nodded. "Yes. An admirable lady. She is doing good
work at the school."

"Could she be of any help to us?"

"No. She is too young. She didn't come to the convent
until ten years after my friend was born. And she knew of
no stories or gossip about a nun or novice who had given birth
there."

"I was afraid that might be the case," Maulbertsch admitted. He gestured me toward a chair, went to his desk,
picked up a book, and pulled his chair toward mine. "Here
is what I found." The book was about a foot and a half tall,

eight inches wide, and an inch thick. It looked old, its dark leather cover worn. Some of the gilt on a large cross embossed on the front cover had chipped away.

Maulbertsch opened it and slowly flipped through the first few pages. The paper had yellowed, and the pages had been written on with different inks and in different hands over the years.

"I've been so busy I haven't had time to look at this yet. This is the roster book for the convent. As you can see, the records go back many years, to the last century, when the order was established. Each page lists the names of the nuns who resided in the convent on the first of the year." He handed me the book. I started at the beginning, turning the pages gently. Each leaf was lined with names, some written in a flowing, large hand, others in more-cramped writing. The pages were dated from the middle of the last century to the beginning of our own, then up to the year of my own birth. The ink, faded on the early sheets, grew darker as I turned the leaves. Pity flooded through me as I thought of these women, all of whom had dedicated their lives to serving God in this house, the early ones believing that the sacrifices they had made—love, marriage, children—would strengthen the order for many centuries to come. None had suspected that their home would be destroyed in the name of modernity.

Maulbertsch took the book from me. "The pages of interest are back here. Now, what year was your friend born?"

"He is thirty, he believes—so 1756."

"We'll start there." He turned the large pages until he reached that year. "What were the initials on the medallion?"

"K.S." My pulse quickened. Was I going to find Vogel's

mother at last? I peered over the top of the book at the page, but could not make out the scribbled writing while reading upside down.

"Let me see. Seventeen fifty-six. Here it is. Yes, the Abbess Elisabeth. She has written her own name at the top of the page. Hilda Gassinger, Annaliese Tiel. Wait, here is a K, Klara. No, her last name was Mader. Hmmm." He looked up. "No one with the initials K.S., I'm afraid."

I tried to hide my disappointment. I looked at the page. The list he had read through took up only three-quarters of the sheet. "Is that all of them? There aren't very many. I thought it was a rather large convent."

He ran his finger down the list. "Twenty. Perhaps we should look at the next year." He turned the page. "Wait, you are right. There are more names on the back of the page." I fought the urge to grab the book out of his hands and look for myself. He studied the names. "Ah, yes, I see," he murmured. "The abbess decided to split the convent's inhabitants into two groups," he explained. "The front page is a list of all the nuns. The names here on the back are of the novices. There was a large class that year. There are ten names."

"Is there a K.S.?" I tried not to shout.

"Barbara Eder, Renate Born, wait—here it is, Seipel—no, her first name is Charlotte. Katrin. Katrin Spiegel. This might be the one we are looking for." He turned the book to show me. "Let me look further through the book to see what happened to her." He pulled the book back and flipped through the next few pages.

I sat quietly, trying to contain my excitement and temper. It was well known that when dealing with bureaucrats, one must do things their way, otherwise one's query would take twice as long. A novice! That made sense. A young girl—unsure of her vocation, vulnerable to the seductions of one of the rich patrons of the convent—had sinned, and had been forced to give the babe up for adoption and then to leave the convent. That would explain why Josepha Hassler had not heard gossip about a nun giving birth to a child. The girl had been a mere novice, quickly forgotten by the permanent members of the sisterhood.

Maulbertsch closed the book with a loud thump. "Yes, I believe we've found her. Katrin Spiegel, from the south of the Simmering district. She became a novice at the beginning of 1756. She must have become pregnant soon after. When did you say your friend was born?"

"November, he believes."

"She was probably required to leave the convent after she gave birth," Maulbertsch continued. "Her name is not in the roster for the following year, nor for any of the years afterward."

"Yes, the timing makes sense," I said. "How can I find her?"

"She probably went back to her people in the village. I'd wager she must have married, so she would have a different name now. Let me look some more. We have copies of all the marriage records from the churches in the area. I'll have a clerk look through them."

I thanked him profusely and headed toward the door. I turned back when I heard him chuckle.

"That's why I love this job," he said. "One never knows

what one can dig up from these old records. We were lucky today, Da Ponte."

I raised an eyebrow.

"It was just chance that I had that roster book. When the convents and monasteries were dissolved, the junior minister in charge of the reform kept most of the records. He's a bigwig now, you wouldn't have had much chance getting to see that book if he had had it."

"What's his name?" I asked.

"Gabler. The one who is to be the emperor's new ambassador to the Court of St. Petersburg. Christof Gabler."

My mind raced as I left the main court of the Hofburg and walked over to my office in the theater. The baron had all of the convent records? I pulled my cloak closer around my chest and tried to dispel the eerie sensation that gripped me. Of course. Pergen had told me that as a junior minister, Gabler had been involved in many of the emperor's pet reforms. Surely it was just a coincidence that I should find the medallion from the Sisters of the Blessed Virgin convent while living in his house.

Once at my desk, I shook off thoughts about Vogel's mystery and settled in to work. I wanted to sketch some ideas to replace the pantomime scene before I told Mozart about Rosenberg's injunction against the dances. I had scribbled down ideas for only ten minutes before the door opened and Troger entered.

"Well, Da Ponte? Have you found our spy?" He smiled scornfully and sprawled in the chair I keep for guests.

"I'm working, Troger," I said. "Come back in two hours, I'll give you a full report."

He slammed his fist on my desk. My inkwell bounced. "You'll tell me now!"

I threw down my pen. "Very well, if it means you'll leave me alone. You know Pergen promised that I would be able to work unheeded."

"What have you learned? Who is the killer?"

I paused.

"You know nothing!" He laughed and shook his head.

"I need more time. There are several suspects. I just haven't had the opportunity to gather enough evidence to determine who the spy really is." I thought of Ecker's defensiveness, Rosa Hahn searching the baron's desk, Bohm's refusal to answer my questions, and the argument I had overheard between Caroline and Rausch. I was not sure if I wanted to tell him about the notebook I had found.

"You'd better hurry up. Prince Auerstein is getting impatient. He wants to see someone hang for his son's murder." His smile chilled me. He picked one of my books off my desk and riffled through it.

"I did find something—"

He looked up sharply. "What?"

"Are you and Pergen absolutely certain that this spy killed the boy?"

"Isn't it obvious? Information has been leaked from the Gabler household to the King of Prussia. An innocent boy is murdered in the same house. There must be a connection."

"But isn't it possible that there are two crimes here,

committed by two people? Someone is spying on the
baron for Frederick, and someone else killed the Auerstein
boy?"

He quirked an eyebrow. "What are you saying, Da Ponte?
What have you found?"

I told him about Florian's notebook: how he had dropped
it the day I met him; how I had set it aside, and had just found
it. "It contained copious notes on the comings and goings of
members of the household. Some of the entries seemed to
be a record of payments of some sort." I did not tell him whose
initials were associated with the payments.

"Blackmail? Where is this notebook? Let me see it."

I willed my eyes not to glance over at the cupboard, where
the notebook sat safely in my cloak pocket. "I don't have it
here. It's back in my room at the palais."

"You idiot! The blackmailer could easily find it."

"It's well hidden, I assure you," I said.

Troger threw my book onto the desk. "It probably means
nothing," he said. "If the boy was blackmailing someone in
the house, it must have been the spy."

I shook my head. "I don't think so. I think he discovered
something else, some secret that someone is trying to hide,
and that person killed him to end the blackmail." My stomach churned as I thought about Caroline.

"Your theory doesn't explain the documents missing from
the baron's office," Troger said. "I still believe Auerstein discovered the spy, and the spy killed him to protect his identity."

"That's the simple answer, perhaps," I said. "But I think
you and Pergen are mistaken."

His face twisted in anger. "Listen to you, suddenly you

are an expert on police matters! You worm! You are lucky the count even gave you the chance to investigate this. I would have taken you out and had you tortured that night. After a few hours you would have confessed that you spied for Frederick and murdered the boy."

My pulse began to race. "You know I am innocent!" I cried.

"What does that matter? We would have solved the case, then and there. But no, we had to play this stupid charade. And now you dare to think you are smarter than we are?"

I fought not to wilt under his glare. "You should treat me with a little more respect, Troger," I said quietly. "I know that the emperor himself recommended me for this investigation."

He rose and towered over me. "You think the emperor will protect you, Signor Poet?" He sneered. "He needs Prince Auerstein's support for his land reforms. The prince is clamoring for a solution to the case. You have accomplished nothing." He lowered his voice. "Picture this. In a few days, Count Pergen and I deliver the Prussian spy to His Majesty. He is stunned to learn that it is his very own theater poet. He is heartbroken that he has so grossly misjudged the man, yet he must act for the good of the empire. He orders a quick trial and execution."

I shivered.

He laughed as he walked to the door. "You are running out of time, Da Ponte! Bring us some useful information, before Pergen decides to end this stupid experiment."

"Who was that?" Mozart asked as he came through the door.

I took a deep breath to compose myself. "No one important," I said. "Come in, Wolfgang, have a seat."

"Have you talked to Rosenberg? What did he want?"

"You are not going to like this," I said. "He told me to
cut out the pantomime."

"What? Why? Because of the cost of the dancers? There
are dancers in the ballet company—we can easily use those."

I held up my hand to stop him.

"He says the emperor does not allow ballet in his operas."

"What? I've never heard of that. And this isn't a ballet
like in Paris, anyway. It's a scene of a wedding celebration,
for God's sake. Everyone dances at weddings!"

"I know, I know," I said. "I told him that."

"It's a joke, right? He wants us to change the whole scene
two days before the dress rehearsal?" Mozart paced up and
down the small room, red-faced with anger. "Did you tell
him the ballet was necessary to the dramatic action?"

"I explained it all to him, but he did not want to listen,"
I said. "He is determined to ruin the opera any way he can."

Mozart's eyes narrowed. "Who told him about the pantomime, anyway?"

I sighed. "Probably one of the singers. Mandini, or Bussani. You know Bussani is part of Casti's clique."

"Damn these Italians!" Mozart shouted. "Oh, not you,
of course, Lorenzo. Salieri, Casti, the whole cabal, they've
worked against me since I arrived in Vienna. They're trying
to poison Rosenberg's attitude toward me. They think I'm
some sort of peasant—"

I leaned back and let him talk. I did not want to tell him
that the cabal was really arrayed against me, that Rosen-

berg's attack on *Figaro* was really just another attempt to get Casti my job.

"What are we going to do?" Mozart asked wearily.

"I've sketched some ideas to replace the pantomime," I said, handing him the sheets I had written before Troger had arrived.

He waved my hand away. "I don't want to replace it! It's perfect the way we wrote it."

I nodded my agreement. We sat for a moment, thinking.

"Can you go to the emperor with this, Lorenzo?"

"I don't know, Wolfgang—"

"You've told me about how he supported you against Salieri that time. Go to him and tell him what Rosenberg did."

I hesitated. Given my discussion with Troger, I didn't feel this was the best time to run to the emperor with a complaint.

"What do you think? Will you do it?" Mozart looked at me expectantly. "I suppose I could try myself, if I could get in to see him."

Just as my heart began to sink, an idea came to me. "Let me handle this, Wolfgang."

"What are you going to do?"

"I'm not sure yet. But don't worry. I'll take care of Rosenberg. Just give me until Saturday."

After Mozart left, I sat for another half hour, working out my idea to foil Rosenberg and Casti. My stomach growled. I wanted to get a quick dinner in the Kohlmarkt and return to work, but Troger's warnings echoed in my ears. I needed to face another unpalatable meal at the palais, trying to get information from the members of the staff. I packed up my satchel and put on my cloak, checking to see that the notebook was tucked safely in the pocket. I picked up my stick and walked upstairs and into the Michaelerplatz. The sky had darkened considerably while I had been working. I turned to hurry back to the palais before the rain began.

A woman screamed. "Stop!" a male voice shouted. I turned to the left to see what the commotion was about. A carriage drawn by two large black horses hurtled toward me. I stood frozen. The woman screamed again. I tried to jump out of the carriage's path, but my legs would not move. My heart pounded so hard I thought my chest would burst before the beasts ran me down. I stared, my mouth agape, as they neared. Just when I felt their hot breath upon me, I fell. Someone grabbed my arms. Pain shot through my body as I was dragged out of the path of the oncoming horses. I felt the wind as the carriage raced by me, its horses whinnying, its driver cracking his whip. I didn't know if my eyes were open or closed. All I could see was a field of gray light twinkling with stars.

"Sir, are you all right?" I felt myself being lifted into someone's arms. Was I dead? I felt a gentle slap on my cheek. My eyes cleared, and I looked into the concerned eyes of a young lackey.

"These damned bureaucrats!" a voice nearby said. "Always in a hurry. This man could have been killed!" Several other voices agreed.

"Are you all right, sir?" the lackey asked.

"Yes, yes. If you would be so kind as to help me get up—"

He helped me to my feet and gave me my stick. My legs

heaved from under me. The lackey held me up. My cheeks began to burn as I saw that my mishap had drawn a large crowd. "You are lucky to be alive, sir," a man called. "The police should do something about these speeders. One day someone won't be so lucky."

I held on to the young man for a few minutes, until my heart had stopped pounding and my legs had steadied. The crowd dispersed.

"Will you be able to get home on your own, sir?" the lackey asked. "Shall I call you a cab?"

I shook my head. "No, it is not far. Thank you for your help. You saved my life." I handed him several coins. When he saw the amount I had given, he grinned and tipped his cap. I leaned on my stick, trying to regain my composure, and watched as he walked away.

"Sir?" I felt a tug at my sleeve.

I looked down into the blowsy face of a market vendor. "It wasn't an accident, sir," she said. She shifted her basket of onions in her arms. "I've been here all morning. He's been driving around the block for an hour. A couple of times he would stop, over there." She pointed toward the Herrengasse. "Then he would go around again. Like he was looking for someone." She paused.

I nodded for her to continue.

"He was sitting over there when you came out of the the- ater, sir. When he saw you, he whipped the horses and came straight at you."

Twenty-one

I stumbled down the Herrengasse toward the palais, clinging to the façades of the small palaces that lined the street, flinching every time I heard the beat of hooves behind me. A light rain began to fall. By the time I had dragged myself up the stairs to my room, I was exhausted. My appetite had disappeared. I took off my cloak and slowly hung it in the cupboard, wincing as I straightened my arm to reach the hook. The shoulder I had injured during my encounter with Pergen's policemen throbbed.

I went over to the desk. Someone had come in and left a pile of papers sitting in the center of the table. They were the scenes from the libretto that I had lent Piatti the other day. To my irritation, I saw that the music master had provided me with comments. Lines of neat, small handwriting covered each page. I sighed. Once a teacher, always a teacher.

I took off my waistcoat and lay on the bed. Every bone in my body ached. Troger's warning rang in my ears. My relationship with the emperor was a good one. He had supported me against my enemies many times. But I had to wonder if there had been some truth to Troger's threats. When matters of state were in the balance, could I really expect my Caesar to continue to protect me?

Perhaps because of my dispirited mood, my thoughts turned to my last days in my beloved Venice. I had lived in the house of a noted political reformer, Giorgio Pisani, and had served as tutor to his young sons. I had fallen in love with a young woman whose husband had left her while she was pregnant. We were happy together. Pisani was running for the office of procurator of St. Mark's. I wrote a poem in support of his candidacy. In the poem, I echoed his calls for political reform and made the mistake of naming three powerful current senators who opposed Pisani's bid for office. My work was a resounding success, read all over the city, by intellectuals and common people alike. Soon after, friends heard that I was to be accused of the crime of *male vita*—living an immoral life. Before the authorities could arrest me, I fled to Gorizia, the closest city in the empire to Venice. I was tried and convicted in absentia, and banished from Venice for fifteen years. If I were to return before then, I would be thrown into a windowless cell to serve out my exile.

My breathing slowed. I floated for a while between unconsciousness and consciousness. For a brief moment, a thought niggled at the back of my brain. Something I had seen—what was it? I was too tired to try to remember. I drifted to sleep.

I dreamed I was making that flight again, escaping from Venice, through the fields of the farms that hugged the bottoms of the mountains. My feet stung with blisters, my clothing hung tattered and wet on my body. My few prized possessions lay bundled in a scrawny sack on my back. Afraid I was being followed by the Venetian authorities, I avoided towns, stealing food from the fields and sleeping in empty hovels. As I threaded my way toward freedom in Gorizia, I was seen, and farmers set their dogs on me. I ran, my legs ready to collapse, until the beasts gave up the chase, and all I could hear was men cursing at me in the distance.

I stirred as the shouting grew louder. Heavy footsteps pounded nearby, men running. I opened my eyes. Where was I? "Help! Come quickly!" A man's voice, one that in my confusion I could not identify. The room was dim. Rain beat against the small dormer window. The next word I heard made my blood run cold.

"Murder!"

I bolted off the bed and raced to the door. Once in the hallway, my mental fog cleared. Bohm and Ecker raced down the stairs. I followed them down to the foyer and into the courtyard. Evening had fallen. The court was lit only by the few torches near the doorways. A cold, driving rain hit me as I ran toward the small group huddled in the center of the yard. My heart leaped to my throat. There, in the same place where the boy had died, Bohm, Ecker, and Piatti leaned over a mound of dark clothes.

"Turn her over!" Piatti cried. "The poor soul!" A small woman, wrapped in a coarse, dark cloak, her head covered by its hood, lay face downward on the stones. She did not move. A dark stain had spread across the back of the cloak. Bohm and Ecker gently turned her over.

"No!" Piatti shrieked. "No!"

"Good God!" Ecker exclaimed. Bohm crossed himself. Piatti began to moan.

I stood as still as a statue. My heart raced. The hood of the cloak fell off the woman's head. I heard a loud groan. The voice was my own. I tasted salt as the rain streamed down my face. I forced myself to look down. Green eyes stared at me without expression. Auburn tendrils lay matted around her head. Her cheeks were pale—paler than they had been the first time I had ever set eyes on her. I moaned. Piatti shrieked again. I fell to my knees.

PART IV

Finale

Twenty-two

"We'll all be murdered in our beds!"

I stood by the library window as Piatti paced before the fireplace. It had been an hour since we had discovered Caroline's lifeless body in the courtyard. The numbness that had overwhelmed me when I saw her lying there had begun to wear off, and I was attempting to deaden the almost physical pain that had taken its place with large quantities of the baron's brandy.

"I don't think the killer is committing these crimes at random," I said. "He is targeting his victims for a specific reason."

Piatti stopped his pacing and took a large swallow of brandy. "But what possible reason could he have, Lorenzo? First the boy, now the baroness. What could they have in common?"

"I don't know." I turned and looked out the window. The rain had subsided, and darkness had fallen. The courtyard was brightly lit by torches, giving me a view not unlike that of the stage of the theater. The body had been covered with a blanket. I watched as the baron and Troger stood over it, huddled in conversation. A constable was directing two young boys to light more torches.

I stared at the small covered bundle. Caroline! My throat thickened. I would never again see her soft smile, smell the lavender perfume in her hair, hear the music of her laugh, or feel the exquisite shock when her fingers brushed mine. I would never have the opportunity to taste her sweet lips.

A carriage pulled into the courtyard. I winced when I saw Pergen climb down from it and approach the baron. The two men spoke for a few moments, then Pergen knelt, lifted the blanket from the body, and crossed himself. He stood and led the baron into the house.

Piatti sighed loudly and threw himself onto the sofa. I studied him. He looked exhausted—his face gaunt and gray, his hands shaking. The slight tic in his left eye throbbed rhythmically.

"You should rest, my friend," I said. "The police will have questions for us tomorrow, I expect. Pull the table in front of your door if you can, if it will make you feel safer." I intended to do the same when I retired for the night.

"You are right," he said. "I need to save my strength. There will be a lot to do. I will have to write music for the funeral." He stared into the fire. "I expect I'll have to start looking for a new position." He laughed bitterly. "The baron is unlikely to keep me on to teach music to the lady's maid!"

I looked out the window again. Troger had disappeared, and all but two of the torches had been extinguished. The miserable constable kept a lonely watch over Caroline's body.

Where had she been going, in the driving rain, all alone, at dusk? To meet Starhemberg? Why had she been wearing a shabby old cloak? Who had waited for her in the shadowy courtyard? Had she recognized her killer, or been surprised by the sudden sharp pain that had caused her to slip to the stones? How long had she lain there, feeling her life drain onto the cold cobbles?

I shook my head. I must not give in to such dark thoughts. I turned back to Piatti. "Have you considered a visit to Italy?" I asked him. "The change might do you good. You must have money saved—perhaps you could find a position closer to home."

His face brightened. "I might do that, Lorenzo. Now would be a good time. I haven't seen my son in ten years. He's almost eighteen now. Soon he'll be married with a family of his own, and I will never have gotten to know him as a man." A stab of jealousy shot through me as he began to muse aloud, making plans. How I longed to return home, to let my beloved city's golden light seep into my soul, cleansing me of grief!

"I shall go write to my wife," Piatti said. He stood and placed his brandy snifter on the mantel. "Are you coming up, Lorenzo?"

"No, I'll stay for a while." We nodded good night and he left.

The sound of horses' hooves drew my attention to the courtyard once more. My chest tightened as I watched a hearse pull up. The driver and another man climbed down from the cab. They removed the blanket from Caroline's body. I wanted to run down and embrace her, but all I could do was watch as they slowly wrapped her in a large white cloth. Tears filled my eyes, but I could not look away. The constable opened the back of the hearse, and the attendants lifted her and placed her inside. The two men climbed up to the cab, and whipped the horses. The hearse pulled away.

I watched the vehicle move out onto the street. A wave of anger surged through me. I turned from the window and put my glass on the table. For the first time since I had entered this house, I was grateful to be here. I would find whoever did this, and I would happily watch as he swung from the gallows.

Twenty-three

The next morning I rose early, my heart heavy. Somehow I managed to wash, dress my leaden limbs, and make myself somewhat presentable. I saw no one as I left the palais. I hurried across the cobbled courtyard and went into the street. The day was sunny, but the streets were muddy from last night's storm.

At the Hofburg, I stopped and left a message, then went to my office, worked for two hours, and walked back out into the Michaerlerplatz.

As I turned to go back to the palais, a small man wrapped in a thick cloak crossed my path, his head hunched close to his chest. I stepped back to let him pass. He kept walking without a word, never looking up at me. His body and gait seemed familiar. It was Ecker. I looked around. No one I knew was in sight. Now was my chance to follow the furtive little secretary. I looked over and saw him pass under the archway that led from the plaza to the Augustine church. I quickly followed.

Ecker hurried past the Spanish Riding School stables and the large plaza outside the Imperial Library. I followed at a safe distance in case he should turn around abruptly. The streets had come to life. As I passed the old Augustine church, a group of monks tumbled out its door, blocking my path. I stood aside to let them pass. When I looked up, I was relieved to see Ecker at the end of the street. He was heading toward the old hospital, where I had met Josepha Hassler. I ran to make up lost ground.

Ecker did not turn into the hospital complex. Instead, he cut straight across the top of the area, and took a left onto the Karntnerstrasse. The wide street was lined with market stalls. It seemed every cook in Vienna was doing her shopping this hour. I quickened my step, afraid to lose my quarry. He walked in the direction of the Stephansdom and then turned down the Annagasse. I waited a few seconds and then followed, passing by the pale gold, spare façade of Count Esterházy's city palace. I paused in the shadow of the old Church of St. Anne on my left and peered down the street. Ecker had stopped before a building several doors down on the right. I drew myself closer to the wall of the church as he quickly looked around him and entered the building.

I hurried past the church and crossed over to the other side of the street. I stopped in front of the beerhouse at number fourteen. A large pile of rags sat near the door, waiting for pickup by the junk man. I studied the building next door, the one Ecker had entered. Its façade was nondescript, and there was no plaque on its wall to indicate the building's use. I swore with frustration.

"What? Eh? Who's there?"

I jumped. I looked up at the windows of Ecker's building. Had someone seen me and called to me? I saw no one at any of the windows. I felt something move at my feet. I looked down at the pile of rags. Something was underneath them. Rats, most probably. I shuddered and turned to move across the street. A claw clutched my ankle.

"Alms, sir?" I looked down. An old beggar grabbed at me. He gave a toothless grin. "After all, you woke me up," he said.

I dug a coin out of my pocket. "Are you here all the time?" I asked.

He wheezed. "Yes, sir. The rich people, when they come out of the church, they take pity on me." He pointed to the beerhouse behind him. "The ones here can be convinced to hand over a coin when they've had enough to drink." He reached up for the coin. I pulled my hand back, and pointed at the building next door with my stick. "What is this building, do you know?"

He spat on the ground before my feet. "Northerners! Heretics!" he said. He grabbed for the coin again.

"What do you mean?" I asked.

"Protestants! The devil's servants! They worship in there!"

My mouth fell open. The beggar pulled the coin out of my hand and buried it in the pile of rags.

"That is a Protestant church?"

"Yes, they come there every day. Very proper, they are.

They never give me any money." He spat again and crossed himself.

I dug out another coin and handed it to him.

"Thank you, kind sir, thank you. God bless you, sir," he crooned, as I turned and walked back to the Karntnerstrasse.

I hurried back the way I had come, my mind swirling with questions. Ecker was a Protestant? No wonder he had become so nervous when I had clumsily attempted to interview him at dinner that first day. If he were discovered, he would surely lose his position as secretary to Baron Gabler. Although the emperor tolerated Protestants, even going so far as permitting them to practice their religion in private, he did not admit them to his inner circle of advisors.

The morning sun shining on the light stone of the Hofburg momentarily blinded me as I entered the Michaelerplatz. The beat of rushing hooves sounded behind me. I scrambled to my right and pressed myself against the wall of the church. I stood for a moment, my pulse racing, then continued on, staying as close to the edge of the plaza as I could.

Perhaps Pergen was right after all—there was a spy at the palais. Protestants throughout the empire admired and supported the King of Prussia. I shook my head. Ecker seemed dedicated to the Gabler family. He had been with the baron for years, and had worked for the older baron before that. He would soon assume the prestigious position of secretary to the ambassador to the Court of St. Petersburg. Why would he give that up to spy for Frederick?

I had thought of no logical explanation by the time I

reached the palais. I expected to see police carriages, but the courtyard was empty. Someone had scrubbed the stones clean. I let myself into the foyer. Everything was still. Melancholy returned as I climbed the stairs to my room. Would I ever return to my simple lodgings, to my normal life?

I entered my room and swore softly. The girl had not been in to make it up while I had been gone. Ashes sat in the cold fireplace, the bedclothes lay rumpled where I had left them, and dirty water sat in the basin. I wanted to wash some of the dust of the morning from my face. I took the empty pitcher. I could get some hot water down in the kitchen.

I had gone down one flight of stairs when I met Rosa Hahn at the landing. The housekeeper's thin face was pale and drawn. She looked at the pitcher in my hand.

"Do you need water, signore?" she asked.

"Yes, I was just going to the kitchen to fetch some. I'd like to wash, but Antonia hasn't been in to clean my room yet."

She shook her head and frowned. "That silly girl, she is useless. She is probably in her room, moaning over the death of the baroness. She uses everything as an excuse to avoid work." She took the pitcher. "I'll get you fresh water, signore. Do you need a clean towel?"

I nodded. She turned and headed down the hallway, toward Caroline's chamber. I followed reluctantly. I did not want to see that room, with its silky green walls, ever again. Rosa stopped halfway down the hall, however, before a small set of double doors. She pulled out a chain with several keys attached and searched through them. A low moan came from within the closet. Rosa's hands froze. "Did you hear that, signore?"

I nodded.

"Aahh!" The cry was louder, higher pitched.

"Open the door, quickly," I said.

She fumbled through the set of keys, finally finding the right one. Her hands shook as she tried to put the key in the lock. "Someone is dying in there! The murderer! He has struck again!"

My heart thumping, I took the chain from her and placed the key into the lock.

"We shouldn't open the door, sir, we should call the police," she whispered.

"Someone needs our help," I said. I turned the key, but the door would not open.

"Are you sure this is the right key?" She nodded. I turned the key again. Still the knob would not turn.

No further sound came from the closet.

I shook the key. I twisted the knob. Nothing. I stepped back, and pushed myself against the door. Pain shot through my injured shoulder. The door popped open, revealing a large closet lined with shelves full of white linens.

I looked down at the floor. My stomach turned over. Rosa gasped. We were too late. Antonia lay on the floor, her skirts pulled up around her waist. Dark spots stained her undergarments, and blood ran down her leg. Her large blue eyes stared vacantly at me, reproaching me for my failure to save her.

Twenty-four

I dropped to my knees. Rosa crossed herself and began to mutter a prayer. I took Antonia in my arms. She felt as delicate as a tiny bird. My eyes began to water. Who was this monster, preying on the young and innocent?

The eyes blinked. A moan.

"She's alive!" Rosa crossed herself again.

"Hurry, bring Dr. Rausch here," I said to her.

"I do not think—"

"Now! She could still die!"

Rosa stared at me, sighed, turned, and ran down the hall.

Antonia's eyes searched my face. "Antonia. What happened? Who did this to you?" I asked. She did not answer, just continued to stare at me, her breathing shallow and raspy. I leaned in close. "Tell me, who did this?"

"Christof." Her voice was so quiet, I wasn't sure I had heard her.

"Christof? Who do you mean?"

Her head sagged to the side. "Florian," she whispered. "Florian."

Auerstein? Was she so close to death that she was imagining things? "No, Antonia, Florian is dead. He cannot have attacked you."

"He knew."

"What did he know? Antonia, please, dear God, you must tell me. He could kill again," I pleaded.

She turned her face back toward mine. Her lips moved as she struggled to expel the words. "Christof. Florian knew," she whispered again. She moaned. Her eyes closed again. I brushed my hand against her white cheek. Her skin was cool and clammy. I pulled her closer, trying to keep her warm.

The few minutes I sat there holding her seemed like hours. She did not speak again, and I did not press her, for it seemed that every breath was a struggle for her. My imagination ran wild as I tried to interpret what little she had told me. Had the baron tried to kill her? Why? What was it that Florian Auerstein knew? Something about the baron? Had Christof Gabler killed Florian?

"What is it, Da Ponte?" Urban Rausch entered the closet. Rosa remained in the hallway. "Put her down on the floor, please." I gently laid Antonia on the floor, stood, and backed out of the small room. Rausch knelt and began to examine the girl, whose eyes remained closed. Rosa stood stiffly next to me, a look of distaste on her face as we watched Rausch work.

"You said she had been attacked," the doctor said, looking up at Rosa. Her face flushed. She opened her mouth.

"I was the one who made the assumption, Doctor," I said. "Are you saying that Antonia is merely ill? Surely the blood—"

"The girl has lost a baby, that is all."

Rosa gasped.

"She obviously started to bleed and crawled into the closet to hide," he said. "Take her to her room. I'll find Bohm and tell him to come up." He headed across the landing, toward the baron's chamber.

I pulled Antonia's skirts down around her legs and lifted her, then followed Rosa up the stairs. Antonia had been pregnant? Who was the father? I struggled to remember what she had told me. Florian had promised to take care of her, that was it. Had he really promised to marry her after all? We reached Antonia's room. Rosa opened the door. I carried the girl inside and placed her on the small bed. Her breathing was still shallow, her skin still pale. A thin blanket lay rumpled at the end of the bed. As I pulled it up to cover her, something fell from its folds and clanged to the floor. Rosa picked it up.

"Where could she have gotten this?" she asked, showing it to me.

My eyes widened. "It belongs to a friend of mine," I said, taking Vogel's medallion from her. I slipped it into my pocket. "It disappeared from my room a few days ago."

"Antonia is the thief!" Rosa rushed to the cupboard and threw it open. "The baron's little gold clock. That pink cap the baroness was missing a few weeks ago. Oh! The wicked girl! Here is my mother's shawl! I thought I'd never see it again! I'll see her dismissed for this!"

"Dismissed for what?" Bohm stood at the doorway. Rosa

crossed the room to confront him. Antonia stirred on the bed, moaning softly.

"Your daughter has been stealing things. I agreed to take her on when you arrived to serve the baron, but I will not tolerate this behavior in my household!"

I drew a sharp breath, waiting for the sullen valet to explode. Instead, he shoved Rosa to the side and knelt at the bed. He stared at his daughter's pale face, then reached under the thin blanket and took her hand. To my amazement, he began to weep. Rosa and I stood awkwardly as the big man's shoulders trembled with grief.

"Anna. My Anna. What have they done to you?" he cried.

I caught Rosa's eye and nodded toward the door. As we stepped into the hallway, Marianne ran toward us. "Signore, a message just came for you." I unfolded the paper and read. Maulbertsch had located Katrin Spiegel. Marianne peered into Antonia's room. "What is going on? Is Antonia ill?"

The housekeeper sniffed. "She was pregnant. She lost the child." She turned to me. "Excuse me, signore, there is work to do." She hurried down the hall.

"It is true, Signor Abbé?" Marianne asked. I nodded. Her face crumpled. She began to cry.

I took her arm and steered her down the hall. I settled her on the bench in the alcove and sat beside her, taking her hand. After a few minutes, she pulled a handkerchief from her pocket and wiped her eyes. "Oh, signore, this is terrible news. My poor mistress, I have done her a great wrong."

"You believed she killed Florian," I said.

She nodded. "One day a few months ago, I caught the

two of them in her chamber. Her dress was unbuttoned, her hair loose. They were embracing. Neither of them saw me.

"After that she became very secretive. She usually told me everything. She stopped buying new hats and dresses, and insisted I mend her old things, even those that were in tatters. I suspected he was blackmailing her, threatening to tell the baron that she had slept with him."

"Would he have been so foolish, to taunt his patron with that information?" I asked.

She waved my objection away. "He was the heir of Prince Auerstein. He knew that even though he was twenty years younger and a mere page, he outranked the baron."

I nodded for her to continue.

"After Florian died, my mistress seemed relieved, almost happy even. I believed his death was probably an accident. Then—"

"You saw her ribbon in my pocket."

"Yes. She had been wearing that bonnet the morning of the day Florian died. She gave it to me the next morning, telling me she had lost one of the ribbons, and asking me to change them. Then I saw the missing ribbon in your pocket."

"How did you know where I had found it?"

"I suspected you were here for another reason besides poetry lessons. The baroness had never mentioned any desire to learn poetry. Johann had said you knew a lot of important people through your job at the theater. I suspected you were here to investigate Florian's death."

I shook my head. What a muddle I had made of everything! I could not even fool an innocent lady's maid.

"You imagined that she had lured Florian to the library,

there was a struggle, the ribbon was torn off her cap, and she threw him out the window?"

She chewed on her lip. "Yes, something like that."

Florian must have accosted Caroline in the library that morning, before I had arrived in the house, and torn the ribbon from her cap.

"Where was she going the night she was killed? Do you know?" I asked.

"She was very happy after Florian died. I guessed she had taken a lover." She smiled forlornly. "For a time, I thought he might even be you, signore."

I put my head in my hands.

"She asked to borrow my cloak. A lady cannot go out on the streets alone, but no one troubles a mere servant," Marianne continued. She put her hand on my shoulder. "Please don't judge her harshly, signore. She was desperately lonely. And as you've seen today, her husband took pleasure in humiliating her."

I lifted my head. "What do you mean?"

"Antonia. He slept with her. He must have fathered her child."

I gaped at her. "How do you know this?"

"Antonia told me herself, signore. She bragged about it, about how often he made love to her." She shook her head. "Foolish girl."

"But—I understood she loved the Auerstein boy. I thought they might be lovers."

"No, signore. She told me Florian tried with her once, but couldn't do it slowly. He ended up with his pants all wet." Her cheeks reddened.

"But she was so insistent that he was going to marry her," I protested.

"Just a dream of hers, signore, I imagine."

I did not know what else to say. The two of us sat quietly for a few minutes. Marianne wept softly. Bile rose in my throat as I recalled my encounter with the drunken baron in the library. *If she does anything to jeopardize my career, I'll kill her.* He had been unfaithful to his wife. He had fathered Antonia's child. Had he also committed two murders?

Twenty-five

Two hours later, I shifted uncomfortably in the seat of a hackney cab as it rumbled through the southeastern suburbs of the city. I had paid little attention to the scenery on my journey. My mind was filled with thoughts about murder.

Christof Gabler was the father of Antonia's lost child, Marianne was certain. Had Antonia, upon learning she was pregnant, turned to the person she considered her only friend in the household—Florian Auerstein? It was likely. She had confided the identity of her baby's father to him, and he had "promised to take care of her," as Antonia had so vehemently declared at the first dinner I had shared with the staff. She had believed he intended to marry her himself, and claim the child as his. But what if that was not what he had intended? Had he instead blackmailed his patron, planning to give the money to Antonia so she could leave the palais and start a new life when the child was born? *Received 30 florins from C.G.* Could the initials in Florian's notebook, the record he kept of blackmail, those I had been so quick, because of my own emotions, to ascribe to Caroline, belong to her husband instead? Had the baron killed Florian because of the blackmail? Had his wife found out about it, and had to be killed also?

I glanced out the window of the cab. The village of St. Marx came into view. The spire of its neat, small church and the bulbous dome of its poor relief hospital nestled into rolling green hills.

My heart lurched as the cab hit a rut in the road. I grabbed the bench beneath me to steady myself, then returned my gaze to the view outside. The cab rolled by farm after farm, row after row of small green seedlings grasping for purchase.

Ten minutes later, we reached the gates of the emperor's new cemetery, established just two years ago. In the past, Vienna's dead had been buried within the city walls, in church crypts and small cemeteries. Modern science had concluded that the accumulation of so many bodies—in Vienna, over ten thousand new ones each year—was unhealthy to the living residents of the city, so the emperor had ordered new cemeteries to be created out in the suburbs, where land was available and the population was less dense. He had even gone so far as to ban the burial of coffins. Wood took up a lot of space in cemeteries and was expensive. Instead, corpses were to be sewn into linen sacks and lowered into common graves.

The people of Vienna had accepted the new cemeteries, but had rebelled against the banning of coffins. After a few months, the emperor had relented and restored the option of individual plots and burial in coffins. The enlightened

thinkers of Viennese society, who agreed with the emper-
or's public health motivations, usually chose the newer sack
and common grave for burials, leaving the old methods to
the uneducated and superstitious.

The cemetery was quiet this afternoon. A lone black crow
sat on the iron gate. I wondered if Caroline's body lay in one
of the common pits, her beauty covered for eternity by a rough
linen sack. I did not know what plans had been made for
her funeral, and I did not feel it was my place to ask the baron.
Icy fingers clutched my heart as the cab rolled by the cemetery. My eyes filled with tears, and in the privacy of the cab's
interior, I allowed myself to grieve freely.

After about ten minutes, I dried my eyes with my handkerchief and returned to my previous musings. I was certain
the baron had killed Florian Auerstein and Caroline, but I
had no proof. If I accused him, I would be asking Pergen to
take my word against that of the protégé of the most powerful politician in the empire. I had to face the truth. No one
was going to believe my charges against the brilliant Christof
Gabler, in mourning for his own young protégé and his
beautiful wife. Accusing him would mean the end of my life
in Vienna. To take on such a powerful man, with his many
friends and sponsors? I would be mad to even consider it. I
knew in my heart that while my own patron, the emperor,
gladly supported me in my battles with my enemies in the
theater, he would not take my side in this fight. All of Vienna would turn against me. I would lose my position in the
theater and would have to flee yet again, to build a new life
in another city.

I gazed blankly out the window at the never-ending farm-land. But what about the victims—the boy, too young to die, and my own beloved Caroline? In my heart I could hear them crying for justice. I was the only one who could see to it that their murderer was punished for his crimes.

The wheels of the carriage turned, taking me toward my destination. The wheels of my mind turned, taking me to-ward a decision that I did not wish to make.

Twenty minutes later, the cab arrived at a small village. I instructed the driver to pull up near the church in the mid-dle of the main street, and asked him to wait for me. The church was surrounded by the large dwellings of the com-munity's founding families, prosperous shopkeepers and im-portant landsmen. I hoped that one of these was the address I sought. But when I hailed a passerby and asked directions, he pointed me down the road, toward the outskirts of the village.

My heart filled with dismay as I approached the cottage. It was a small, shabby affair, but I could see that the tiny garden out front was neatly kept. Green flower shoots were breaking through the ground. I knocked on the door. A mo-ment later, it was opened by a woman in her late forties, her graying hair tied neatly up in a bun. Two small children re-garded me seriously from the safety of her skirts. Behind her I could see a younger woman seated by the hearth, nursing a baby.

"Good afternoon, sir," the older woman said. "Can I help you?"

Now that I was finally face-to-face with her, I did not know what to say. I gave a small bow. "Good afternoon, madame. Are you Katrin Aigen, formerly Katrin Spiegel?"

Her face grew wary. She nodded.

"I've come about your son," I began.

She gasped, and clutched the doorjamb, trying to keep herself steady. Her face was white. The two children began to cry.

"Matti? Are you here about Matti?"

Matti? Who was Matti? Perhaps it was the name she had given Vogel before she gave him up for adoption.

"Yes," I said.

She shrieked. "He's dead, isn't he?"

I gaped at her. "I—"

Before I could finish, she fell to the ground in a dead faint.

Twenty-six

"Who are you? What did you say to her?" The young woman rushed to Katrin and knelt beside her. "Don't just stand there like an idiot, help me!"

My tongue was tied with embarrassment. I put down my stick and helped the girl lift her mother, who was regaining her senses. Together we led her over to the chair by the hearth. As the daughter fussed over her mother, I looked around the room. Unlike the outside of the house, this main room was cheery and neat, with flowered curtains hung at the windows. Over in the corner, the baby wailed from the cradle into which his mother had dropped him when Katrin fainted.

"Mama, are you all right?"

"Some water, please. That's all I need." The girl hurried to the back of the house. Katrin's eyes wandered around the room, confused, and finally lit on me. "Matti," she moaned.

She began to cry. The girl returned with a mug of water and knelt beside her mother. Katrin took a long swallow.

"Who is Matti?" I asked the daughter.

"My younger brother. He is in the army. Surely you know that?"

I chided myself for my clumsiness, for blurting out as I had, frightening these poor women. I shook my head.

"You are not from army headquarters?" Katrin asked.

"No, madame, I am here on another matter." I introduced myself.

"What could the theater poet want with me?" Katrin asked.

I looked over at the girl, who was listening intently. "Perhaps if I could speak to you alone, madame? My errand is confidential."

The girl snorted. Katrin squeezed her hand. "It's all right. Take the children outside. I'll listen for the baby." The girl glared at me, but called to the two toddlers, wrapped them in bulky woolen cloaks, and ushered them out the door. She paused to give me one last cold stare on her own way out.

"Now, sir, if this is not about Matti, what is it? You said you wanted to speak to me about my son."

"Yes, madame. About your other son. Johann."

She looked at me, confusion all over her face. "Johann? I don't have a son named Johann."

My heart sank. Had I come this far to find Vogel's mother only to have her deny ever giving birth to him? I reached into my cloak pocket and pulled out the medallion. "This belongs to you, I believe."

Her eyes widened as she turned the medallion in her hands. "Where did you get this?" she whispered.

"It belongs to a friend of mine, a man named Johann Vogel. He found it among his adoptive mother's things after she died." I described the muff, the ring, and the book to her. "I found this medallion inside the muff, and used it to trace you." I hesitated. She had bowed her head and was staring at the medallion. "I hope that you do not find my being here a terrible intrusion," I said. "My friend is desperate to find his birth mother. He was unable to search himself, so I agreed to help him."

She looked up at me. "Oh, sir! Seeing this has brought back so many memories, both good and bad. My little boy! To think he is all grown-up. I thought I would never see him again. But—"

"He is eager to meet you," I said.

"But you don't understand, sir. You have made a mistake."

"Madame, I assure you, he only wants to meet you. He does not expect any money," I lied. It was obvious there was no money here to save Vogel from his prison sentence.

"He is not my son," Katrin said.

"But I don't understand. The medallion—those are your initials, are they not?"

She nodded. "Yes, the medallion is mine. Thirty years ago, I was a novice at the convent of the Sisters of the Blessed Virgin. I was fifteen years old. I had no desire to become a nun. I was in love with a local boy. We wanted to marry." Her voice hardened. "My father hated Anton, I don't know why. He would not let us get married. He knew that in a year I would be sixteen, that I would not need his permission.

He wanted to lock me away, separate us forever. He went to the old priest at the church here. Together they arranged to have the abbess take me on as a novice in the convent."

She took a sip of water.

"I worked in the infirmary as part of my training. The convent took in a lot of unwed mothers, as you probably have learned." I nodded. "I loved nursing, especially taking care of the babies before their adoptions were arranged. One of them in particular touched my heart. A little boy. I remember he was not adopted right away. I took care of him for several months." She smiled at a distant memory. "I remember his chubby hands and fat cheeks," she said. "Whenever I had spare time, I would pick him up, rock him, and sing to him." She lifted up the medallion. "He loved to grab at this. I used to take it off and swing it in front of his face, watching him follow its gleam and trying to catch it."

Disappointment washed over me.

"After four months, the abbess was finally able to arrange an adoption for my little friend. On the day he was to leave, one of the nuns brought me a new suit in which to dress him, and a box. She told me it contained the few items his mother had left behind. I peeked inside it and saw the muff, the ring, and the book. I didn't think these were things that would help him in his new life. He was a baby, he needed a plaything. So I pulled the medallion off my neck, and quickly sewed it into the lining of the muff. I guessed that his new parents would find it when they returned home with him, and it would be too late to bring it back to me. I hoped they would let him play with it."

I sighed. "I apologize for coming here like this, and for

frightening you. May I ask you—did you ever meet the boy's birth mother?"

She shook her head. "A few months after the baby left, my father died in an accident. I knew by then that I wanted to be a wife and mother, not a nun. I left the convent, married Anton, and started a family of my own."

"When you took care of the child, did you ever hear any mention of his mother? Did the nuns say anything about her?"

She shook her head once more. "No. No one told me anything. I never knew her name, or where she came from. I have no idea what happened to her."

Twenty-seven

When I arrived at the theater Saturday morning, the main hall buzzed with the excitement and trepidation that only a full dress rehearsal can bring. The candelabras had already been lit, and the candles belched wispy smoke overhead. On the stage, a wardrobe mistress was hastily stitching the hem of Nancy Storace's dress as the prima donna ran her voice through the scales. The orchestra members were subdued, concentrating on tuning their instruments instead of trading bawdy jokes back and forth, as they had done at previous rehearsals. Thorwart, the assistant theater manager, bobbed up and down, greeting and seating the privileged patrons and nobles who had been invited to get the first view of the opera.

Mozart was already there, dressed in the rich red suit and gold-laced hat he usually saved for performances. I had put on my best suit, also, worn as it was, for it is often said that a man's clothing can be a suit of armor. I had told Mozart of my plan to thwart Rosenberg's edict against the ballet in the third act. His eyes had widened, then he had laughed and hurried to give instructions to the singers.

Now I sat in a seat a few rows in front of the stage, off to the side, where I could observe both the rehearsal and the reactions of the guests who had come to watch. Rosenberg and Casti had arrived shortly after we had begun; Salieri had hurried in ten minutes later. Within two hours, Mozart had led the singers through the first two acts with only a few missed cues and forgotten lines.

As the opening to the third act sounded, I looked over to the side door of the theater. I hoped that the recipient of my invitation to the rehearsal had agreed to come, and that he would arrive in time. We were only at the beginning of the act; there were plenty of scenes before his presence was required.

The singers moved easily through the act. Mozart had made Kelly see reason, and the impudent tenor sang his role as the judge without a stutter. A few scenes later, the cast exited the stage, leaving it to the two female leads, Nancy Storace and Luisa Laschi. As Beaumarchais's Countess Almaviva and her maid, Susanna, the two sopranos looked beautiful in their costumes, Laschi clad in a lavish, jeweled white gown and Storace, although the bigger star of the two, wearing the simple costume of the lady's maid. Their voices soared in a duet, in which they plotted a tryst for the maid in the count's garden.

"What a gentle breeze there'll be this evening," Laschi sang.

"A breeze . . . this evening," Storace echoed.

"Beneath the whispering pines," they both sang.

"He'll understand the rest," they agreed.

The women were composing a note to trap the count in an act of infidelity with the maid. I smiled at the irony—my beautiful poetry and Mozart's lush music portraying two scheming women. I had to admit to myself that it was a stroke of genius on both our parts.

As the scene concluded and the ladies received their bravas from the guests in the audience, I glanced over at the theater door. Still no one. My stomach began to churn. The end of the act was now only a few moments away. I turned my attention back to the stage. A group of peasant girls, one obviously a gauche boy dressed to appear as a girl, presented flowers to the countess. The count and his nosy gardener arrived onstage, and the gauche peasant girl was revealed to be the amorous page the count had banished from court in the first act.

I looked over at the door again, straining to hear any indication of an arrival outside, but the noise from the stage drowned out all other sounds. I glanced to my right, at my trio of enemies. Rosenberg frowned at something on the stage. Salieri sat quietly, his usual bored expression on his face. Casti, however, was laughing along with the action. I smiled to myself. If he knew I was watching him, he would be sneering instead, just to spite me.

By now the budding soprano Anna Gottlieb, playing the young daughter of the gardener, had convinced the count to allow the page to marry her. Francesco Benucci, singing the title role of the valet, Figaro, entered, and launched into a musical battle of wits with the count. I looked over at the door. Still no one. My hands grew cold.

Suddenly the music and singing stopped. The time for the act's finale had come. My heart sank. I had been so sure my plan would work, I had not concocted a second strategy. Mozart turned to me from his seat at the pianoforte, his eyebrows raised in question. I gestured for him to stall for a few minutes. He turned to the stage.

"Let's take a five-minute break. Everyone stay onstage, please."

Rosenberg stood and loudly cleared his throat. "Herr Mozart, continue with the rehearsal, please. Your opera is very long, and my time is short this morning." Casti shot me a grin.

Mozart looked over at me. My heart thumped so loudly in my chest I could swear everyone in the theater heard it. I froze, unsure of what to do.

"Herr Mozart?"

Mozart shrugged at me and turned back to the orchestra. He raised his hand and waited a long moment. As his hand lowered, the flutes, cornets, and strings began to play the first measures of the lilting march that opened the finale. Just then, the door to my left opened. I exhaled loudly. The orchestra members who faced the door stopped playing. Mozart, his back to the door, continued to wave his hand.

Rosenberg leaped to his feet. "Herr Mozart, stop, please!"

By now everyone in the theater had risen. Mozart and I both stood and bowed as the emperor, accompanied by a few courtiers, entered the room. Rosenberg rushed to greet him, and led him to a seat in front of his own. Casti approached the emperor and kissed his hands. "Please continue, Mozart," the emperor said.

The orchestra began the scene again. The chorus entered, the men dressed as huntsmen, the girls in long, flowing gowns. Two of the maidens sang a song praising Count Almaviva. The rest of the chorus joined in. When they had finished, Mozart put down his hands. The orchestra fell silent. Onstage, a wedding ceremony took place. Nancy Storace gesticulated wildly as she passed the amorous note to the count, Stefano Mandini. He waved his hands over his head. They looked ridiculous, like giant puppets on a children's theater stage.

The emperor snorted. He began to stand. Rosenberg jumped up. "Stop, everyone!" The emperor turned to Casti. "What is this?" he asked.

Casti rose and gave a fawning bow. "I do not know, Your Majesty. Perhaps if you asked the theater poet—"

"Da Ponte? Where are you?" the emperor called. I got to my feet, grabbed my libretto, and hurried to him.

"What is this?" he asked, gesturing toward the singers on the stage. I said nothing, just handed him the pages from the libretto. It was my other copy, which still contained the scene Rosenberg had thrown into the fire.

The emperor scanned the pages. "This calls for dancers," he said. "Where are they?"

I shrugged and looked over at Rosenberg.

"Where are the dancers, Theater Director?" the emperor asked.

Rosenberg's face whitened. "Your Majesty, I considered

it best to remove the ballet," he sputtered. "As you know, the opera company has no dancers."

"Can't they be borrowed from one of the other theaters?" my wise Caesar asked.

"Yes, Your Majesty, but I thought you—"

The emperor waved his hand. "Then get Da Ponte as many as he needs," he said. He called over to Mozart, who had been standing at the pianoforte. "Mozart, skip this scene and continue. Dancers will be here later, you can rehearse the finale then."

Mozart bowed, stole a glance at me, sat down on the bench, shuffled through his score, and gave instructions to the singers and orchestra. The emperor settled back into his seat. The music began. Rosenberg summoned Thorwart and whispered in his ear. The assistant theater manager hurried out the door.

I smiled.

Twenty-eight

The emperor stayed another hour, during which I entertained myself by glancing every so often at my adversaries. When the emperor applauded a scene, their faces fell in unison, and when he stood to shout "Bravo!" at the end of a difficult aria, three sets of lips tightened into thin, pinched lines. When the emperor left for the Hofburg, all three scurried after him.

Six dancers from the imperial ballet arrived by one o'clock, and we skipped dinner to work with them. By three, the long day was blessedly over. The singers and orchestra dispersed. Mozart and I left Thorwart to close up the theater and walked into the late-afternoon sun.

"Did you see Rosenberg's face?" Mozart clapped me on the shoulder. "I thought he was going to lose his breakfast then and there."

I laughed.

"You are a genius, Lorenzo! What made you think to just invite the emperor to the rehearsal and see the butchered scene for himself? I would have stormed over to the Hof-burg, demanded an audience, and tried to make my case."

I smiled. "It was a risk, but I know him well," I said. "I knew that he would think the scene was ridiculous without the ballet. Besides"—I grinned wickedly—"why go behind Rosenberg's back to embarrass him when you can do it to his face, with the emperor and the entire cast present?"

Mozart laughed. "I feel good about this opera, Lorenzo. I think we'll have a hit on our hands in a few weeks!"

A sudden weariness swept over me. "I hope so." I sighed.

"What's wrong, my friend?" Mozart peered into my face.

"I'm tired, that's all," I lied.

"Whatever happened with your barber? Did you find his mother?"

"No. I've followed lots of leads, all of which have gotten me nowhere. I think I'm ready to give up trying."

"You did your best. That's all he can ask of you," Mozart said. "Are you sure that's all that's wrong?"

"Too much work, not enough time," I said.

He hesitated. "If you don't mind my saying so, Lorenzo—you should find yourself a nice wife. Stop running from this lady's maid to that singer. Find someone to make a life with. Things become much simpler with a wife. You know what I always say—a bachelor is only half alive!"

I laughed as he slapped me on the back.

"You know, I think we have achieved the near impossi-ble, Lorenzo." Mozart chortled. "That rare moment when a good composer, one who understands what great theater is, meets an able poet."

"Able?" I teased. "Is that all I am?"

"No!" He laughed. "You are that true phoenix—the perfect partner! A brilliant librettist *and* a brilliant conniver!"

My cheeks grew warm with pleasure at his praise. He pulled his watch out of his pocket. "I had better get home. I promised Carl a ride on Horse this afternoon."

We embraced briefly, then I stood watching as he walked, whistling, down the Kohlmarkt, his hands in his pockets.

I turned and trudged down the Herrengasse to the palais. The relief and excitement I had felt when the emperor ordered Rosenberg to bring in the dancers had dissipated, and a strong sense of disappointment and melancholy overcame me. I had been so sure that Katrin Aigen was Vogel's mother! Now I was back where I started, with no other leads to follow. I did not look forward to visiting Vogel in prison and telling him I had failed him. And I had yet to decide whether to tell Troger that I suspected the baron had killed Florian Auerstein and Caroline.

The street was crowded this late sunny Saturday afternoon. It seemed all of Vienna, at least those without carriages to take them out to the Prater, had decided to stroll. I stayed as far to the right as I could, close to the buildings. I knew in my current mental state I would not be alert to a carriage rushing at me suddenly.

"Signor Da Ponte?"

I looked up from my thoughts to find a man, a stranger, had come from behind me and was matching my step on my right.

"Yes?" As I turned to him, I felt a sharp object push against my left side. A strong arm grabbed my left elbow. The man on the right pushed closer to me.

"Keep quiet, Signor Poet. Just keep walking."

My heart raced as I recognized the voice and guttural accent.

"What do you want with me?" I asked, my voice trembling.

"Just keep walking, signore, and don't call attention to yourself. You will regret it if you do."

We veered sharply into a long alley. They pulled me several feet around a corner. The tall walls of two noble palaces pressed in on the narrow alleyway. The ground was strewn with garbage, dumped from the kitchen of the great houses. I gagged at the stench. The noise of the street could not be heard back here. All was quiet except for the sound of someone playing a pianoforte high above in one of the homes.

"What do you want?" I cried. "I have just a little money." I drew out my coin purse and threw it on the ground. "Take it and let me be!"

The man with the accent pushed me against the wall. His companion reached down and pocketed my purse.

"Go keep watch," my assailant told him. He turned his attention back to me.

"Weren't you warned to keep out of business that doesn't concern you?" he asked me. He shook his head. "But you Jews can't help yourselves, can you?" He punched me in the stomach.

Pain shot through me. I groaned. "Who sent you?"

He laughed. "You know who did." He punched me again.

I fell onto the muddy ground. My hands clutched at something slimy. I shuddered and let go.

"Goddamn Jew!" He kicked me in the side.

I tried to curl into a ball to protect myself, but I could not move. The pianoforte tinkled from above. He kicked me again, then again. I recognized the tune, a sprightly aria from Mozart's last opera. My attacker leaned over and turned me facedown, pressing my mouth into the nearest pile of garbage. I gagged. He twisted me back around to face him. I tried to open my mouth to cry for help, but I could not move my lips. The music stopped. He mounted me and sat on my aching stomach. He pummeled my face with his fists.

"Filthy goddamn Jew! Think you're better than the rest of us!"

A warm, salty liquid came from my mouth. The pianoforte resumed, its player repeating the passage I had just heard.

"Come on," I heard my assailant's companion call. "That's enough."

"In a minute," my attacker said. He leaned over me, his putrid breath in my face. "One more minute." He smiled evilly, and reached inside his cloak, pulling out a halberd. My eyes widened.

"Who's the better man now, Signor Abbé?" he said, sneering.

"Come on!" His friend's voice was more urgent. "Someone will hear us. We're not paid to kill him!"

My assailant raised the halberd above his head. The music stopped again. I saw the yellow of his rotten teeth, then a field of stars. I fell into blackness.

Twenty-nine

I don't know how long I lay there before consciousness returned. I gingerly pulled myself up on my hands and knees and groped for my stick, which I found in a pile of trash a foot away. My face felt wet and sticky. I rummaged through my cloak and found a handkerchief. When I pulled the clean cloth away from my face, I saw blood and dirt all over it.

My entire body groaned as I pulled myself to a standing position. I stumbled as I slowly made my way out of the alley. The few passersby on the now quiet Herrengasse stared at me as I trudged by, but no one stopped to ask if I needed help.

My stomach churned with worry. How had my assailants discovered that I was born a Jew? I had not practiced that religion for twenty-three years, not since the monsignor of Ceneda, named Lorenzo Da Ponte, had baptized my family so that my father could marry a Christian woman. It was he who had seen that I was given an education. I had eagerly taken our patron's name, and would always be grateful to him for changing my life. I had never told anyone here in Vienna that I had been born in the Jewish ghetto. I shivered as I wondered who had paid the man to beat me, and how he knew so much about me.

After what seemed like an eternity of slow, painful steps, I reached the palais. My hands shook as I fitted my key into the lock, opened the door, and entered the foyer. I dragged myself up the stairs.

"You killed her!"

The shout came from the left, the baron's office. I hurried as fast as my aching legs would take me down the hallway. The wide doors stood open. The baron stood in front of his desk, his hands outspread before him. Bohm, both hands holding the old sword that had hung over the mantel, pointed the tip at his employer's neck.

"I don't know what you are talking about," the baron said.

Although his back was to me, I could tell that Bohm's arms were shaking. The baron winced as the sword tip grazed his cravat.

"You killed my Anna!" Bohm shouted.

The baron raised his hands higher. "I know of no one named Anna," he said.

"You should have been arrested by now!" Bohm cried. "You should have hung as a traitor to the empire! When they came to me and offered me the money to steal information from your desk, I saw my chance to avenge her! You would be blamed, your career ruined, your life and your family's lives destroyed, like you destroyed mine."

My mouth dropped open. At that moment, the baron saw me. His eyes widened slightly.

"I don't know what you are talking about, Bohm," he said. "Who is Anna?"

"My wife!" Bohm cried. "You killed her. You and your emperor. We were happy, me, Anna, and Antonia, living in the cottage out at Schönbrunn. I managed the grounds for the old empress. She appreciated my work so much she left me a pension of six hundred florins a year in her will. Then you and the emperor canceled all the pensions! I was left with nothing!"

The baron nodded for Bohm to continue.

"My cottage, all of the beautiful things the empress had given Anna and little Antonia, I had to sell them all just to move us here to Vienna to find a new position. Anna took it hard. The night before we were to leave, she hanged herself in the kitchen." He pushed the point of the sword closer to the baron's neck.

The baron caught my eye. I made a small gesture. He could not risk a nod, but managed to raise his eyebrow imperceptibly.

"You allowed that boy to seduce my daughter," Bohm shouted.

The baron swallowed hard. He held his hand up. "I did not—"

"He filled her head with dreams, so he could ruin her!" Bohm said. "It is all your fault!"

I stepped into the room. "Don't worry, Bohm! He will pay for all of his crimes!" I shouted.

Bohm jumped and whirled around. The baron grabbed the hilt of the sword and twisted it out of the valet's hands. He threw it to the ground and pushed the startled Bohm against the desk, pinning his hands behind his back.

"Quick, Da Ponte, some rope, in the cupboard there!"

I ran to the cupboard and flung open the doors. Piles of documents stood neatly on the top two shelves. A pile of rolled maps sat on the bottom shelf.

"I don't see any rope—"

Bohm twisted and kicked at the baron. "You deserve to die for what you did to me!" he yelled.

"In the drawer, at the bottom," the baron said. "Hurry!"

I pulled open the wide drawer and grabbed a coiled length of rope. I ran back to the desk.

"That chair, bring it here, quickly."

I hurried across the room and grabbed a wooden chair that sat in the corner, then dragged it over to the desk. The baron pushed Bohm onto the chair. The valet began to weep.

"Hold his hands behind the chair while I tie him," the baron said. My shoulders ached as I pulled Bohm's wrists together. His anger spent, he offered no resistance.

"Anna, Anna," he sobbed.

"Did you kill my wife?" the baron demanded.

"No, no. She was innocent. I only wanted you. I swear. I've killed no one!"

The baron turned to me. "Good work, Da Ponte," he said. He rubbed his neck. "Find Ecker and tell him to send for Troger."

I nodded and headed to the door.

"No, wait a moment," the baron called. "Before you go, tell me—what did you mean when you said that I would pay for all of my crimes?"

I stood silently for a moment. I made my decision and opened my mouth to speak.

Thirty

"Sir! Are you all right?" Ecker hurried into the room before I could utter a word of accusation. He looked around the room: at Bohm, tied to the chair, weeping uncontrollably; at me, battered and bruised, standing with my mouth wide open; and at the baron, who had picked up his father's sword and was carefully replacing it in its place of honor over the mantel. "What happened?"

"I'll send for Troger," I told the baron. He nodded, and I fled the room.

Rosa Hahn was coming up the stairs from the foyer as I arrived at the landing.

"Signore, what is going on up there? What is all that noise?" She gasped as she saw my face. "What has happened, signore? Who did this to you? Was it the murderer?"

"It's Bohm. He's attacked the baron."

"Is the baron all right?"

"He is fine," I said. My legs would no longer carry me. I sank to the steps.

"Signore, you are injured!" She hovered over me.

"I'll be fine, Rosa," I said, waving her away. "Please, would you go into the street and get a boy to run to the Hofburg? Tell him to fetch Captain Troger from Count Pergen's office. He can ask one of the guards how to find him."

She nodded. "Go down to the kitchen, signore. I'll wash those cuts for you when I return." She ran down the stairs and out into the courtyard.

I pulled myself up and slowly made my way down to the kitchen. The large room was empty, but the fire was burning and it was warm. I sprawled in the chair by the hearth and closed my eyes. My mind was in a whirl. Bohm was the spy. He had nursed a grudge against the baron for his role in the emperor's pension reform, and had come to Vienna to seek vengeance for the suicide of his wife. Had he planned to kill the baron? Perhaps, at the beginning, when his mind was still clouded with grief at the loss of his wife. The King of Prussia's agents must have kept watch on the household, and seen the arrival of Bohm as a chance to plant a spy. The valet had cooperated, hoping that he could incriminate the baron and see him accused as a spy for Frederick. When Antonia had lost the child, the sight of her lying deathlike on the bed had made him lose his senses.

"Now, signore, let me see." Rosa entered the kitchen. She winced as she looked at my face. "What happened to you?"

"Some ruffians robbed me in an alleyway."

She poured warm water into a bowl, dipped a cloth in it, and gently began to clean the dried blood off my face. My body relaxed as her competent fingers dabbed at my injuries. The water and her touch were soothing.

"Oh, I'm getting all wet!" she exclaimed. She rolled up the sleeves of her dress. "I have some herbal ointment here, signore. I'll rub it on these scrapes. Just put your head back a bit. Yes, that's good." I closed my eyes and enjoyed the feeling of her fingers dancing over my skin, deftly rubbing the grease into my sores. I inhaled deeply. Her skin smelled like lemons.

She moved my head to the side, turning it so it faced her inner arm. I opened my eyes for a moment and studied the spatula-shaped dark purple birthmark on her upper arm. Something niggled in the back of my head. Where had I seen that mark before?

"What has happened with Bohm?" she asked me.

"He blamed the baron for causing his wife to commit suicide," I explained.

"Turn your head to the right, signore," she said.

"He had worked for the old empress and she had left him a pension. The baron was one of the ministers who canceled all those pensions when the empress died. He—"

All at once it came to me. The last time I had seen a mark like that I had been sitting in a similar position, being shaved by Vogel that last day in his shop. My pulse quickened. *Look for the woman who spilled the wine,* Florian Auerstein had told me when I demanded he tell me what he knew about Vogel's birth mother.

I sat up straight and clutched Rosa's forearm. She jumped back, startled.

"Madame," I asked. "Are you familiar with a convent called the Sisters of the Blessed Virgin, here in the city?"

Her face whitened.

"You see, I've seen a birthmark like yours before," I said. "It was on the arm of a man who was born in that convent, thirty years ago."

She gasped.

"A man you know well. Johann Vogel."

She moaned and swayed, grabbing onto the back of my chair.

I jumped to my feet. "Wait here, Miss Hahn," I said. "I have something to show you."

I hobbled to the door and up the stairs, my pulse racing with excitement. I had found Vogel's mother at last.

At the first landing I ran into Piatti, who was wearing a cloak and carrying a valise.

"Lorenzo, good, I'm glad I bumped into you. I'm taking the coach tonight to Trieste, then on to Bologna. I wanted to say good-bye." He peered at my face. "Good Lord, what happened to you?"

"I can't talk right now, Tomaso," I said. "What time are you leaving?"

"In a half hour. I was just going to wait in the library until my carriage came."

"I'll be up in ten minutes," I said. I climbed the stairs to my room, grabbed Vogel's box, and hurried back down to the basement. Piatti had told me that Florian spied on everyone in the house, especially the women. He must have been peeping at Rosa while she was undressing one day and had recognized the birthmark as being similar to Vogel's.

I turned into the kitchen.

"They told me he was dead! They told me he was dead!" Rosa, her face red with anger, beat her fists against the chest of the man who held her by her upper arms.

"Calm down! You know I did what I had to do at the time!" Urban Rausch said. "I wasn't ready for marriage thirty years ago."

"You told me you would marry me after I had the baby!"

"I remember no such promises," Rausch said. "I told you I would pay for you to have the baby at the convent."

"No!" Rosa shrieked. "You told me we would marry! After the baby was born, you never came back. The nuns told me the baby had died. I was all alone, with nowhere to go."

"Nonsense!" Rausch said. "I paid the abbess very well to make sure that you were offered a post working at another convent. Get control of yourself! I am not to blame for your lifetime of unhappiness!" He pushed her off him. She stumbled and fell to the floor, sobbing.

Rausch noticed me at the door. "What are you gaping at, Da Ponte?" he asked. His mouth contorted in an ugly expression. "You couldn't mind your own business, could you, you goddamn Jew! I should have ordered those men to kill you, not just beat you."

I stared at him. "How did you know I was born Jewish?" I asked.

"I carry on a small private practice in addition to my research. I have patients in high places. When you came here, I asked around about you. I knew you were spying on me, trying to prove that Vogel was my son." His laugh was harsh. "Apparently everyone in Vienna knows that the theater poet is a Jew passing as a priest!"

Rosa pulled herself up onto the chair. "You had him beaten, you lied to me—all to protect your reputation so you could marry that Heindl woman," she said.

"I've been a poor relation to my ward and her husband too long," Rausch said. "Always having to beg for funds to complete my manuscript, to buy books for my research. Franziska supports my work. I wasn't going to let it come out that Vogel was my son. I'll admit I made a mistake when I was a student, carrying on an affair with my mother's chambermaid, but why should I still have to pay for that? Franziska would have broken off our engagement if the news had come out. I've done right by you. I took a risk, bringing you here and getting you this job when your convent was closed. And didn't I give you hundreds of florins to make up for the past?"

"Florian told me my son was still alive," Rosa whispered.

"He saw your birthmark and remembered that Vogel had one of the same type in the same place," I said. I turned to Rausch. "The baron had the records from the convent where Vogel was born. He must have gone through them and found Vogel's birth certificate, with your name and Rosa's on it."

"Yes," Rausch admitted. "He showed them to me one evening. I was astonished that the result of my little mistake was actually here in this house, threatening my future. We both agreed that it would do neither of us any good if my past came out. He burned the birth certificate in the library fireplace."

"Florian must have been eavesdropping," I said.

"He told me there were records that showed my son was still alive," Rosa said. "He teased me, wicked boy! He refused to tell me what he knew."

"That's why you were searching the baron's desk that evening," I said. She blushed. I turned to Rausch. "The boy must have told the baroness about it. She insisted you admit your paternity." Rausch shook his head.

"Don't lie to me, Doctor. I overheard your argument with her. A few days later, she was dead."

"You think I killed her?" Rausch was indignant. "I loved her!"

"You encouraged me to lend him the money," Rosa cried. "You wanted him away from here, in case I found out—and then you urged me to press the lawsuit against him. My God! I sent my own son to prison!" She began to weep again.

"Why are you crying?" Rausch said. "You are not so innocent in all of this." He laughed. "You lusted after him! Everyone in the house could see your desire all over your face. You never even recognized that he looked a bit like you, in his nose and his lips, or that he had my hairline."

As I stood there, their voices receded. Rausch's mention of recognition renewed the niggle in the back of my mind I had had the other night. I had seen something that I recognized, something that didn't make sense—

A moment later my mind was inundated with images. Neat, cramped rows of handwriting in a small notebook. Pages from my libretto, covered with comments. A red-faced man rushing into the library. A quizzical eyebrow as I chatted in the courtyard. A worn, carefully repaired coarse cloak, its hood covering a small, delicate head.

I slipped out of the room and climbed the stairs. I now knew who had murdered Florian Auerstein and Caroline.

Thirty-one

I stood in front of the library door, my heart pounding. I quietly pulled open the door. The sun had set, and only a small lamp on the table lit the room. Although the windows were closed, the heavy velvet drapes had not been drawn. Tomaso Piatti stood at one of the tall bookcases, his attention deep in the baron's collection. He drew out a volume and stuffed it into his valise.

"Tomaso," I said.

He started, but quickly regained his composure. "Oh, Lorenzo, it is you! Why are you standing there in the shadows?"

I glanced at the valise.

"All right, you've caught me, my friend. But you must feel the same as I do. These magnificent books are wasted here. In all the years I've been here, I've never seen the baron read a single book. He won't miss these."

"You killed Florian and Caroline," I said.

Piatti sighed. "Ah, Lorenzo. I wish you hadn't come up

here after all. Things would have been much simpler if you had fallen in front of that carriage the other day." He closed up the valise. The tic in his left eye had disappeared.

"You were blackmailing Caroline." I pulled the little notebook out of my pocket.

"I was right after all. I knew you had it," Piatti said. "I looked everywhere in your room for it. How did you know it was mine?"

"I didn't. I assumed it was Florian's. He dropped it that day in the library. I only realized a moment ago that it actually belonged to you. Everyone told me how sloppy Florian was. Even you told me that the music assignments he turned in to you were full of inkblots. The notes in the book were too neat to be his. I recognized your handwriting, from the comments you wrote on my libretto."

Piatti shook his head. "I am a natural teacher. I couldn't resist marking up your work. How stupid of me!"

"It was Caroline who was paying you, not the baron?" I asked.

"Yes. I saw her one day in the Prater. She took the closed coach. I saw Starhemberg climb out of the carriage. I could tell from the look on his face they were having an affair. I saw a chance to get some money from her." He straightened and looked at me. "You wouldn't believe the pittance they pay me! I trained at the best conservatory in Italy, and they pay me like I am the cook, insist I eat with the servants!"

"Was Florian blackmailing you?"

"He stole the notebook from my room. He confronted me with it, threatened to tell the baron. I needed this job,

Lorenzo. My wife and sons back in Bologna depend on the money I send home."

"Did he demand money to keep quiet?"

"No. He had already had the book for a few days before you came. I offered to pay him to give it back, but he preferred to play with me. He teased me, talking about what he would do. Finally, I had had enough."

"You were looking for him that day I first met you. I remember you rushed in, angry at someone."

"After you left that day, I confronted him here. I demanded he give the notebook back. He taunted me. He jumped up on the windowsill and pretended he was a judge, sentencing me to life in prison for blackmail. He told me he had decided to give the notebook to the baron."

"So you pushed him out the window."

He lifted his valise off the table.

"After Florian fell, I rushed down and searched his body. I couldn't find the notebook. Then I remembered that you had been here. I had heard you two arguing. When the police came, I told them you had threatened Florian and run from the house. When you came the next day, I thought you might have the notebook. That's why I searched your room. But I couldn't find it."

"So you began to feel you were safe, until that day that Marianne and I returned from our visit to Vogel in prison."

"Yes. I believed the boy's father must have taken the notebook when he came to collect his things. No one would be able to tie it to me. I heard you tell Marianne to go to the police. I panicked. I thought perhaps Florian had told her about me, or she had overheard something."

"She believed her mistress killed the boy," I said sadly. "You waited for your chance. You must have seen a figure in a coarse cloak leave the house. You rushed down and stabbed her, thinking it was Marianne."

"I was distraught when we turned the body over and I saw that I had killed the baroness by mistake."

I remembered our night together here in the library after Caroline's death. What a fool I had been! I had supposed that Piatti had reached his breaking point, that he was terrified of the murderer. I had even advised him to go home to Bologna!

"You gave me good advice, my friend. I am going home to Italy." He took a few steps toward me, the valise in one hand. "Come with me. We will both be revered in Bologna. Your work will finally be appreciated, Lorenzo."

"You know I cannot."

He studied my face. "You loved her! She was the woman you were mooning over!" He laughed. "Poor Lorenzo! Let me tell you, my friend. You had no chance with her. She whored only with the highest aristocrats!"

Rage surged through me. I lowered my head and charged at him, hitting him squarely in the chest and knocking the valise out of his hands. His surprised grunt sounded faintly through the roaring in my ears. We wrestled. I pinned him against the wall of bookshelves. Pain shot through my leg as he kicked me. I let go of his arms and stumbled backward.

He turned and pulled a heavy volume from the shelf and with both hands hurled it at me. I ducked. The book struck my shoulder and thudded to the floor. He pushed me aside and rushed to the door. I ran and threw myself at him. We slammed to the floor in front of the sofa. His face was red, his eyes wild. We grappled and thrashed around on the small rug. "You can't escape," I said, panting. "The police are downstairs."

He kneed me in the groin. I howled with pain. He stood, raced to the window, and leaped onto the wide sill. I grunted as I pulled myself up. As I ran to the window, I tripped on the edge of the rug. The small table next to the sofa toppled over. The little Harlequin figurine cracked into pieces on the floor.

I heard voices in the hallway. Piatti reached up and unlatched the window. I crawled over to the sill. "No!" I screamed. "I will see you hang!" I grabbed his left leg and pulled. He clung to the drapes with both hands. The soft evening breeze wafted into the room. I pulled harder.

The drapes crashed down on top of me, taking Piatti with them. We rolled around in the soft velvet. He pulled away from my grasp and lifted himself to his hands and knees. I groped at him through the tangle of heavy fabric. He climbed back onto the sill. The door opened.

"What the hell is going on here?" The baron, Troger, and Ecker stood in the doorway, gaping. I freed myself from the drape, reached up, and clutched at Piatti's leg. My arms throbbed with pain as he pulled himself closer to the window.

I gasped. "He murdered Caroline and Auerstein." Piatti kicked at me. I lost my grasp and fell backward. The baron and Troger ran to me. I scrambled around and tried to grab Piatti's leg again, but I was too late. He pushed the window open wide and jumped.

Epilogue

A soft snow fell as I followed the surge of people leaving the theater into the Michaelerplatz. A small group of aristocrats, the women shivering although dressed in luxurious furs, waited nearby for their lackeys to bring the carriages around. One of the men caught sight of me and waved me over.

"Bravo, Signor Da Ponte!" he cried, pumping my hand. "I cannot remember the last time I enjoyed an evening at the opera so much!" His friend shook my hand and congratulated me. The ladies tittered and fawned over me a bit, asking me how long it had taken me to write the libretto, what it was like to work with such a talented composer, and how it felt to be the toast of Vienna.

A Rare Thing, the opera I had finally found time to write

for my Spanish friend Martín, was the hit of the Court Theater's season. After it had premiered in November, tickets had been in such demand that hundreds of people were turned away from every performance. I was making a nice profit on requests for copies of my libretto. Everywhere one went in the city one heard our arias being sung. Society ladies dressed and did their hair to imitate the costumes and styles in the opera. I had even seen a few lady's maids wearing their tresses à la *A Rare Thing*.

My reputation had soared since the premiere. I was in high demand among the composers in the city. Rosenberg had called me into his office to congratulate me, and even Salieri had written from Paris, proposing that we should work together again. My only regret was that Casti was not around to witness my triumph. Last summer, the fool had written a long poem poking fun at the Empress of Russia and had presented it to the emperor. My Caesar had not been amused, since the empress was one of his closest allies. Casti was quickly given a large purse and invited to take his leave from Vienna.

Over the last nine months, I had slowly recovered from my ordeal at the Palais Gabler. For a long time, my dreams were haunted by Piatti's screams as he fell from the window. I often woke up in a cold sweat, my heart pumping wildly, imagining that I heard that dreadful thud when he hit the stones. He had not died immediately. Although his body was broken and the doctors proclaimed there was no hope for him, he had lingered a few days. After his death, his son had come from Bologna to claim the body. I had met him briefly—a sullen young man with none of his father's charms.

Two days after I recognized Rosa Hahn's birthmark, the housekeeper had petitioned the court to release her son from debtor's prison. I don't believe that learning the identity of his birth parents has brought my barber the happiness and riches he had imagined when he asked for my help that fateful day in April. True, Rosa forgave the debt he owed her, but Urban Rausch had refused to legally acknowledge that he was Vogel's father.

The pompous doctor had married his rich widow in June. Vogel and Marianne were married a few months later. Vogel's business is thriving, and I recently learned that Marianne is expecting their first child in the spring. I had taken Rosa to meet Josepha Hassler at the Deaf School, and that good lady was happy to take the housekeeper on to her staff.

As far as I know, Gottfried Bohm is rotting in prison, awaiting trial for his attempt to kill the baron. Marianne had invited Antonia to live with her and Vogel, but the girl had run away after a few months. I had helped Marianne search for her for days, but we could not find her. I hoped that she had found her way back to her old home somehow, and had been taken in by her mother's family. The streets of Vienna are no place for a young girl to be on her own.

I could not bring myself to tell Troger that Ecker was a Protestant. He and the baron left for St. Petersburg last month.

As for my opera with Mozart, *Figaro* had premiered a week after I confronted Piatti. Although I was sleeping poorly and still ached from my encounter with Rausch's men, I did not miss the performance. The house had been full, and except for some hissing from the galleries, the opera had been well received. The audience had demanded that many of the arias be encored, and Mozart had taken numerous curtain calls. Yet by June, merely a month later, Vienna had lost its enthusiasm for *Figaro* and was ready for the next new thing. The opera has been performed only five times in the last six months, and no performances are planned for this new season.

Constanze Mozart had given birth to a son in the middle of October. Three weeks later, I had had the sad task of mourning with my friends at the Stephansdom, after the babe succumbed to the dreadful suffocation spasms that take so many newborns. I had been so busy with new work the last few months that I hadn't been able to see the Mozarts, but I had heard from Rosenberg that they had left a few days ago on a visit to Prague. It seems *Figaro* is popular there, and Mozart had been invited to conduct a performance.

As the summer turned to fall and then to winter, I slowly stopped mourning Caroline. My memories of her faded, and it was only when I caught the scent of lavender on a woman passing by that I felt a stab of grief. Perhaps Mozart had been right when he told me to find an uncomplicated woman and settle down. I was too much like the boy in my aria, the one I had read to Caroline and Marianne the first day—in love with the idea of love.

My relationship with the emperor has grown even stronger since Casti was dismissed. He had thanked me for helping to solve the murders, and had jokingly offered me a position in the new investigative service Pergen was setting up. I had laughed and quickly demurred. Since then, I have heard whispers about strange goings-on in Pergen's office.

Many men were being hired; much money was being spent. I tried to avoid being drawn into such discussions.

Occasionally I would think, though, about my experience at the Palais Gabler, and dark suspicions would cloud my mind. Who had hired Bohm to spy on the baron? Had it really been agents of the King of Prussia, or had someone with another, more complex agenda placed him in the household? I wondered if I had not been a pawn in some larger game Pergen had been playing with the emperor. I remembered the baron telling me that night in the library that the emperor had insisted I play detective so that he could save the expense of creating a professional secret police department.

It was natural for a minister like the count to want to expand his area of influence. And Pergen had never given me any details about the documents that had disappeared from the Palais Gabler. Had Pergen himself paid Bohm to spy on the baron, in order to show the emperor that he was under threat, and needed a secret police force? Perhaps when Piatti had killed Florian Auerstein, Pergen had argued for greater authority. But maybe the emperor still would not listen to him, and, to save money, had suggested that I investigate the crime. Had Pergen willingly gone along with his sovereign, certain that I would fail, and that the emperor would finally agree to fund a secret police force? My mind would invent scheme after scheme. Then my head would clear, and I would laugh at my imaginings.

I smiled as another group of well-wishers congratulated me on *A Rare Thing*. I stood in the cold for a bit longer, warmed by the soft velvet coat of my new suit under my cloak.

When the crowd had finally dispersed, I crossed the plaza and headed down the Kohlmarkt toward my lodgings, the wheels of the fancy carriages clattering all around me. I could not help but think again of Venice, where late at night, after the theaters had let out and the revelers had straggled home, the only noise a solitary pedestrian can hear is the rhythmic gliding of the gondolas—

I shook my head. Enough. I pulled the collar of my cloak up to shelter my neck and walked on, toward home.

AUTHOR'S NOTE

Mozart's mature years in Vienna were a time of transition for musicians and composers. In 1761, twenty years before Mozart rebelled against his father and took up permanent residence in Vienna without a job, Joseph Haydn began his long employment with the family Esterházy. Although he held the post of director of Prince Nicholas Esterházy's large musical establishment, Haydn was treated as a servant: required to wear livery, attend daily upon his master, compose what his employer required, and refrain from travel without the prince's permission. Twenty-eight years after Mozart's death in 1791, three wealthy noblemen would promise Beethoven a lifetime stipend, with no strings attached, if he agreed to remain in Vienna and compose whatever he wished.

Vienna in the 1780s was the perfect place for a musician to break with tradition and attempt a career at what we would now call freelancing. A forward-thinking monarch, well read in the works of the Enlightenment, had recently ascended the throne. The power of the old, landed aristocracy was being superseded by a rising class of new nobles, who were merchants, bureaucrats, and professionals rewarded with a title for service to the Habsburg monarchy. A thriving middle class thirsted for new products to buy and new entertainment to enjoy. Vienna was a bustling world capital.

Another artist attracted to the opportunities in Vienna was Lorenzo Da Ponte, a native of the Veneto, born a Jew but who converted to Christianity as a youth, a lover of poetry and literature, who had been banished from Venice for his political activities. He is the hero of this book, rather than Mozart, for many reasons, chiefly that too much is known about the composer and too little about the librettist. And the librettist has a grievance against history—if his name is included on a modern-day opera program it is usually as an afterthought, in much smaller type than Mozart's; when lines from the operas are quoted, the words are generally attributed to the composer; and when scholars admire the plotting of a certain operatic scene or an elegant turn of phrase in the libretto, they prefer to believe that Mozart had been standing at Da Ponte's side, dictating over his shoulder as the poet wrote. I thought it time to give the librettist a voice.

All of Da Ponte's character traits, habits, past experiences, and passions described in the book are factual. His misfortune concerning his teeth, his love of fine clothing, his quickness to anger, and his equally ready desire to help those in need have been documented by biographers. His story about finding books in his father's attic comes from his memoirs, and he tells us that he kept a small selection of works from the great Italian poets with him at all times. I've incorporated excerpts from the *Rime sparse,* by Petrarch, Da Ponte's favorite poet, into his lessons with the baroness and Marianne. And I've also given Da Ponte a chance to read one of his own poems, the aria *Non son più cosa son, cosa faccio* from *Figaro.*

Many of the characters in *The Figaro Murders* are historic figures: Joseph II was a mentor to both Mozart and Da Ponte, and both men remained in Vienna probably because of his interest in their careers. All of the emperor's reforms mentioned in the book were enacted. Frederick of Prussia attempted repeatedly to weaken Joseph's power against the other princes of the Holy Roman Empire, and worked to stymie the emperor's territorial ambitions. Count Johann Anton von Pergen was a longtime member of the Habsburg bureaucracy. At the time of the action of *The Figaro Murders,* he had recently been appointed minister of police. His power would grow over the next few years, as Austria went to war with the Ottoman Empire, freedom of speech was curtailed, and many of Joseph's reforms were repealed.

Count Franz Xavier Rosenberg-Orsini (Rosenberg in the book) was the director of the emperor's opera company and one of Joseph's closest advisors and confidants. His friend and Da Ponte's nemesis, Giambattista Casti, was famous throughout Europe for his poetry, librettos, and wit. It is not known whether Rosenberg and Casti were in fact in league to get Da Ponte relieved from his position as theater poet, but Da Ponte was certain they were, and complains about them in his memoirs. Antonio Salieri was the court composer at the time *Figaro* was written. All of the singers in the novel, including the irrepressible Michael Kelly, were members of the original cast of *Figaro*. Da Ponte's friend and the composer of his great hit *Una cosa rara* (*A Rare Thing*) was Vicente Martín y Soler. I've shortened his name to Martín for ease of reading.

I've invented the character of Troger, Pergen's assistant, as well as all of the people Da Ponte meets during his search for his barber's mother. Readers familiar with *Figaro* will recognize the inhabitants of the Palais Gabler as the characters from the opera.

Many of the scenes in the book are based on actual occurrences. The riddle Florian tells Da Ponte is one of a set that Mozart, dressed as a masked Oriental philosopher, presented at a party in the Hofburg in February 1786. The full set of riddles is presented and analyzed by Maynard Solomon in *Mozart: A Life* (HarperCollins, 1995). The tenor Michael Kelly claims in his memoirs that he performed his rôle in *Figaro* with a stutter. He also really did parody Da Ponte onstage during a performance of the librettist's opera *Il demogorgone*, although the performance actually occurred in July, after the premiere of *Figaro*. The episode where Rosenberg bans the dance scene from *Figaro* comes from Da Ponte's own memoirs.

The city of Vienna is much changed since Mozart's time. However, although the modern traveler must avoid the Ringstrasse—which was developed in the nineteenth century when the old city walls were torn down—and must turn away from the many bewigged salesmen in breeches and coats hawking tickets to Mozart/Strauss concerts, it is still possible to turn down a street or enter a courtyard and be transported back to the eighteenth century. All of the streets I have Da Ponte travel still exist today, and I have placed both librettist and composer in the homes it is known they lived in while writing *Figaro*. (Mozart's apartment is now the Mozarthaus Vienna, a museum dedicated to the composer's time in the city.) The theater where Mozart and Da Ponte worked was torn down in the early nineteenth century, but several paintings from the 1780s show it in the Michaelerplatz, to the right of the old wing of the Hofburg. I imagined office space in the old building for both Da Ponte and Rosenberg. The Palais Gabler is a pastiche of many architectural elements from various palaces near the Herrengasse—the façade from one, the courtyard windows from a second, the bubbling fountain from a third. There was no convent in 1786 named the Sisters of the Blessed Virgin, but there were many like it that were closed by Joseph II, and many nuns who lost their homes. I invented the custom of giving a medallion to each novice in the convent. And finally, because I had not yet visited Venice when I wrote this book, Da Ponte's longings for his home are informed by Peter Ackroyd's *Venice: Pure City* (Vintage Books, 2010).

The Viennese public did tire of *Figaro* soon after its premiere, and it was not performed in Vienna again until 1789, when it was revived with some changes to the arias. It was performed twenty-eight times after that until Mozart's death, in 1791. During his lifetime, Da Ponte was better known for writing *Una cosa rara* than for any of the three operas he wrote with Mozart. *Figaro* was revived sporadically during the nineteenth century, but was generally unpopular with audiences who were attracted to operas of the bel canto and romantic styles. In the early twentieth century, several conductors began to perform *Figaro* again, and the opera became very popular after the end of World War II. It is now one of the most performed and beloved operas in the world. A current-day staging of *Una cosa rara*, on the other hand, is a rare thing indeed.

The academic and popular literature on Mozart, Da Ponte, and their operas is vast. For readers who want to learn more about Da Ponte, a good biography is Sheila Hodges's *Lorenzo Da Ponte: The Life and Times of Mozart's Librettist* (University of Wisconsin Press, 2002). Da Ponte's memoirs, translated by Elisabeth Abbott, have been published by New York Review Books (2000). For Mozart, I recommend starting with his letters. The collection translated and edited by Robert Spaethling, *Mozart's Letters, Mozart's Life* (W. W. Norton, 2000), is nicely annotated and allows the reader to encounter the composer in his own voice. A fine introduction to the operas themselves, including musical analysis, can be found in Andrew Steptoe's *The Mozart–Da Ponte Operas* (Oxford University Press, 1988). Nicholas Till's *Mozart and the Enlightenment: Truth, Virtue, and Beauty in Mozart's Operas* (W. W. Norton, 1992) ties all of Mozart's operas to the intellectual history of his era. A much longer list of sources I have consulted during the writing of this book may be found at my Web site, www.lauralebowbooks .com, or on my author page on Goodreads.

I hope that reading *The Figaro Murders* will encourage those who have never encountered the opera to do so. If you are new to opera and to *Figaro* in particular, I recommend that you begin with a video of a performance, since the opera's plot is complex and best understood when seen onstage. Many excellent performances are available.

What is ahead for Lorenzo Da Ponte? As he mentions in the epilogue, Mozart and Constanze have left for Prague, where *Figaro* is a hit. They will return to Vienna with a commission to write an opera based on the Don Juan legend, and Mozart will again call upon his friend Da Ponte for a libretto. After a successful run for *Don Giovanni* in Prague, the emperor will order a performance for Vienna. And while librettist and composer are at work adapting the opera to the more sophisticated tastes of the Viennese audience, bodies will start turning up in the streets of the capital . . .

I am grateful to the following people for their assistance and support: my agent, John Talbot; Keith Kahla and Hannah Braaten at Minotaur; first readers Marjorie Smith and Joan Yesner; and my husband, Bill, without whom nothing I do is possible.